S0-ASG-294

"Thou hast freed Excalibur!"

"Whoa!" said the lad, examining the gleaming sword. "Awesome!"

"By pulling Excalibur from the stone, Arthur," I said, "you have set your foot upon the road you were destined to travel."

"I figured I'd take it to the market, see if I could sell it," Arthur said.

"*Sell* Excalibur?"

"Uh-huh."

"For *money*?" I cried.

"Well, unless someone's got a really good lute to trade for it."

"A lute? To *trade*?"

"But I'd rather go for the money," Arthur said. "This sword looks pretty valuable. I'll bet I could get enough dough to outfit the whole band, don't you think?"

"*What* band?"

"Well, okay, I don't have a band yet. That's in the future. I figured I'd go on the road alone first, build my rep, get some steady gigs, and then acquire the band. I'm going to call it Arthur Pen and the Dragons. What do you think?"

"*What?*"

"Or maybe just Arthur and the Dragons. Or Arthur Pen's Dragons? I dunno yet."

LOGAN-HOCKING
COUNTY DISTRICT LIBRARY
230 E. MAIN STREET
LOGAN, OHIO 43138

Also Available from DAW Books:

Places to Be, People to Kill, **edited by Martin H. Greenberg and Brittiany A. Koren**
Assassins—are they born or made? And what does an assassin do when he or she isn't out killing people? There are just some of the questions you'll find answered in this all-original collection of tales. From Vree, the well-known assassin from Tanya Huff's *Quarters* novels . . . to a woman whose father's vengeful spirit forced her down dark magic's bloody path . . . to an assassin seeking to escape his Master's death spell . . . to the origins of the legendary nin-sha and the ritual of the hundredth kill . . . here are spellbinding tales of murder and mayhem of shadowy figures who strike from night's concealment or find their way past all safeguards to reach their un-suspecting victims. With stories by Jim C. Hines, S. Andrew Swann, Sarah A. Hoyt, Ed Gorman, and John Marco.

Pandora's Closet, **edited by Martin H. Greenberg and Jean Rabe**
When Pandora's Box was opened, so the ancient tale goes, all the evils that would beset humanity were released into the world, and when the box was all but empty, the only thing that remained was hope. Now some of fantasy's finest, such as Timothy Zahn, Kevin J. Anderson & Rebecca Moesta, Louise Marley, and Sarah Zettel have taken on the task of opening Pandora's closet, which, naturally, is filled with a whole assortment of items that can be claimed by people, but only at their own peril. From a ring that could bring its wearer infinite wealth but at a terrible cost . . . to a special helmet found in the most unlikely of places . . . to a tale which reveals what happened to the ruby slippers . . . to a mysterious box that held an ancient, legendary piece of cloth . . . to a red hoodie that could transform one young woman's entire world, here are un-forgettable stories that will have you looking at the things you find in the back of your own closet in a whole new light. . . .

Army of the Fantastic, **edited by John Marco and John Helfers**
How might the course of WWII have changed if sentient dragons ran bombing missions for the Germans? This is just one of the stories gathered in this all-original volume that will take you to magical place in our own world and to fantasy realms where the armies of the fantastic are on the march, waging wars both vast and personal. With stories by Rick Hautala, Alan Dean Foster, Tanya Huff, Tim Waggoner, Bill Fawcett, and Fiona Patton.

FATE FANTASTIC

EDITED BY
Martin H. Greenberg
and Daniel M. Hoyt

DAW BOOKS, INC.
DONALD A. WOLLHEIM, FOUNDER
375 Hudson Street, New York, NY 10014

ELIZABETH R. WOLLHEIM
SHEILA E. GILBERT
PUBLISHERS
http://www.dawbooks.com

Copyright © 2007 by Tekno Books and Daniel M. Hoyt.

All Rights Reserved.

DAW Book Collectors No. 1419.

DAW Books is distributed by Penguin Group (USA).

All characters and events in this book are fictitious.
Any resemblance to persons living or dead is coincidental.

If you purchase this book without a cover you should be aware that this book
may have been stolen property and reported as "unsold and destroyed" to
the publisher. In such case neither the author nor the publisher has received
any payment for this "stripped book."

The scanning, uploading and distribution of this book via the Internet or any
other means without the permission of the publisher is illegal, and punishable
by law. Please purchase only authorized electronic editions, and do not partici-
pate in or encourage the electronic piracy of copyrighted materials. Your
support of the author's rights is appreciated.

First Printing, October 2007
1 2 3 4 5 6 7 8 9

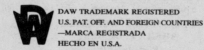

DAW TRADEMARK REGISTERED
U.S. PAT. OFF. AND FOREIGN COUNTRIES
—MARCA REGISTRADA
HECHO EN U.S.A.

PRINTED IN THE U.S.A.

ACKNOWLEDGMENTS

Introduction © 2007 by Daniel M. Hoyt
Ascent © 2007 by Julie E. Czerneda
Approaching Sixty © 2007 by Mike Resnick & Barry N. Malzberg
But World Enough © 2007 by Sarah A. Hoyt
Consigned © 2007 by Thranx, Inc.
My Girlfriend Fate © 2007 by Darwin A. Garrison
A Rat's Tale © 2007 by Barbara Nickless
The Bones of Mammoth Malone © 2007 by Esther M. Friesner
Death and Taxes © 2007 by Kristine Kathryn Rusch
Fate Dogs © 2007 by Robert A. Hoyt
The Man With One Bright Eye © 2007 by Joseph E. Lake Jr.
A Tapestry of Souls © 2007 by Paul Crilley
The Final Choice © 2007 by Phyllis Irene Radford
The Prophecy of Symon the Inept © 2007 by Rebecca Lickiss
Choice of the Oracles © 2007 by Kate Paulk
Camelot's Greatest Hits © 2007 by Laura Resnick
Jack © 2007 by Dave Freer

CONTENTS

INTRODUCTION

Daniel M. Hoyt

I was fated to write this introduction. I think the first time I became aware of it, I was sixteen. I remember it quite clearly. I was at a carnival one night, under a full moon, there was a palpable tension to the air, and then this wizened old woman with straggly white hair and a jagged scar slashed across one eye walked right up to me—

Well, you know the story.

"It was inevitable."

"An ironic twist of fate."

"Self-fulfilling prophecy."

For denizens of high-tech societies that generally eschew the notion of mysticism, modern humans seem to have an odd fascination with fate. The concept itself is rooted in ancient man's desire to explain things and events he couldn't reconcile intellectually. After thousands, maybe millions, of years, we still haven't shuffled off the pervasive instinct to fall back on fate as a last-resort explanation.

Even prophecies, cousins of fate that are essentially stories of preemptive rationalization, seem to survive well beyond their inception. Maybe they're just fated to survive. Or maybe once we acknowledge them as prophecies, we *make* them survive, *because* they're prophecies. Whatever the reason, they survive, sometimes for several millennia. Many ancient religions—and even new ones, for that matter—have prophecies central to their belief systems. Nostradamus, less than five hundred years ago, charmed the French court with prophecies that are still believed by many today.

Ironically, even when prophecies fail to come true, we refuse to reject fate. Instead, we twist the results and rationalize them in some other way, yet cling to the underlying concept of fate.

Equally ingrained in our subconscious seems to be the notion that fate may not always be fixed. Every now and then, we're allowed to reject our fate, to twist it around to suit our own needs. Once. Just once.

And it's there that we find the truly interesting stories (for we are storytellers, and always have been) about fate. It's right there, when we allow ourselves to believe that we're not merely a society of automata absentmindedly marching toward our deaths according to some cosmic blueprint. There we find the stories that make us believe in life, in free will, and—maybe because they're exceptions to it—in fate.

There we find the stories that make us human.

Okay, maybe I never met a woman at a carnival when I was sixteen imploring me to write an introduction about fate. What *did* happen, though, is that sixteen very talented fantasy and science fiction short-story writers have come together to explore fate, as only they can.

From Julie Czerneda's sublimely multilayered reflection of our relationship with fate, to an academic consideration of fate and consequences as only Kris

Rusch can present it, to Dave Freer's thoughtful collision of mythology and morality, you'll find fate examined from unique and unexpected angles.

On the lighter side, consider Darwin Garrison's amusing take on dating one of the three Fates, or Robert Hoyt's tongue-in-cheek look at hot dog street vendors through a stockbroker's eyes, or Laura Resnick's retelling of the Arthurian legend, set to music.

You can't go wrong with Mike Resnick or Barry Malzberg; together, they take on gambling and the Kabbalah. Or try Alan Dean Foster's thought-provoking ascent into Hell. Esther Friesner's trademark wit shines with her tale of a soothsayer, lemmings, and a frozen tundra. Irene Radford reminds us that even Fate has rules.

In these pages, you'll find wonderful stories that will delight you and challenge your own notion of fate. I know you will.

It's fate.

ASCENT

Julie E. Czerneda

I was born to kill.

There was no other purpose to my existence. No other was required. I knew my life's role as few ever did and it brought me, if not joy, then a steadfast measure. That which took me to that destiny I sought and embraced. That which did not, or worse, could distract, I avoided or ignored.

Until I met Zephyr on the Dedmas Cliff.

"Oh, do come on!" The shout skipped along the cliff face. Those seabirds still unaroused by our ascent rioted in a blur of wing, feather, and raucous cry.

I tucked my head toward my chest to shield my eyes from beak and justified temper, my fingertips digging into stone, holding still until the last bird launched from its hole. Spitting guano from my dry mouth, I waited another breath, then lifted my head.

Four round downy heads looked back at me from their crack, eyes unblinking.

I smiled at the chicks.

"C'mooonnn!"

Three chicks shrieked as I climbed after my companion.

Companion?

Thorn. Irritant. Bully. Prod.

Companion, I told myself, easing up the crumbling cliff.

Nimble where I was ponderous. Agile where I was methodical and slow. Above all, that gentle touch where I was force incarnate.

As if reacting to the thought, my fingers closed too firmly and my left hand fell away from the cliff, filled with pulverized stone.

Hanging for an endless moment from my other, more reasoned right hand, I contemplated the problem.

"Use your feet."

My companion was swift of thought, too, while I needed to view a thing from all its sides, consider consequences, and only then act. He dropped to my side as though we laid on a floor and only pretended waves and jagged rock teeth waited so far below.

He tapped my legs sharply. "You've two of them. Remember?"

He was life.

I was death.

Destinies neither of us chose.

My feet, obeying him before me, found a deep crack—and the chicks I'd spared, I realized too late, licking any evidence from my teeth. Zephyr turned strange when I did such things. Strange and cold and wary.

It wasn't fair, I thought, my free hand finding and holding—more carefully now—the stone. There was nothing of Zephyr that changed how I regarded him.

"Keep moving, lummox," he urged with a chuckle. "There's a ledge broad enough for even your haunches almost in reach. I'll go ahead and start some jaff."

I was bred to end a threat.

They'd tipped me overboard in the cold shadow of the cliff, their small ship more fragile than I, more at risk within the surge and froth of ocean. I'd been buffeted too, slammed by dark boiling waves as my outreached hands fought to take hold. But they'd known I could endure what they could not, so they'd turned their ship toward safety with cries of relief that echoed the birds wheeling far above.

They'd never reached it. The hold I found had been their ship. Wood was nothing to the hands I'd been given. When a wave heaved me up and away, my hands had stayed clenched around a strip of newly splintered plank, the small ship already listing well to one side and beyond salvation.

Their cries had turned to futile curses.

I'd reached the base of the cliff and begun my climb without witness.

How had Zephyr known to find me there?

"Nice view."

He made conversation. I made the jaff myself, putting a thick pinch of leaves from the pouch at my waist into the flattened sphere that was both pot and cup, holding it open against the nearest of many rivulets draining down the cliff. The water had rained on an unseen land, from clouds as far above us now as the ocean lay below. I wondered if the result would taste foreign.

I crouched over the pot, rocking it from side to side to draw the most from the leaves. There wasn't room to move otherwise. With my back against the continent, my feet dangled out over what I'd climbed these long hours.

"You're planning to share, I hope?"

Without a word I held out the battered pot. Zephyr laughed and shook his head, eyes agleam with mischief. "I couldn't. From the look of you, you need it more than I. Go on. If I get as slow and weary as you, I'll take my turn."

He was anything but weary, restlessly pacing the part of the ledge not covered by me. His hands, delicate and sure, moved like the birds whirling through the air below. As if he thought he could fly.

"So, what's it like up there?"

I put my lips to the spout and let the cool, bitter liquid drip into my mouth. Slow was better. The virtue within the leaves was absorbed best by the tongue. Mine was swollen, its cracks taking fire from the spice. I persisted, drop by drop. I'd been taught to embrace pain.

Taught by it.

Taught to embrace it, I told myself, staring out at the ocean. Pain was a tool. I understood its use.

Zephyr straddled my legs with his. I couldn't see past his slender form and frowned at this trivial victory. "What's it like?" He was pointing up. "Surely you know."

I didn't need to know, so I kept the spout to my lips.

"Aren't you the least bit curious?"

I was made invincible.

I'd pulled myself from the surf at the base of the

infamous cliff and begun my ascent. The battering waves had tried to brush me aside; they found easier work eroding the layers of softer stone. The wind, rising up the wall with its load of icy spray, had tried to numb my flesh. Easier to chill the birds riding the updraft.

I had looked no farther than my next grip. My destination would matter when I reached it.

As we'd approached through morning mist, hearing the roar before seeing our goal, the Dedmas Cliff had suddenly punched through the clouds, an immensity of black tilted seaward as if about to crash down on the ship. Those who'd brought me had exclaimed in awe. Up close, its surface was rotten with crumbling, newer stone. Through those gaps the exposed bones of the world jutted at sharp angles, defying the ocean's power.

For now. Other such bones lay wave-washed and defeated at the cliff's foot.

The cliff was nothing more than my road. I'd ignored the exclamations of the soon-to-be dead and studied the surf. And as I'd begun my climb, I'd never looked to the top or thought of what was to come.

Until Zephyr's soft cheery voice had whispered in my ear, "Well met, lummox!" Then he'd asked, for the first time, "Do you know what's up there?"

"Wake up! C'mon!"

I blinked open my eyes, scrubbed flakes of dried jaff from my lips with the back of one hand. I must have dozed. No matter. Even the body they'd given me appreciated rest after a day of such climbing. Another day to go. Or rather, night.

I blinked, then squinted. The sun had dropped below

the sullen clouds, riding the horizon. Its light skipped and danced over the waves. When I rose to my feet with a grunt and turned to face the cliff, the sun peered over my shoulder and found glints of crystal in the rock. They looked like eyes.

Zephyr was on the move, his quick toes nipping into the smallest crevice, his delicate fingertips caressing the cliff. He'd shaken his head at the scars I left in my passing.

I hadn't asked for such mammoth hands and feet, with their ever-sharp talons that made it impossible to keep from tearing my own clothes. I hadn't asked for arms to match, or shoulders too wide for the doors others used.

I hadn't asked for a nightmare's face.

"Hope you can see in the dark, friend lummox," Zephyr called from above.

I was destruction.

When Zephyr had appeared beside me on the cliff, nimble and happy and sly, I'd thought him a dream. Not that I'd been encouraged to fancy, but the playground of my thoughts had outlasted the rest. He'd acted like a dream, too. Unsurprised.

Unafraid.

I'd forgotten what it was like, to have company who didn't fear me.

Or hurt me, when they still could.

The novelty had stayed my horrible hands, not that I could have touched him. From that meeting, he ascended beside me with the grace of a swimmer, every gesture with purpose, every reach without flaw.

While I climbed with raw power, ruining the stone.

*   *   *

"Over here!"

Zephyr balanced on a thrust of sheer rock, waving one hand vigorously at me. I didn't like it when he risked himself, though he had the skill to do so. I'd learned, however, that he wouldn't be ignored. With a sigh, I abandoned the straight ascent and edged sideways.

"Hurry! I tell you it's remarkable!" He disappeared from view.

Distraction.

Yet I found a crack to take my right foot, forced my right hand into another, eased myself over the dark spire. My belly, scaled and rough, left its mark on the softer stone. This, a rib of the world, ignored my passing.

Zephyr's so-remarkable find was another fall of water, nothing more. The cliff was laced with such. Elsewhere, water clung to the rock in seeping stains or evaporated into a cloying spray. This ribbon was wider than others; judging by the growth of small, feathered green through the stone, more permanent. Its crystal strands made a sound as they writhed past and down, like the cold chatter of teeth.

My companion leaned precariously close to its near side. "Stick your head und—" The exhortation became a gurgling laugh as Zephyr took his own suggestion. I waited in dread for the waterfall to wash him from the cliff. The spray-washed surface was treacherous and slick. But he might have been a fish bounding upstream for all the water's plunge affected him. After a moment, he surfaced and shook his head, drops flying like pearls from his hair. His teeth flashed in a smile. "C'mon! You stink. You don't want to get to the top like that, do you?"

I looked into the cloud-hidden heights where this waterfall had been spawned.

I didn't want to get to the top at all.

Having said it, if only to my innermost self, I trembled.

I was taught to obey.

When old enough to understand such things, I was told my life's purpose: to kill our enemy, those who dwelled above us, who wove spells within the clouds for this land's ultimate destruction. Until that moment, I would live in the arena where training would hone the physical tools given me. I did my best, always. In the early years, the broken bodies of my instructors would be dragged away after each session. More precisely, what remained of those bodies, since I ate what I could before they were taken from me.

There was no other food given me; I asked for none.

The time came when there were bodies, but no longer instruction. I recall a vague curiosity. Had I learned all they could teach or was I being sent those who would not themselves learn?

Not that I asked or was answered.

I was tested; it was always the same. Each time the moon hid her face, regardless of the weather, I was to climb the wall of the arena, using only my hands, until I reached the mark scratched in the stone. Halfway up. There, I was to stay. Moon after moon, year after year, eventually, inevitably, my hands would grow numb, my arms spasm, and I would fall to the sand. I wasn't punished. No need.

Failure meant I'd stay here.

Inevitably, the time came when I held to the wall, conscious only that my body would die before my hands would let go. I remember being content if that were so.

They'd looked down on me from above; faces that came and went with the days. Then one came who was different from the others. He'd stared down at me with hollow eyes and told me my goal. I would ascend the unclimbable Dedmas Cliff and kill all who'd believed themselves safe living atop it.

They'd brought me models of the cliff face. I'd studied them until I knew its stoneworks more intimately than those of my arena. They'd provided rocks like those I would encounter. I'd slept with them under my body and held them in my hands until that grip felt more natural than an empty palm.

The time came when they'd opened the gate of my arena and my journey began.

I recall a vague joy it would soon be over.

"Sure you don't need help?"

Zephyr's breath entered my nostrils and mouth, warm and fresh. I saw my eyes reflected in the dark gleam of his. "You look," he added consideringly, "stuck."

What had appeared in the models as a vertical gash in the cliff, a promising path through a section that leaned out over the surf, had narrowed into a trap. I leaned my head against the wall behind me, twisting my neck to assess the possibilities. If the gash had been a chimney, the sharp bend overhead would pin and collect smoke, let alone a climber. Maybe I could reach outside, try to pull myself out and past the obstruction . . .

Zephyr had followed my gaze. "That won't work," he decided. "You'll have to go down and try another path."

My feet were against the other wall; the force of my legs pressed my back and shoulders against this one. I'd inched my way in similar fashion with success until now. I tested the cracks above with my fingers; rock crumbled at my touch. The fragments clicked and tapped and spun away into the dark. We were halfway up the cliff now. Had the moon been shining, I might have seen the distant blur of white that marked the waves now far below.

Undeterred by our height or my situation, Zephyr used me as his personal stair. Standing on my bent knees, he reached to slap his slender palm against the inward lean of stone. "Face it. They made you too big." A rebuke, as if he'd expected better.

I sighed. I was as I was. I didn't belong here; he did. Where I struggled, he moved without effort. On passing the mark I'd set myself, the height above which I knew my body could not survive a fall, he'd become even more careless. No, not careless. Casual, as if there was no place safer.

Now he bounced on my knees. "You taking a nap? I tell you, friend lummox, you're stuck. The only way out is down."

The only way I couldn't go. Down was away from my goal. To move in that direction was to negate my life's purpose.

Did Zephyr guess what that was?

I became patience.

The beslimed lower reach of the cliff had almost defeated me before I'd properly begun my ascent. What use was strength denied a grip? I'd clung to the first hold I'd found, able to resist the suck of wave and the flood of spray rushing down the wall. Knowing I'd be vulnerable to their force when I reached for another, I'd taken my time, and stared through the froth to study the cliff, considering this path and that. I'd ignored the rain when it began, drunk my fill, welcomed the flashes of lightning. Finally, satisfied, I'd chosen cracks for my fingers, felt barnacles crush under my palms and the soles of my feet, and climbed.

Once past the domain of water dwellers, I'd moved steadily, with growing confidence. The rain had ended, leaving its tears along the stone. Soon I'd reached the lowest of the narrow sloped ledges crammed with nests. The debris and guano made for treacherous holds, the adult birds had screamed their rage, but I'd smiled. I'd grabbed what warm life couldn't fly away, made short work of it.

Been distracted.

Breath, soft on my ear. "Well met, friend lummox."

Blood had dripped from my chin and coated my chest, made my hands wet and slippery as I'd turned to find the source of the voice. My first thought had been to destroy. My second, to feast.

Until I'd looked into his face.

"You're being stubborn."

The gash was deep, so deep my outstretched fingers couldn't feel its end. I flexed my knees to dislodge Zephyr, then shifted sideways, into the shadow.

The air was stilled here, sound muffled, so I heard the deep steady thud of my own heart. My training had not included medicine or other knowledge, but I knew hearts, how to stop them, how to pull apart their lean dense meat, their taste. I knew lungs and intestines and the startling softness of brain within its bone case.

I possessed such parts. *That didn't make me alive.*

"And what have we here?" I felt Zephyr squeeze by me, his hands feather-soft and warm on my forearms and shoulders. For an instant I could see him, despite the shadows, as light from some unseen source found his face. "Clever lummox. You found a passage!" A surge of movement and he was gone.

I braced myself within the rock, alone in the dark. The cliff engulfed me, as if I rested within its cold, hard womb. I could stay here, listening to my heart, until I starved and died.

Would that be murder enough for my makers?

"Are you coming?"

Why did he insist I survive?

I stirred myself to follow Zephyr.

I was intended to prevail.

They'd never told me whom I would face atop the cliff. Either they hadn't known, or they'd believed it was a foe who could be defeated by talon and fang, overwhelmed by brute force. I'd been given no other weapons, no defense except the body they'd made me and taught me to use.

I remember wondering if I was their first attempt.

"Now that's a view!"

I rocked my little pot of jaff, pretending, to myself at least, my hands were no longer shaking, trusting the rest and spice would restore the strength I'd left in that dreadful hole.

What had been for Zephyr a quick and easy scurry up a shaft, its sides roughened into a natural ladder, had been for my larger, heavier, stiffer self a traumatic birth. I'd had to dig my way through the last of it, force a passage with all the power this body possessed, losing ground with each exhalation as the tightening walls refused my lungs room to expand, leaving blood and scale behind as the rock resisted my every move.

I didn't quite believe I'd escaped.

I put my lips to the spout, unable to hold it steady as the first drips entered my mouth. I licked the burning liquid from my lips and understood something for the first time.

I could fail.

"There!" Zephyr's slender arm shot out like a spear. "The harbor lights at Darphos! Come, lummox. Take a look."

The harbor I'd left the night before held no lure. I took my time finishing the jaff, then put the sphere back in the waist pouch. I'd lost flesh, but not this, during my struggle.

A struggle that had brought me to this wide ledge beneath an overhang of stone. Close to a cave, but the floor was polished smooth, warning it would offer no protection from wind-driven rain or runoff from above.

"It must be a wonderful place, this Darphos." Zephyr continued, gazing outward into the night. "What do they make there? You know a people by what they make."

They'd made me.

Had the people above made him?

I was terror.

My first instructor had dropped to his knees before me, young and new as I'd been, pleading in a language I didn't know. I recall being uncertain. It was the last time I'd felt thus. They'd descended from the walls with prods and hooks to teach me the cost of indecision.

My next instructor had cried out at the sight of me, but she'd been proud and strong. She'd taught me the cost of failing to anticipate an attack.

The other faces had blurred over the years; perhaps someone else had kept count.

When they were to take me to Darphos, to board the ship that would carry me to my fate, I'd felt a stir of curiosity. The world outside my arena was a mystery, populated my dreams with wonders.

My first steps into that world had taken me through the deep, pitted gates to a dusty road. The road had sliced a barren landscape to the horizon, straight as the flight of a bird. At the beginning of that road had waited a pair of great horned beasts cloaked in gleaming metal. They'd been harnessed to an ebony cart set with flags whose searing colors twisted and flailed in the wind.

The beasts had screamed at the sight of me and tried to bolt.

So I'd traveled to Darphos with my head and taloned hands wrapped in black cloth, my huge feet hidden in bags, my grotesque body crouched within a box. The world's wonders remained no more than dreams.

Safe from me.

"Rest, friend lummox, while I name the constellations for you."

I leaned my head against the cliff, my feet hanging in the air, and listened to the warm lilt of Zephyr's voice. I knew the names well enough. One of those who'd walked the upper walls of my arena had taught me, having nothing else to do. No one escaped my arena; no one tried to enter. I'd taken the names in silence and, each night when I'd laid my aching body on the bloodied sand to sleep, cursed them in the privacy of my thoughts. I'd cursed their freedom, their clarity, and most of all, their unblinking witness.

They'd glowed brightest on those moonless nights, while I held to the wall by my talons; they'd watched me fail.

Yet, as Zephyr pointed and named, reciting some fool's tale for each, those shards embedded in the body of the sky became unfamiliar. His voice had a strange power over me, erasing the past, offering . . .

Distraction.

I stood and reached for the overhang, driving my fingertips into its silent stone. By that grip alone, I pulled myself upward and away.

My life had a purpose. He made me forget that.

"Ready to go, are we?" Zephyr laughed. He used my body as his ladder, my head as a step. It was like being climbed by a mouse. Once above me, he leaned down, eyes like stars. "View's better higher up anyway."

I was given a purpose.

It had been so clear at the bottom. Climb to the top of the Dedmas Cliff and kill those I found. I'd assumed I was to feed as well, though I'd wondered if the cliff dwellers would taste foreign or if all blood and flesh was the same once dead.

When Zephyr had arrived, my self-appointed companion, nothing was clear except his presence.

Had I been lonely?

His presence and the towering cliff. They were one in my mind; two halves of a whole. I would have climbed forever, to have him with me.

Was I happy?

Questions I'd never considered. Dangerous, distracting questions.

I began to fear the people of Dedmas had a defense after all, and it climbed at my side.

"There you go. Morning. Time for some jaff, I'd say."

I didn't stop, despite Zephyr's cheery suggestion. The sun was rising, its rays touching the ocean beyond, the island of Darphos, other lands beyond that. It did nothing to brighten or warm the cliff's face.

I climbed faster, reckless, losing my grip and regaining it, driven.

Zephyr easily kept pace beside me. He looked less happy. "You should stop, friend lummox," he urged. "A drink, at least."

I paused to tilt my head into one of the many rivulets streaming from above, catching the water in my mouth. It tasted of soil and mineral; I spat out grit.

"Good. Good. Now take a look. Don't waste this light."

I pressed my face against the rough stone, eyes closed, and reached for a new hold.

His voice, soft in my ear. "For me. Please. Look. So few have seen this."

I could endure any pain, but not his plea. I lifted my head and looked at him, my cheek scraping the rock.

He smiled and flung out his arm as if to encompass all of existence. To forestall an even wilder gesture over nothing, I wedged my leg and shoulder into a crevice and turned so I could look.

We were higher than I'd imagined. Pinwheels of white flashed over the ocean—birds, too distant to see as individuals, dancing in the air. Puffs and streaks of gray hung above them, below us—clouds, I realized.

I looked beyond, and saw that Darphos and what I'd thought to be other islands were connected, one land. Connected to this cliff as well. And this cliff . . .

· It was the base of a mountain, a mountain with sheer, white-clad shoulders that extended as far as I could see.

Nearer was a cup of verdant green, laced to the black rock by vine and artful stonework and a glittering river of white that tumbled into the air. Other cups, like inlaid emeralds, studded the upper rim of the cliff where it joined the mountain. A vertical world, complete unto itself. Beautiful and inviolate.

Where I was to kill.

Zephyr leaned close, blocking my view.

"You do remember, don't you?" he asked.

I had no past.

They'd taken that before they'd taken my body. My earliest memories were of heat and fumes and darkness. I remembered fighting to breathe, then pain coursing through me with each beat of my heart, as if my blood had become fire. My first conscious act had been to scream.

Though I hadn't heard my voice over theirs.

Some unknowable time later there'd been light. I remembered it as dim and moving, as if seen from the depths of the ocean. But no ocean burned like this. Even then, young as I'd been, I'd understood I was being remade and wondered why.

When they gave me a reason, I remembered being grateful.

"You can't stay here."

I ignored Zephyr, who'd tried everything short of falling to gain my attention. I needed to think.

I ignored him, but all my thoughts were about him. My odd companion was the key. Somehow, I knew it.

I puzzled at the shape of his face, its smooth curved lips and wide, gleaming eyes. I considered the free and joyous way he climbed, the strength that must be innate within those deceptively slender limbs.

I no longer wondered why he was here, with me. He belonged to that world, to those emeralds tucked within rock. I was a threat; he was their response.

But he was not here, I decided, to delay me. Or even harm me. He was prince of the cliff. At any time, had it been his intent, he could have led me to a trap or tricked my hands loose from the wall. He had not. In fact, I realized, frowning, he'd saved me twice.

"You're thinking very hard, friend lummox," Zephyr commented. He let go with one hand, swinging idly from the other, his toes tapping against the rock. A perilous game, this high, unless somehow sure of safety.

Or without need of it.

"Clever lummox," he smiled, patting my knee.

I didn't feel clever. I felt as though every reach and hold and pull of the ascent to this moment had ground itself into my flesh, torn my hands and feet, worn my body to the breaking point. My purpose, the goal of my life? The scheming of distant specks. They hadn't seen this place. They hadn't seen themselves from it. They'd feared what they couldn't know.

I felt unmade.

"Almost there," soft on my ear.

I clutched the cliff, flattened my body against it, afraid to take too deep a breath and fall.

"C'mon, friend lummox," Zephyr coaxed. "You're too near to stop now." His fingers collected drops from the wall and flicked them at me. "Thirsty?"

I licked the moisture from my lips and froze. The

water fell from above, from those cups of green. How simple to poison it . . . add a spell of confusion . . . cause attackers to have visions . . .

Mine laughed. "So now I'm a vision?" Zephyr poked me with his toes. "Take that."

Not a vision. A manifestation. *But why this clever, dear sprite of a being?*

Zephyr cupped my face with both hands, brought his so close I could see myself in his eyes.

It was impossible; he stood on nothing.

Yet I didn't fear he'd fall.

"You know," he said gently. "You've known from the first moment you saw me."

He came closer and closer, until the moment came when there was no difference between us and I felt his life fill this body they'd made.

"My life," I said, knowing it was true.

My life as it would have been, should have been, had they not stolen me from this cliff and made me a weapon against my own.

I gazed at the nearest emerald cup, far overhead, imagining its wonders.

One last time, I tightened the fingers they'd given me, crushing the rock held by their hands, hands that dropped free.

Then, being Zephyr, I spread my arms and laughed as I fell.

APPROACHING SIXTY

Mike Resnick and Barry N. Malzberg

"Kabbalah" is a word I can barely pronounce, let alone spell, something like the name "Artismo," which was the appellation of a fancy allowance horse more years ago than I would like to think, or "Secretariat," which was a great horse but had the letter *a* where the *e* should be or vice-versa.

This book containing the Kabbalah is one composed of signs and wonders, mysteries and omens, as my brother-in-law Jake tells me when he hands it to me at a family dinner. This is just as the losing streak approaches sixty, which probably qualifies for the *Guinness Book of World Records*.

At thirty I gave up the *Form* and the *Telegraph* and went to the *Green Sheet*. At forty I started phoning Creepy Conrad and giving him my credit card number in exchange for what he promised was surefire information. At fifty, I even went to *shul* and nagged Jehovah a bit. But as I approached sixty, I was out of alternatives and ready to grasp at anything.

"It could be called an apostasy, Demetrius," says Jake, who spent seven months studying to be a rabbi, before they threw him out when they found him in bed with not one but two blond shiksa bimbos, "to offer you a book of instruction in Kabbalah for a mere losing streak. But I can see that your distress has gone beyond the obvious to the malignant. Following the sport of kings is a dangerous profession and I intuit that you are weak with need." Probably he also intuits it from the two thousand bucks I owe him and can't pay.

There is nothing for me to say in response to this. I could berate Jake for his condescension (but not until I pay him the two large). I could object to his patronizing, to the fact that he has always treated my presence in the family as something of an embarrassment and that he considers my profession with the horses as a disgrace (at least during losing seasons).

But I can also understand that in many ways I have caused Jake and Nate at least as much concern and trouble as they have caused me. So I take the book, a rather limp number, from his extended hand and say, "I am always grateful for advice, Jake, even though I can make no commitment."

"You listen to me," he says, a long-lost rabbinical fervor seeming to crease his features. "You're not supposed to even study this unless you are a man and you are over forty. Women and immature males are excluded. Children are excluded. This is considered too dangerous for a younger man, one whose flames have not been properly coaxed and controlled."

"I am over forty," I reply. "I am in fact forty-nine years of age, as well you know, since I've been part of this family for more than twenty years. My flames are coaxed and controlled"—his sister the yenta can testify to this, and often does, whenever she can find an audience. "In fact, at this moment my flames are in need of spontaneous fuel. Have you ever lost fifty-nine of *anything* in a row? Can you even imagine how this feels?"

It is odd that I make the remarks at that time in that way, because the book itself, this mysterious Kabbalah text which Jake has handed me, seemed to be emitting a strange warmth of its own, an uncomfortable heat that passed from the binding into my hand the way that a rein can slip into the hand of a jockey.

"Do I understand consequence?" replies Jake, and I can tell he's gearing up for a long-distance oratory. "My entire life is consequence. So is yours. So is everyone's, as the Kabbalah makes clear. We are the creations and extensions of a celestial order we can barely understand."

There is much more of this, Jake the accountant often returning to his rabbinical roots when properly encouraged (or even discouraged), but I will pass on the remainder of that conversation, and also on the remonstrations of my wife, Sylvia, and my other brother-in-law, Nate, the nearsighted and color-blind custom tailor, who are both highly displeased when they obtain knowledge of what Jake has placed in my hands.

Sylvia of course has lived with low and high disgust for many decades and has learned resignation, but Nate is blunter and more direct. "Give that back to me," he said, spying the book in my hand and instantly deducing the reasons for its presence.

"It's *my* Kabbalah!" I say. "Go get your own!"

"You're such a *meshuggener pisher* you think the Kabbalah's a book, like the Bible or something by Abba Eban. It's the *knowledge,* the mystic system *within* those pages."

"The book, the knowledge, it's all the same," I say. "It's a system, like betting claimers who are moving down in class, or doubling up on front runners when the track comes up muddy."

"Jake again!" mutters Nate. "What does he think he's doing? Give it back at once!"

"Stay calm, Nate," says Jake, overhearing the conversation. "Demetrius is in need of aid at the present time and this may be a way of bringing him back to the fold."

"Didn't you hear him?" screams Nate. "He thinks it's God's betting system! You are as crazy as you were when you tried to crawl into the ark during Yom Kippur fifteen years ago!"

Well, it goes on like this for hours, but I do not return the Kabbalah, and eventually Nate and Jake decide they have fulfilled today's quota of acrimony and they go home to their wives, and I will now engage in what the Kabbalah text—which I look at briefly in the late evening before putting it to the other side of the bed—calls a necessary pause, an important transition, and point to subsequent events at Aqueduct Race Track in South Ozone Park in the borough of Queens, New York, which followed from my acquaintance with the Kabbalah as the night does the day.

As one of only two or three thousand people in this era of off-track betting who still attends Aqueduct on a regular basis, actually entering the premises, I carry my burden of being exceptional with fair grace and no little trepidation. Fifty-nine consecutive losses will not induce the humility which already comes from being one of only two or three thousand.

Book in hand, eighteen hours after my conversation with Jake, I am standing by the rail watching the horses, nonwinners of two, stagger onto the track. I consult the book denied flaming men and all women and use it to induce a psychic moment.

I pour over the words. I try to make sense of the commands. I attempt to order the mathematics.

And then, suddenly, a very clear voice within my head says: *Five.*

I look around. "Who said that?"

But there is no one near me.

I look at the tote board in the infield and rub the book for good luck.

Five.

The number 5 horse is 17-to-1. I borrow a *Form.* His name is Quanto La Gusta, and he has lost fourteen in a row since winning a claimer at Finger Lakes, which hosts such poor horses that you could throw a saddle on Jake and *he* could come in third if the track wasn't too muddy.

I reach into my pocket. I've got $1,650 left, all the money I have in the world. When I lose this, my profession is done, and I will either have to get an honest job or go to Big-Hearted Ernie, who charges 20 percent interest per day. I look at the board again. The number 5 horse is up to 22-to-1.

"You're sure?" I whisper to no one in particular.

Five, says the voice with the confidence of one who has never lost fifty-nine in a row,

The horses are coming onto the track, and I decide I can wait no longer. I leave the rail, make my way through the crowd, and stand in line at the $50 window. And as I do so, I look at the parallel line to the next $50 window, and I see a Hassidic Jew standing right opposite me, wearing his signature black *shtrieml,* a round fur-trimmed hat decorated with a

feather. He is humbly reading a Kabbalah text, and
he is wearing the humblest $900 black alpaca coat I
have ever seen, and there is an incredible shine on his
humble $300 shoes, and I realize that I have been
wandering in a fool's paradise, that the true answer
was here all along. I want to tell him to hide the text,
that we don't want anyone else figuring out how to
get a direct line to God, because if even half a dozen
big plungers learn the secret, Quanto La Gusta could
go down to 4-to-1 by the time they reach the gate.

I avert my eyes, because I don't want anyone to see
me staring at the book and wondering what I am staring at, and I whistle to myself and gaze alternately at
the ceiling and my feet until I am finally first in line.

"What do you want?" says the clerk at the window.

"I want number 5, thirty-three times," I say.

He looks at me like I'm crazy.

"You're sure?"

"Thirty-three tickets on Number 5, right," I say.

He shrugs and punches a button and out pop the
tickets. I share a secret winner's smile with the Hassidic Jew, and then I go back to my spot at the rail,
right by the sixteenth pole, and wait.

"The horses are at the post!" announces Marshall
Cassidy over the public address system, trying to put
a little excitement into his voice even though this is
just a nothing race for nonwinners of two, and two
thousand pairs of binoculars are lifted into position.

"And they're off!" yells Cassidy.

Quanto La Gusta breaks in the middle of the pack,
but Jose Santos quickly hustles him up to the front,
and as they hit the far turn with half a mile to go he's
seven lengths ahead of the field, and I am cursing
myself for not finding this remarkable book ten
years sooner.

By the head of the stretch he's ten lengths in front, and I can see that he's not even breathing hard—and then, as quickly as he opened up on the field, he begins to shorten stride, and his lead goes from ten lengths to six to three to one to nothing in less than a furlong. As they pass me, with a sixteenth of a mile to run, he's already eighth, and by the time they hit the finish line he is eleventh, and the only horse he has beaten is one that broke down on the backstretch.

I stare dumbfounded at Quanto La Gusta as he trots back on his way to the barn, and I cannot believe it. God *told* me he couldn't lose.

I decide to ask the old Hassidic Jew what went wrong, but he is nowhere to be seen. Finally, on a hunch, I go to the cashier's window. Sure enough, the old man is walking away with a wad of hundreds that would choke Quanto La Gusta.

I walk up to him.

"Excuse me," I say, "but I notice you use the Kabbalah text . . ."

"Yes, I use a Kabbalah text," he answers with a twinkle in his eye.

"And you just won?"

"Baruch Hashem!" he says happily. Praise the Lord.

"Did He whisper a number to you?"

"That's how it works," says the old Jew. "He whispered *seven*, plain as day."

I frown. "You're *sure?*"

He smiles and holds up his bankroll.

"I don't understand it," I say. "I used the book, and He told me to bet the number 5 horse."

The old man extends his hand toward my book. "May I?"

I hand it over to him.

"Well," he says, still smiling. "That explains it."

"Explains what?" I demand.

"I use the *Sefer Yetzirah,* the Book of Creation," he explains. *This,*" he adds, handing the book back to me and trying unsuccessfully to hide his amusement, "is the *Sefer ha Mafli,* the Book That Astounds."

"There's a difference?" I ask.

"The *Sefer ha Zohar* is the Kabbalah for *trotters.*"

He is still chuckling to himself while I try to remember Big-Hearted Ernie's phone number.

BUT WORLD ENOUGH

Sarah A. Hoyt

"The Gods sell all that they give."
—Fernando Pessoa

The one-eyed man sat at the table and rolled the knucklebones of the sacrificed ox. Outside, the wind blew from the mountains and the dry and cold winter of Bythinia settled upon the land. Hannibal Barca's house was deserted. Hannibal had made his way down from his bedroom, with its wide balcony and easy point of access to the vast, empty kitchen, where he sat at the much scrubbed pine table, and rolled his knucklebones by the light of the dying fire. And still he couldn't get an answer.

He'd sent the servants out, long ago. No reason to endanger them as well as himself. At any rate, they were foreigners who could not speak the Punic language and who had no personal loyalty to him, but served only for coin.

And yet, it seemed like only yesterday that Hannibal had commanded the loyalty of crowds, multitudes, of armies and followers. If he closed his eye now, he could almost see behind it, Carthaginians and Africans—

31

and Celts and Greeks too—marching side by side, in massed ranks, a hundred thousand of them marching, with horses and elephants over the Alps, attempting the impossibly daring feat of conquering Rome itself.

Was it the echo of their footsteps he heard when he rolled the knucklebones and heard them hit the scrubbed pine table with a hollow sound? Was it the sound of their shouts in the wind?

No. He pulled his cloak tighter around himself. He knew his hair was streaked with more white than black, his once sharp features made blurry by age and wrinkles. And he knew his arms could no longer hold the sword throughout endless combat. And his legs would no longer allow him to ride over half a continent . . .

And yet, he thought, frowning into the dying fire in his fireplace, and yet, the gods had promised him a great empire. How could he achieve it now? What did it all mean?

He rolled the knucklebones and stared in confusion at the result. The combination of bones, the way they'd fallen, meant nothing. Or nothing he could understand.

He gathered them again into their ivory cup, and flung them once again onto the table. Tanit had promised. And now she must answer him.

"Hannibal," Hamilcar's voice echoed, anguished, somewhere above his nine-year-old son.

Hannibal felt his father's calloused hand on his arm. The emotion in his father's voice shook him. He fought back from the intense light and confusion in his mind, struggled for control of the legs that had given out under him. He held on to his father's hand, drew himself up. He opened his eyes.

And faced the sacrifice—a young bullock that the priest of Tanit had butchered upon the altar. The altar was in a courtyard, where the whitewashed walls of the other rooms of the temple—the reception room, the holy inner room, the priest's area, formed three sides of it. The fourth side was open, on the side of the mountain that faced the city of Carthage.

Brilliant sunlight of summer shone from whitewashed wall upon whitewashed wall of the great African city, making it glare like a shameless jewel. Amid the houses, people moved, dark haired and light of limb. Farmers and merchants and scholars. Phoenician and Libyan and Carthaginian and half a dozen other nationalities.

Beyond the city, in the sparkling blue bay, boats of many lands sat at anchor, come to sell and buy and trade with the greatest traders on Earth.

In that moment, a great engulfing love for Carthage came to Hannibal. He understood, just enough, dimly, to know it wasn't his, but the love of something . . . something that linked to him, that was in his mind, that made him long for Carthage as men longed for women, as a hungry child might long for a sweet. *All this,* a voice in his mind said. *All this might have been lost. And more.*

It wasn't a voice, really, more of a buzz, a tension, a feeling like . . . like what happened when thunderbolt threatened and your hair stood out from your head. Hannibal's head seemed to vibrate with it, to become filled by it. And his legs failed him again.

"Hannibal," his father, Hamilcar, said. This time he was grasping his son by both arms, trying to make him stand.

As from a great distance, Hannibal heard the priest speak. "It will be demons. You didn't have a child pass through the fire and now demons will take your oldest son. You mark my words." .

Nonsense, the voice-feeling in Hannibal's mind buzzed. *Nonsense. Not demons.*

Things that Hannibal's too-young mind—more schooled, as well-born Carthaginians were, in the traditions of Greece than those of his own people—had never known flooded him. He looked around, the scene diffuse in his sight as though a dazzling light shone behind his eyes. His head pounded with an ache that wasn't an ache.

This morning he'd come to the sacrifice glad only that his father thought him old enough to go with him. Now he knew everything about it in a way he could never have dreamed. They were here to offer sacrifice and beg the lady to grant his father, Hamilcar, and his brother-in-law Hasdrubal a good start to their new colonies—what they hoped would be their new empire—in Spain. Hannibal had just been admitted to the rites, though perhaps a little too young for them.

The linen robe they'd made him wear, so different from the Greek chiton he normally wore at home, seamless and long-sleeved, had made him feel stupid when they'd walked to the temple. It no longer did. He knew it was proper to wear Punic attire to address a Punic goddess, come to Carthage from ancestral Phoenicia with Queen Dido centuries ago. And he knew the voice in his head was the goddess addressing him—him, personally.

He would have been overwhelmed by the honor, only the goddess didn't seem to be trying to honor him. She, whose image was so sacred that she was usually represented by a circle with two lines for up-raised arms, had a message for him. A message she'd been trying to convey when, as the bull lay dying, she'd entered his mind and made his legs weak and his head spin.

But the message wasn't real words, and Hannibal had to struggle to make them words. It was, Hannibal suddenly understood, the problem of an eternal being trying to speak to a mortal one.

"Now he'll twist in a fit," the priest said. He was a small, bald man, his eyes narrow and spiteful. "And he'll forever be possessed by demons."

"Not . . . demons," Hannibal managed. The words seemed to take up his whole breath and he had to struggle for more.

". . . too young for this," Hasdrubal said. "He's just too young."

And no doubt, Hannibal thought, running his gaze over his brother-in-law's black-bearded countenance, middle-aged and already running to fat, *it would suit Hasdrubal very well if I were too young. It would suit him even better if I were truly in the grip of a demon.* Because Hannibal was the oldest son of the great general Hamilcar. The real heir to the great fortune of the Barca family. His brother Hanno was but an infant, and yet subject to the many forms of demon likely to take a baby suddenly in the night. Until their late births, Hasdrubal, handpicked by Hamilcar to marry his oldest daughter, had been Hamilcar's right hand and stood in place of an heir to him.

This Hannibal knew, suddenly, without surprise, though there should have been surprise. Up till now, it had never occurred to the boy that Hasdrubal would benefit by having him out of the way. He'd always thought Hasdrubal merely a kindly older man, with sons close to Hannibal's age.

Now, as he struggled for breath under the weight of revelations, Hannibal looked at his father—an older man, tanned and beaten by a thousand storms, a million battles. Hamilcar had fought the endless, punishing war against the Romans. And he'd come home to quell a military revolt which had cost him the life of his second in command and best friend, Gisgo. Now, his hair white, his eyes burning with bitterness amid a nest of wrinkles, he looked at his oldest son, the hope of his old age.

Hamilcar was setting out, away from Carthage, away from the Senate of Carthage which had thwarted his campaign against the Romans through insufficient funds. The Senate, which had caused the mercenaries to revolt by trying to cheat them of their pay at the end of the war. He was setting out, at an age when most of his peers would be settling into contented senescence, cradling grandchildren on their arms, to try yet again to create a place where he could stand free and defend himself without the constraints of the weak-kneed Senate.

And Hannibal knew what the goddess had told him, in the words that were no words. *You must go to Spain with your father. You must not leave him. You must learn from him the art of war. You must attack Rome, relentlessly.*

"Why?" he asked the clear air, the voice inside his head, the terrace-built houses of Carthage. "Why?"

Because you will create a great empire, an empire that will mold all of the future, the voice in his head said. *Because you will be remembered forever. Immortal. Like Dido.*

"Why?" the boy asked again even as his elders looked at him, with varying degrees of amusement and shock. The priest was babbling something about speaking to no one.

Because it is your fate, the voice said.

And with that, Hannibal's mind and eyes cleared, his legs stood beneath him, his once more. And he looked at his brother-in-law, at his father, at the still babbling priest.

"Quiet," he said to the priest. His voice echoed with the steel and fire of battle, with the command of a great general. It was his father's voice in the piping tones of a young boy. The priest stopped, mouth agape. Hannibal turned to his father, whose hands were still on Hannibal's shoulders, holding him up. "I am well, Father, it is only that in the moment the sacrifice died I knew my fate."

"Your fate?" Hamilcar asked, letting go of Hannibal's shoulders.

Hannibal nodded. "My fate is to go with you to Spain, to learn to command your army from you. And when I'm a man, I shall make war on Rome. Rome shall never know peace while I live. And I shall make Carthage a great empire that will echo to the end of history and make men remember—"

Hannibal realized suddenly what moved his father, and he smiled.

"—your name forever."

There was a moment of silence, and Hamilcar looked at his son, eyes wide. For just a moment, Hannibal wondered if his father was going to order him put to the fire—his throat slit, his body burned, his ashes buried in the shrine of the goddess—as was often done to children who proved defective. They were given as sacrifice, to keep the other children healthy.

But then Hamilcar threw his head back and laughed,

an uproarious laughter rare in the man who had spent his entire life battling ruthless enemies, half of them within his own city. "The goddess has given you a grand fate, has she not, Hannibal?" he said.

Hasdrubal huffed impatiently. "He is but a child," he said. "And we are not taking him to Spain with us. He will stay here, with his mother, learn the traditions of Carthage, and become a proper man before he joins us."

And by then, Hannibal thought, Hamilcar would be dead, Hasdrubal would have seized control of the colonies in Spain, and his brother-in-law would be Hamilcar's heir for good.

"No," Hannibal said, the force of his new knowledge behind him. "No. You will take me."

And his father, a smile playing on his lips, looked at Hasdrubal. "Do not forget," he said, "who is the head of the family and the general of all-mighty Carthage." Then he smiled at his son. "I think I will take you with me, Hannibal. I think I will."

Hannibal bowed solemnly. "Then I can promise you I'll always be an enemy of Rome," he said. As he spoke, he could feel the goddess withdrawing from his mind, leaving behind the feeling of a job completed.

"You are out of your head," twenty-five-year-old Hannibal told Hasdrubal. "To be accepting Roman treaties."

They were in Hasdrubal's house, a broad house, built of stone and whitewashed, like the houses of Carthage, with a vast terrace open to the breezes of the Mediterranean.

Hasdrubal sat on this terrace, upon a low-slung chair with broad arms. He wore Greek clothing—as did they all except when addressing the gods—which in his case consisted of a very fine chiton of what seemed like a most delicate peach color and—from the bit showing on his left shoulder—either silk from the orient or the finely spun byssos from the isle of Amorgos, for which the ladies of Greece pined and swooned. The himation was of just as fine stuff and embroidered all over with tiny red flowers.

He'd been reading a scroll when Hannibal stormed in, and now he let the scroll fall from his fingers and looked up at Hannibal, a half smile with which an adult might indulge the tantrum of a spoiled child on his lips. "Hannibal," he said in a voice of soft censure.

Hannibal threw his head back and squared his shoulders. "No, answer me this, *brother*." The title, which under the law he was supposed to use for his brother-in-law, dripped from his tongue laced with sarcasm, reminding Hasdrubal that however close to the family he might be, he was no Barca. "I heard you received Roman envoys. And you agreed to conquer nothing north of the river Ebro. Why are you accepting limitations from the Romans on the building of your own empire, *brother*?"

Hasdrubal sighed. He rose from his chair with a jangle of the silver bracelets on his arm. He pulled the himation looser over his broad paunch. "Hannibal," he said. "You are young."

Hannibal glared. He could feel the glare burning out of his eyes. "I might be young, but I'm my father's son," he said. "My father would not want us to deal with the Romans. Ever."

"Your father," Hasdrubal said, speaking softly, "dealt with the Romans, Hannibal. He signed the treaty of Catulus, ending the war."

"But you would sign a treaty without even warring." Hannibal paced in front of his brother-in-law, who stood stock-still and watched him, frowning. "You signed the treaty in vile submission before anyone demanded that you submit."

"Hannibal," Hasdrubal said, and put his hand on Hannibal's shoulder where his short soldier's garment—his chalmys—fastened, leaving his skin uncovered and his shoulder and arm free to wield his sword. "We have enough of an army to worry the Romans. We have enough of an army that they're not demanding we leave Spain. That, I know, is in great part your doing. You've trained them. You've led them. And the Romans are not trying to attack us. They merely want assurances we will not attack their precious Saguntum, the city they consider a friend of Rome; all else, we're free to do. Unspoken in the treaty is the understanding that we're allowed to control the rest of the territory south of the Ebro. They will not hinder us in this. And then, perhaps, we can strike at Rome. Or perhaps simply squeeze her out for commerce."

Hannibal glared at Hasdrubal and shook Hasdrubal's hand from his shoulder. He could understand the truth of his brother-in-law's statement. He could understand the facts behind his talk. In some ways what Hasdrubal proposed was more of a Punic way. To slowly strangle the enemy with commerce. To reduce the enemy to dependence with smart bargaining.

But it was not what Hannibal wanted. And it did not accord with what he remembered of the goddess inside his head. *You will create a great empire,* she'd said. *Your name will be remembered.*

If they went with Hasdrubal's plan they would eventually win out. Or at least, perhaps they would. The Romans were in many ways a plodding people, less flexible and certainly less adept at winning the loyalty of those in whose lands they had colonies.

Carthage stood at least an even chance of taking over Spain, of colonizing the vast land and converting the Greeks and Celts already living here to the Carthaginian way of life and Carthaginian culture.

But by the time that soft victory came, Hannibal would be long dead, his name forever forgotten. "It is not what my father would want," Hannibal said. "It is not what my brothers would want. My brothers and I—"

"Your brother Hanno is sixteen, Hannibal, and your brother Mago is twelve and still with his teachers. What can they have to do with this?"

And now Hannibal lost the temper he had long held back, and stomped hard with his sandal-clad foot upon the polished rock of Hasdrubal's terrace. "They are sons of Hamilcar, as I am! And they know he would want us to make incessant war upon the Romans!"

"No," Hasdrubal said softly. "No, Hannibal. You want that. Your father never did. And Hannibal," Hasdrubal drew himself up, pulling himself so that despite his growing corpulence he affected a military and proud bearing. "I am the commander of the armies, by election. And you are just my younger brother-in-law."

Hannibal took a good five breaths, in offended silence, before he could collect himself enough to storm out of Hasdrubal's house in a temper.

The temper carried him all the way into his own house, where he ignored the soft voice of his wife,

Imilce, calling his name, and ran up the stone stairs to his own quarters, his own room. There he took deep breaths to calm himself, but in vain.

Instead, he started pacing, hands clenched. He'd made the army. He'd made it what it was. An amalgamation of mercenaries, of Libyans, of recruits from nearby friendly Celtic tribes, it stood at near forty thousand men and it was far from the ragtag mercenary force his father had once commanded against the Romans. These men knew Hannibal, had seen him grow up and trusted him, were loyal to him with their own lives.

He'd always thought that was the gift of the goddess to him, that he had the ability to lift men's hearts and souls, to win them to his side with his words, and they would follow him with enthusiasm. He certainly was better than his father at it.

And yet the one man that Hannibal couldn't persuade was Hasdrubal. And Hasdrubal had been elected to command the army when Hamilcar had died, because Hannibal had been only seventeen and was too young to be in charge. Now Hasdrubal was in charge until he died. And though he looked older, and going to fat, he was only twenty years older than Hannibal. By the time he died, Hannibal himself could be well advanced in middle age, and not in the state to make any of the war on Rome he'd promised the goddess he would.

Leaning on the cool wall of his chamber, he pressed his closed fists hard against his temples, where pain burned as though something were trying to burrow in. Or his anger were trying to crawl out. He pushed his hands hard, knuckles biting into his skin. *Please,* he thought. *Please. Lady. I want but to serve you.*

But how can I when this . . . soft merchant bars my way and would barter away our chances at an empire?

From outside the house came the sound of screaming, a sound that grew nearer. Someone pounded on the front door. It was opened, then closed again, hurried steps upon the stairs. Imilce screamed, a short scream, and then, "I'll tell him."

His room door opened. "Hannibal, Hannibal," Imilce said. "Your brother Hasdrubal is dead."

Hannibal opened his eyes and brought his hands down. "Hasdrubal?" Hasdrubal had looked no more likely to die soon than he'd looked likely to take flight. "Dead?"

"A Celt killed him," Imilce said, her dark eyes brimming with tears, her dark hair disheveled as though she'd torn at it, though she'd had little contact with Hasdrubal. "With a silver knife."

"Hasdrubal?" Hannibal asked again. "Dead?" In his mind he thought of the goddess reaching out her powerful arm. Now Hannibal would be the commander of the armies. And he could do her will.

"There are Romans," Imilce told Hannibal as he returned, muddied and bone-tired from his campaign north, as far as the river Douro, to consolidate his holdings and solidify his domain over the loose confederation of tribes that occupied that wild land.

It was fall now and the steady-falling rain of that region, with the bone-chilling cold that accompanied it, had got into Hannibal's body so much that even the week back to his more southerly domains, as he approached Cartagena, hadn't seemed to dispel the chill. Indeed he'd ridden back faster than he surely should, more desirous of warmth than even of his wife's company.

Now he stood in the entrance room to his house, his brother Hanno just behind him, still chilled and covered in mud. He wanted his bath and his bed. He wanted Imilce and calm. Instead there was this.

"Romans?" he asked.

"A delegation of them. All very proper," Imilce said. "Important people."

"What do want they with me?" he asked. That the Romans might be alarmed at his relentless campaigns since Hasdrubal had died, he didn't doubt. That they might find this sudden Carthaginian obsession with war and fighting—when before they'd been ready to deal—disquieting, Hannibal could well imagine. But why would they send him a delegation? Did they not know, was it not the word everywhere, that he was a sworn enemy of Rome?

"They will wait," he said, "until I've had my bath." He walked past Imilce before she could object, and all the way up the stairs to his chambers, where the servants had set warm water and oils and his clothing. He unwound his cloak from his chilled body and bathed, with the aid of two body servants.

When he was done, he rejected the clothes laid out for him—a chiton and soft himation, which he might very well have worn in the house. In their place he demanded just the rough wool chiton that he wore in battle, and which he fastened to his shoulder and side with a serviceable fibula. He'd go to see these Romans dressed as a soldier.

Outside his door, already bathed and similarly dressed, Hanno waited.

Together they went to face the Romans, who looked

like fat merchants and who introduced themselves as
Publius Quintus Sanguntinus and Marcus Illius Sextus.

Imilce, ever the housewife and hostess, had served
them olives and pomegranates served in silver dishes
mined from the region. One of the Romans had
dripped pomegranate juice down the front of his tunic,
staining it purple.

"You wish to see me," he said, sitting down.

"Yes, my lord," Sanguntinus said. "We come at the
behest of the Roman people."

"The Roman people will always have my ear," Hannibal said. And said it without irony. After all, hatred
was, much like love, a devotion, a constant attention
to the other.

Sextus fidgeted. "We would like to request, my lord,
that you not . . . that you leave Sanguntum in peace.
For it is a friend of Rome."

Sanguntum. Several discordant thoughts ran
through Hannibal's mind. Sanguntum was, after all,
on the south side of the Ebro, and Hasdrubal had said
that the contract left that to the Carthaginians. And
the Romans were asking for peace for Sanguntum.
That meant that they believed he would be within his
rights to attack it.

He stood up and smiled. "I will grant you, gentle-
men, that I've not in the least changed my intentions
toward Sanguntum this last year."

One of the Romans opened his mouth as though to
ask what those intentions were and what it all meant,
but Hannibal was smiling, the smile so broad on his
face that it almost made his features crack. "But
you've waited long, and you're probably tired. Let me
call my wife, and she will make sure slaves bring you
wine and food and whatever else you desire."

They couldn't ask while he was being hospitable, and in two hours they were too drunk to ask. By the time they sobered all they would remember was that Hannibal had been hospitable, and therefore that he could not possibly mean to attack Roman interests. They would only remember he was a friend.

"And what mean you to do about Sanguntum?" Hanno asked while he and Hannibal walked amid Hannibal's olive trees.

"I mean to take it," Hannibal said. "It is to the south of the Ebro, and even by Hasdrubal's dealing, ours to take."

Hanno gave Hannibal a worried look. "The Romans aren't likely to take it calmly."

"The Romans," Hannibal said, "can take it as they will."

"Carthage has been given an ultimatum by Rome," Hanno said, breathless, coming into Hannibal's study, where Hannibal was playing with his year-old son, Hamilcar. "They said they can let fall from their breast either war or peace."

Hannibal scarcely looked up. His decision, if such it was, had been made long ago, when the goddess had told him that his fate was to always be an enemy of Rome. "Well, then we'll snatch at the war and let the peace go." He positioned Hamilcar on his knee and bounced him up and down gently. The baby smiled, letting a thin tendril of drool fall, which Hannibal wiped with the back of his hand.

Even while doing it, he was aware that his brother had stopped, unnaturally still, like a statue.

"But," Hanno said, "you can't mean it. We've lost two wars against Rome. We are not prepared . . ."

Hannibal smiled. "But we are. I've had it all

planned a long time. We will do what no one has ever done. We will march into Italy and attack Rome."

"Into Italy?" Hanno asked. "What ships will take us there?"

"None. We will march by land, over the mountains."

"You are mad, brother."

Hannibal looked up. "If madness is greatness, then I am. The Celts cross the mountains all the time to raid the northern part of Italy. Don't fret. It can be done." He grinned wide. "We shall do it with elephants."

Hanno backed up blindly, to sit on a chair near Hannibal. "With elephants?" he said.

Hannibal laughed at his tone of surprise, and on Hannibal's knee Hamilcar giggled the rounded giggle of a contented baby.

My son will be master of an empire, Hannibal thought. The goddess had promised, and he trusted.

Hannibal crossed the mountains with horses and elephants and forty thousand followers. Some elephants and some men had died in the crossing, but Hannibal could hardly regard that as important. His decision had been made long ago, and if the goddess was with him, then these losses were inconsequential.

As though to prove his blessing from Tanit, almost immediately men from nearby tribes attached themselves to him. They more than compensated for the ones he'd lost. He pushed on.

In the marches of the Arno, he lost an eye to a chill that became a raging fever. This, though marring forever the countenance that his wife had loved, also meant nothing. He must continue. It was his fate.

He plundered Arretium. The city of Capua, second

only to Rome in glory, deserted Rome to stand by Hannibal's side. Latins, Umbrians, Sabines, and Picentines stood against him in vain.

In Rome, human sacrifice was practiced for the first time in centuries—two Gauls and two slaves were killed to appease the gods. It meant nothing. They could not stand against the power of Tanit.

On the shores of Lake Trasimene, he won a great victory and near Cannae in early August—with Magus's help—he defeated the Roman legions and cut them to pieces.

But the Romans were in Spain now, and laying waste to the careful empire that Hannibal had started building there. And Hannibal didn't have enough men. Never enough men.

It was then that he started using the knucklebones, from an animal sacrificed to Tanit. He would roll the bones and read the result. Since the goddess was no longer in his head, he had to roll the dice to find what she meant him to do.

He rolled the dice when, early one summer, news came to him that his wife and son had been killed by a fever—a result of the chaos of war in Spain. And the knucklebones told him to press on. He expounded to the goddess on his lack of men, on the fact that not enough Celts were crossing over to his side and that the Italianate tribes remained deaf to his appeals.

But the knucklebones said, *Press on.*

He rolled them again when Syracuse rebelled and aligned itself with Carthage. And again when news of his brothers' deaths reached him. And again when the pestilence swept the Carthaginian camp and destroyed their fighting force, leaving Hannibal with even fewer men.

And he rolled them, yet again, when, trying to protect Capua, he attempted to divert troops from laying siege to his allied city by making sorties on Rome itself, with his elephants. This failed. The Roman Senate apparently knew that the walls were far too strong to be breached.

At long last, bitter at heart, Hannibal left Italy. He left it to defend Carthage itself. The knucklebones could not be lying. As they could not be lying when they told him that he must sue for peace after his defeat.

Hannibal hadn't understood—he still didn't understand—but he knew the goddess would not deceive him.

An enemy of Rome, not forgotten by the wrath of her people and her rulers, he moved from principality to principality, trying to hide, trying to live a little longer, trying to spy an opportunity from which to charge again. Because it was his fate to make war on Rome and to win and to create a name for himself.

In Bythinia, at the end of the world, the winters were as cold as the summers were parched, and before the snows fell, blanketing the mountains, the wind came, carrying just a few flakes, biting to the bone of the old man Hannibal had become.

For a couple of years—he disdained to count the years of his exile—he'd lived here, with his comfortable house that contained nothing of himself, served by men who worked for the money alone and did not know, nor did they care, whom they served.

And then there had been rumors of Romans. Romans had tracked him down and with Bythinian complicity—or indifference—paving their way, they had gathered in the nearby city. One by one they'd trickled up, over the last few days. There was a veritable detachment of them surrounding his home.

They thought—and he couldn't say they were wrong—that he had been encouraging the king of Bythinia to rebellion.

And now there were dozens of them outside. *Dozens to kill an old man.*

Hannibal had sent his servants away. A great general, as he remembered his father teaching him, risked men when risk was necessary. The rest of the time, he tried to save the lives of those who served him, even if their service involved lighting fires and cooking meat, and their loyalty was to gold and not to him.

All alone here, in his empty kitchen, he rolled the knucklebones. And he got no answer. Or no answer that he could understand. The symbols the bones formed on the scrubbed pine were always the same. The symbol for completion. The image of something done.

Hannibal shook his head. He wasn't done. If he were done, Rome would be defeated and Carthage would be the great power in the world. Or at least that offshoot of Carthage which was his beloved Cartagena in Spain.

But he wasn't done. He got up and poured himself a cup of wine from a flagon hanging on the wall of his kitchen. It tasted sour, not like the wine he'd drunk in Italy while he commanded his troops. But he drank it anyway, against the bone-biting cold.

Without the goddess and her promises, he would have stayed in Cartagena, by the Mediterranean Sea. He could imagine it now—even in this season—bathed by mild breezes and the warm waters of the ocean.

He could imagine the terraced houses—which might now be all destroyed by the Romans—reflecting the sunlight. And children running and playing in the dusty streets.

If he hadn't fulfilled his promise to the goddess, his son might have been one of those children. But no. By now Hamilcar the younger would have had children, and perhaps given his father a cloud of grandchildren to play with and bounce on his aged knee.

Hannibal surveyed his knee where it showed, bony and scarred, beneath his chiton. He drank another cup of wine and tossed the knucklebones again.

And again the symbol was for completed. And for accomplishment. He'd accomplished nothing. From outside, he could hear the steps of his enemies and voices calling as they walked around the shuttered house, seeking entrance.

Was that the front door giving, as they applied shoulders to it? And how long till they decided to set fire the house and roast their old enemy alive? And what could the goddess mean by all of it?

I mean you're done, a voice said. *And well done. You have fulfilled your fate, Hannibal Barca.*

His head hurt, as it had those many years ago in Carthage. His eyes seemed blinded by a light that shone behind them. "I have done nothing," he said, his voice reedy and wavering. "I have done nothing, save cause the loss of Carthage and of all my family."

The light resolved itself into a figure. A female figure, drapery enveloping the voluptuous curves, the arms raised as the arms of the goddess were in the only sketchy representations of her that Carthage allowed.

Hannibal's mouth felt dry and tight. *The wine,* he

thought. *One of the hired servants poisoned my wine.*
It was such a Roman trick to buy the demise of enemies by bribing their servants that he could almost
have laughed. Only he couldn't laugh past the tight-
ness at his throat, and it was too late, and his chest
hurt when he inhaled.

Oh, but you have done everything I told you, Tanit
said, her voice sweet and soft in Hannibal's ears like
the voice of his Imilce in the short years of their life
together.

He tried to shake his head, though it hurt him. He
fought with all his might against the workings of the
poison in his body. He wouldn't die. He didn't have
an empire. He was not ready to die.

By your actions Carthage was lost, Tanit said. *By
your actions Rome learned the power of final conquest,
of total destruction of an enemy. It has shown them
how to be ruthless. And how to win. From now on,
nation after nation will fall under the heel of Rome.
And Rome will last long enough to forever be part of
the civilization of men.*

In his mind's eye, Hannibal saw Roman statues,
Roman clothing, Roman poetry in lands beyond those
he could even imagine. He saw many languages de-
rived from Latin.

But you promised I . . . he thought. He could no
longer talk.

*I promised you would never be forgotten. And you
won't. Wherever Rome is mentioned, so will be the
name of her greatest enemy.*

Hannibal wanted to laugh or cry or scream at the
depth of Tanit's betrayal. But his mind, working fast,
and with all it had left, reminded him that he was
Carthaginian. Carthaginians were first of all mer-

chants. In any deal, you had to make sure that you were getting what you thought you were.

Hannibal and Carthage itself, Hannibal now realized, had been nothing but a sacrifice in the gods' games of power.

But if he'd lost a bargain, he'd lose it like a Carthaginian. He shrugged off his flesh like an ill-fitting cloak and crossed over to the arms of the radiant goddess, laughing at his own foolishness.

He'd got exactly what he'd bargained for.

CONSIGNED

Alan Dean Foster

"Why are you so determined to go to hell?"

Crouched down behind the fold of reef, Menno kept his bubbles small and deliberately unobtrusive as he whispered a reply to Codan. "All my life I was told that I was destined to go to hell. It was a determination that I accepted willingly. What has always astonished me is that no one else shares my desire to do so."

Holding his spear steady as he floated parallel to the sandy bottom, his friend spoke while intently eyeing the parade of passing polosto. "How awkward it must be for you to find that the rest of the world is so terribly afflicted with sanity."

"Always the sarcastic one." Menno joined his friend in patiently watching and waiting as the school of unaware polosto continued to drift nearer. "Sarcastic and apathetic."

"I am not at all apathetic," Codan assured the other hunter. "I am adamantly opposed to the very notion. Didn't you ever realize that the suggestion was not to be taken literally? People are often told to go to hell. None of them ever takes it as a personal challenge.

At least, none until you, my friend." Upon concluding this observation he exploded forward over the top of the reef and thrust madly with his spear. With their cover thus broken, Menno had little choice but to follow.

Even so, he had to admit that Codan had chosen the moment well. The polosto had come in very close to the reef, enabling both hunters to spear good-sized specimens before the school could flee. As the impaled prey writhed on the polished lengths of zek shell, unable to flee or reach around far enough to bite the hunters, the two Tyry enjoyed eating their prey alive. There was, after all, nothing a true Tyry enjoyed more than eating. Beginning with the tentacles, a true delicacy, the pair soon worked their way down to the polostos' internal support, a single expanding spiral of bone.

The rest of the carcasses and all of the polostos' internal organs were saved and stowed in drag-sacks of woven absab weed. These would be towed home to be distributed among members of both males' extended families. Once the two hunters had eaten their fill, they turned away from the outer reef and began the long, steady swim homeward. Timing their departure from the reef to the changing of the current allowed them to make steady and relatively easy progress.

"Why don't you come with me?" Using a right-side tentacle to flick aside a persistent cluster of parasitic keleth worms, Menno swam a little closer to his friend. His strong, broad, four-lobed tail made short work of those keleth who persisted.

"What, to hell?" Using one webbed tentacle, Codan gestured disparagingly. "I wish you would drop this enduring mania, Menno. It was already becoming tiresome years ago." Using his spear, he prodded a likely looking hole as he swam past the opening. If it had been home to a tasty foudan, the angry invertebrate would have displayed itself and its anger immediately, an appearance that would have led to its becoming an instant appetizer. "Much as certain members of the community might wish it, you are not going to hell, however much you persist in pretending to continue to humor their requests."

"Well, don't say I didn't give you the chance." With a half flip of his tail, Menno moved out ahead of his friend.

Turning his head slightly to the right so that he could focus one eye completely on the other Tyry, Codan flicked his own tail and caught up. "What are you talking about? What 'chance'?"

Menno slowed deliberately, dropping down beneath his friend in a gesture of polite deference. They were very close now to the place he had chosen for the attempt. "I'm going. This evening." Raising two of his four webbed tentacles, he extended them rightward. "There."

Backfinning, Codan halted. "Now you're scaring me, Menno. A joke's a joke, but you're not bubbling laughter." Having turned, he now found himself staring in the direction his friend had designated.

Instead of being composed of sand or reef or storm debris, the indicated bottom was smooth and solid; all rock, with nothing growing or hiding on it. Other than a distinct greenish tinge, its most notable characteristic was a remarkably unvarying upward slope.

"I have been all the way to the end," Menno declared proudly. "To the terminus. To the place where the real world ends. The slope continues on and on, the greenstone ascending steadily until it breaks the sky—and passes beyond it to enter hell. I am certain of this."

Turning away from the unvarying slope, Codan stared at his lifelong friend and hunting partner, turning to regard him first out of his left eye, then the right. "You're not joking, are you?"

"I am quite serious." Menno gazed back at him.

Coming close, Codan studied his companion's upper body. "Your eyes are clear and unfogged, so you have not been eating the purple kalis that grows in the lower caves. Your words are precise. Only your thoughts, it seems, betray any madness." Having rendered this opinion, Codan resumed swimming.

Menno caught up to him easily. "Since others told me that I was destined to go there, I have always dreamed of being the first Tyry to visit hell and return."

"Easy to visit." Codan gestured with his left tentacles. "Impossible to return."

"Not any longer. I have devised an apparatus."

That brought Codan up short. "An apparatus?" He held up his spear. "*This* is an apparatus, and a very effective one. But it cannot get me to hell and back. No artificial construct can do that."

"I have prepared for this all my life." Menno's tone was confident, assured. "You'll see. I will show you tomorrow morning. If you won't join me, will you at least come to observe? Without a credible witness there will be none to believe me."

"Bereave you, you mean." Reaching out, Codan draped a tentacle around his friend's upper body. "Be a sensible fellow. We've made a good catch, we're

bringing back ample food to share, and tomorrow is
another bright and beautiful day. Enough of this talk
of going to hell." He made a gesture that was reflective of his innate sardonicism. "We all get there
sooner or later anyway."

"If you won't come . . ." Menno's voice trailed off
tersely as he kicked hard with his tail lobes.

"I didn't say that." Codan rushed to catch up. "I
suppose I must. As a friend and hunter-brother. Someone has to be there to revive you."

"Thanks." Menno entwined one of his own tentacles around that of his friend. "As a moment of histor-
ical importance it will be in need of recording."

"A moment of hysterical importance," Codan cor-
rected him—but gently, for he was truly and hon-
estly concerned.

The morning of the following day dawned clear and
sunny. The atmosphere was bright, cool, and devoid
of current. A perfect day for visiting hell, Menno assured his friend. Or rather, friends, for Codan had
insisted on bringing Kedef along. In addition to being
senior to both of the hunters, among the Tyry Kedef
had an impeccable reputation for honesty. Whatever he
reported would be believed. This was the reason Codan
offered for inviting him, anyway. In reality it was a sub-
terfuge, a way for him to enlist the aid of a respected
elder in trying to talk Menno out of what was seeming
to be more and more an inescapable insanity.

"Even if you could somehow enter hell and survive," Kedef was muttering as the three males swam
parallel to one another in the direction of the greenstone slope, "you are sure to be eaten by a demon."
He turned reflective. "I commend to you the tale of
Ses-Haban."

Ses-Haban was a mythical Tyry of ancient times who had dared to swim high enough to gesture contemptuously at the inhabitants of hell. According to the legend, he had thrust two tentacles completely out of the real world and into that terrible nether realm. What he sensed there was unknown, because as soon as he had done the unbelievable deed, a demon had promptly bitten off both offending limbs.

Singled-minded of purpose and determined to fulfill the urge that had driven him since childhood, Menno would not be dissuaded. "Ses-Haban, if he existed, was unlucky."

"Ses-Haban, if he existed," Codan suggested brusquely, "was stupid."

"Where is this apparatus of which you have spoken?" the elder inquired. Codan did not try to conceal his surprise. Was Kedef showing interest?

"You will see it soon," Menno assured him. "I've had to work on it in secret, when away from the community." Having reached the flow of greenstone, he was leading them downslope. "Jeers and jibes do not bother me, but there are those whose fears exceed their common sense. Had they known what I was about they might have tried to interfere with my work." He twisted his upper body to look back the way they had come. "They might have tried to stop me."

"You can hardly blame people for fearing hell," Codan reminded him.

"People fear that which they do not understand," the other hunter riposted.

"Often with good reason," Codan added. But this time, Menno did not respond.

The entrance to the small cave had been camouflaged with loose reef growth and rock. Working with all four of his tentacles, Menno pulled the rubble aside. From the dark interior he extracted a thick, perfectly transparent tuzaca shell. But it was not the classic spiral tuzaca shape. A deformity had produced a shell that took the shape of an elongated bubble.

Kedef's tone as he studied the product of the younger Tyry's labors was admiring. Codan realized to his horror that the elder's presence was starting to have the opposite effect from what he had intended.

"You have modified this," Kedef declared with conviction as he eyed the unusually formed shell. "In several places, it would appear."

Gratification suffused Menno's reply. "Yes. See here, where I have smoothed the base after removing the animal?"

Kedef's tentacle ends tiptoed appraisingly over the exterior of the crystal clear shell, stopping at a round opening. "And what is this hole for? It is not natural."

"No. I made it. That is where the voyoupa intestine goes."

Shells and intestines. Codan was beginning to wonder if he was going to have to use force to put a stop to this lunacy.

As he and Kedef looked on, Menno extracted another shell from the cavity in the rocks. This one had a lid. When opened, both sight and smell identified the shell's contents. Codan's tentacles recoiled. The shell contained chisith innards. Sticky and stinking, they were violently expelled by a chisith whenever it was attacked or disturbed. Entwined in the viscous strands, a preoccupied predator would pay no further attention to the chisith, allowing that simple creature to scoot safely on its way. What possible use could Menno have for such a pot of scavenged goo?

He proceeded to show them.

Working with a silicate spatula, he daubed chisith innards all over the upper part of his body, careful to stay above his tentacles but below his head. Taking up the large tuzaca, he then carefully pulled it down over his head so that its base rested against the painted line of chisith guts that now encircled his upper torso. The gummy chisith innards gripped the base of the shell. Menno then brought out a long coil of voyoupa intestine. Additional chisith innards were pasted both inside and outside the round opening he had made in the tuzaca shell. One end of the intestine was passed through the hole. More chisith innards were added to the outside. Within seconds it had been tightly sealed in place.

"You perceive how this apparatus works?" he asked boldly. Though muted by the intervening shell that now enclosed his head and upper body, his words remained intelligible.

Codan had composed a choice response, but Kedef spoke first. "I think so, somewhat, but still . . ." The elder's voice trailed off into uncertainty. "I am not sure I understand the proper function of the length of intestine."

"The principle is very simple." Clutching the coil of intestine in two tentacles, Menno used another to hold up the end. "There is no atmosphere in hell. Only searing heat. Studies suggest that a Tyry can endure the increased temperature for some time before it begins to adversely affect the body. But this point is moot in the absence of breathable atmosphere." With his remaining free tentacle he reached up to tap the outside of the transparent tuzaca shell.

"The adhesive chisith insides form an atmospherically tight seal between my upper body and the tuzaca shell. The latter is presently full of perfectly breathable atmosphere. When I venture into airless hell, I will carry my breathable atmosphere with me."

"It won't last you more than couple of minutes," Codan pointed out relentlessly. "Studies suggest *that,* too."

"Which difficulty brings us to the purpose of the voyouda intestine." Once again, Menno waved the open end. "There is a very small hole near the base of the tuzaca shell. Once in hell, it will leak atmosphere. It is designed to do so. As exhausted atmosphere bleeds out, I will use the tube formed by this intestine to suck fresh atmosphere into the shell. Bad atmosphere out, good atmosphere in." He eyed the two other Tyry; one old and thoughtful, the other young and alarmed.

"What if this crazy setup fails on you?" Codan demanded to know. "What if the chisith seal fails, letting the atmosphere inside the shell all out at once? What if you can't suck in fresh atmosphere fast enough to replace the old?"

"Then I will still have time enough to return to the real world." Menno's confidence had not deserted him. Indeed, Codan thought, the closer his friend came to suicide the more assured he appeared to become. "I will only need a minute or two. If it comes to it, I can hold my breath longer than that."

"It is an astounding and bold notion." Kedef hovered in the water above the smooth greenstone, his tail moving lazily back and forth to hold him in position against the current.

Codan turned on the elder. "You are not actually going to give your blessing to this madness?"

Turning to one side, Kedef eyed the younger Tyry with his left eye. "It is not a matter of giving the blessing or the withholding of it. Menno is of age. I cannot and would not try to stop him. Besides, everyone in the community knows he has spoken of a desire to fulfill the requests of many ever since his tail lobes were first formed." He looked back at the obviously proud Menno. "Triumph rewards the audacious."

"There is audacity," Codan pointed out, "and then there is folly." But by this time Kedef was paying him no more attention than was his friend.

So thoroughly had things turned around that Kedef helped Menno to secure the length of intestine to the hole in the tuzaca shell. Codan refused to lend a tentacle to the final preparations. Even at the speed he could swim, it was too far to race back to the community to raise the alarm. He could only hope that the foredoomed experiment would not destroy his friend.

When the last of the preparations were concluded, Menno turned a slow circle in the water. "How does it look?"

"Everything appears tight and secure, young boldness." Kedef's tone was full of encouragement. "How is your breathing?"

Holding up the open end of the voyouda intestine, Menno waggled it back and forth. "No problem."

"Of course there's no problem," Codan growled. "He's still in the real world." But it would not be long until that boundary was tested.

He and Kedef followed as far as they dared. They trailed behind the self-assured Menno as the latter swam upslope with even, powerful strokes of his tail. Soon they were in the shallows, and still Menno continued swimming. Onward and upward. Codan realized that further pleading was of no use. His friend was determined to go through with this. It was, after all, the fulfillment of a lifelong impulse.

Drifting together side by side, he and Kedef watched in fascination as Menno kept swimming, swimming, just kept swimming, until all they could see was the hunter's lower body, then just his tail, and finally not even that. He was well and truly gone. Gone into hell itself. But the end of the long coil of voyouda intestine trailed behind, whipping slowly back and forth in the slight current that marked the boundary between hell and the real world.

"Do you think he's still alive?" Codan finally asked after an interminable several moments had passed.

"I think he must be." There was wonderment in Kedef's voice. "If he had been eaten by a demon, then I would think the piece of voyouda would have fallen back into the water by now. A demon would either pull it out or let it go, but not maintain a constant length. Think of it! A Tyry, moving about in hell itself, observing and recording for the first time! What tales your friend will have to tell us when he returns. What unprecedented sights he will have seen!"

Codan said nothing.

More time passed. It seemed impossible that Menno could have survived so long beyond the sky. The waiting was taking its toll on both him and Kedef. They had been half rocked to sleep by the current when his eyes suddenly dilated sharply.

"There! By the Line of Otos, he's coming back!"

Upslope was indeed the familiar shape of Menno that was coming in their direction. But something was wrong. The atmosphere-retaining tuzaca shell was still in place, glued securely to the hunter's upper body by the gooey chisith innards. The upper end of the voyouda intestine was still sealed to the hole Menno had artfully drilled in the shell. Despite this, the intrepid explorer was not swimming normally. His tail was not moving. Tentacles as limp as strands of ncasa weed, he drifted partway toward them before being caught by the current.

Codan and Kedef did not hesitate. Taking deep breaths in case hell should come after them, they swam rapidly upward, grabbed hold of the motionless hunter, and dragged him down into deeper, safer water.

"Menno!" Codan was tugging and flailing at the tuzaca shell. When it would not come loose, he pulled his knife from his waistwrap and used it to cut through the spongy, solidified chisith. With Kedef pulling, they soon had the shell off. Still Menno did not respond.

When he saw why, Codan whirled and lost the undigested remnants of his morning meal. Even the venerable Kedef was forced to momentarily turn away. Only when both had managed to overcome the initial shock were they able to turn back to regard Codan's friend.

Menno was dead. That had been immediately apparent. It was the particularly hellish means of his passing that had so shocked them. The driven explorer's entire upper body was burned dark, as if he had been shoved into one of the underwater volcanic vents that dotted the far boundaries of the community's territory. His eyes had been boiled away. Codan tried to imagine his friend under that kind of assault, reeling from the unexpected fiery pain as he struggled to make his way back into the water. With his eyes gone

he had probably lost his way, and had only stumbled
back into the real world when it was too late. Stumbled, or fallen and rolled downslope.

But the tuzaca shell, full of cooling, soothing atmosphere, had survived intact and still sealed in place.
What had gone wrong?

"I cannot imagine," Kedef murmured in response
to Codan's query. "I have not the kind of specialized
knowledge necessary to posit an answer to that question." Drifting in the water, the somber elder considered the dead, burned body. "Yet his lower body,
beneath the shell, shows signs of only slight wrinkling.
It is almost as if in some way the tuzaca shell that was
necessary to sustain life somehow contributed to its
destruction. If this attempt is to be repeated, the matter will require considerable further study."

"Further . . . ?" Codan gaped at the elder. "You
don't mean that you're going to suggest that another
Tyry try this?"

Kedef responded with a gesture that was difficult to
interpret. "You are yet young, Codan. A thing once
tried is destined to be tried again. Wiser Tyry than
you or I will discuss what has happened here today
and seek ways of overcoming it. There will always be
those who feel they have no choice but to push at the
limits of the possible. There will always be those who
from an early age will be urged to go to hell, to the
point where they come to regard it as their destiny."

Codan was quiet for a long moment. When he spoke
again, it was with renewed admiration for his deceased
companion. "Well, all is not lost today. In his passing
Menno has provided me with the opportunity to fulfill
a long-held desire of my own. To eat a close friend."

Kedef gestured understandingly. "A laudable, if not

especially revolutionary desire. I will assist with the hauling."

Together they towed the body of the dead explorer back to the community. The story of his valiant effort, temporary success, and subsequent demise was the occasion of much discussion and debate. In the end, the effort was accounted a modest success. After all, there were leftovers.

MY GIRLFRIEND FATE

Darwin A. Garrison

Nelson Wong glanced around the edge of the heavy steel fire door into the sunlit Seattle alley that skirted the uphill side of the parking garage. Less than twenty feet away, partially concealed by a Dumpster in a shaded corner, a pile of cardboard and restaurant garbage moved fitfully in time with a wet snuffling sound.

"Ghoul, you think?" Given the soft, feminine nature of the voice behind him, most men would have felt a warm thrill of excitement. All Nelson could feel at the moment was a light pain behind his eyes and a stomach-churning irritation . . . that, and the overwhelming *wrongness* of a dark fae in the wrong place at the Wong time.

"Well, duh," he whispered back after forcing a derisive snort. "I can feel the disruption from here. Can't you?"

A piqued sniff came from behind his head. "I don't do *vibes,* Nel."

Nelson allowed himself a tiny victory smile. Moira hated being reminded that he was better at this aspect of his part-time job than she could ever be. Considering what a pleasant mess she'd made of his life since turning up, he had to take his satisfaction wherever he could find it.

"You could have stayed in the car."

"All you have are those saccharine anime sound-track CDs. I'd tear my hair out in less than five minutes."

"There's the radio."

"Thirty seconds. Ten if I accidentally tune Stern." A pair of slender arms encircled him, followed by the feel of a well-endowed feminine chest pressing against the back of his oilcloth duster. "Besides," a warm breath whispered into his right ear, "I have to make sure nothing happens to you. Don't I, lover?"

The tongue that darted into his ear worked like a detonator in the plastic explosive of his temper.

"Sweet Jesus!" He threw off Moira's arms and spun around to face her. Without resistance, the spring-loaded heavy door slammed home with a hollow *clang*. "I am *working* here! Can't you be serious for even five minutes?"

"Never," she told him with her trademark half smile, half leer on her full lips. "You're just too damned sexy." It was that same expression, along with her striking violet eyes, glittering golden hair, and sensuous curves that had started the fiasco that currently passed as his life. Now he knew better, although if she had been wearing the same bikini as she had back on that beach in Greece . . .

He shook his head violently to clear that particular memory out of his mind before tilting his head down and pressing the fingertips of both hands to his forehead.

"You are so frustrating sometimes!" When he swept

his hands away from his face, he was able to see Moira's feet poking out from beneath her designer jeans. As in, really see them, painted toenails and all, through the spaghetti-thin crimson straps of her shoes. He looked back up into her eyes, disbelieving.

"You wore *heels* on a hunt?"

Her smile was dazzling.

"Aren't they the most darling thing? I mean, sure, they don't show my calves off as well as the Giorgios but they're so much more comfortable. And the red. I mean, they just draw attention."

"Attention?" Nelson said, still stuck between disbelief and detonation. "You generally don't *want* to draw the attention of the things that I have to deal with. It's bad karma. What the hell were you thinking?"

She pulled her left foot back behind her right calf, dropped her chin, and twisted up in her very best shy-little-girl pose. "I was hoping that . . . after the hunt and all . . . well . . . dancing."

"Dancing?" Nelson wanted to yell, but when Moira did the whole pose thing with the lower lip and the fluttering eyelashes and . . . "O, sweet Mother Mary. Dancing."

"We haven't gone in a long, long time, honey," she cooed as she reached out to take his elbow. "There's this new club in Kirkland. I hear about it all the time. C'mon. Take me after this. Please."

"Look," he began reasonably, "I'm probably going to end up smelling like cordite and sweat before we're done here. That's why I always like to shower after a job. Besides, I don't dance unless—"

He stopped and cocked his head quizzically at her. "Tell me you weren't going to slip me some more of that crap you got from your aunt."

The way Moira's eyes darted to one side along with the flush on her cheeks spoke volumes. Then her eyes flashed back to his as another disarming smile curved her lips.

"Aphrodite's such a dear."

"For crying out loud!" he bellowed, his temper finally fracturing. "How can you justify doing that to me again?"

"It was fun!" she shouted back. "Besides, you can be such a stick in the mud without a little *help*."

"It was a week! When I finally came to my senses, I couldn't walk! You're damned lucky we aren't parents!"

"Like I'd mind!" she snarled back with a vehemence that rocked Nelson back on his heels. "You should try listening to your biological clock tick for three thousand years! There's nothing wrong with—"

A tentative scratching came from the door.

They turned in perfect synchronization and stared.

"Oopsie," Moira whispered. "Was there a handle on the other side?"

"Um, not sure."

"Car, you think?"

"Oh, yeah."

Nelson reached out to guide Moira away from the door and back through the garage toward their car. As soon as he heard the click of her heels against the concrete bustling away from him, he backpedaled himself, swinging his SPAS assault shotgun up from beneath his duster as he moved.

"This is all about to go pear-shaped," he muttered as he jacked a shell into the chamber and aimed the weapon at the door, "I just know it."

*　　　*　　　*

Ten steps of attempted running were all that it took
to convince Moira that Nelson had a point about the
heels. She slipped out of her shoes, snatched them up
by the straps in a smooth twirl, and jogged toward the
car at a much faster pace. Seconds later, Nelson's
SPAS roared to life in the darkness behind her and
she sprinted.

"This is going to be murder on my pedicure!" she
snarled aloud and dodged a roof pillar to follow the
down ramp back to the car. They had parked halfway
between the downhill street entrance and the uphill
side alleyway where they had just spotted the ghoul,
which was the same place where the paper said the
murders had occurred. She had to admit his ability to
pinpoint disruptions was getting better and better.

Now if only he could get paid for doing this Boy
Scout crap.

But as she turned onto the ramp and the car came
into sight, her train of thought shifted radically. The
sight of two female figures standing casually by the
silver Magnum slowed her to a walk. Stopping well
outside of arm's reach, she nodded her head.

"Addie. Cleo. This, um, isn't a real good time."

Addie, the elder of Moira's two sisters, quirked a
wry eyebrow in reply. With her silver hair pulled back
into a severe braid and dressed in a dark blue Armani
business suit-skirt combo, her trim figure practically
screamed authority and competency. Cleo, on the
other hand, was far more comforting in her stylish
torn jeans and jacket, with a bright red Che Guevera
T-shirt peeking out. She had chosen to dye one half
of her normally dark brown bangs neon purple as well.
Moira's little sister gave her a cheery wave along with
an impish teenaged grin.

Looking back to Addie, Moira shook her head. "Really. I mean it. This isn't a good time." Accenting her statement, the SPAS barked again on the level behind them, followed by a string of Chinese expletives and the sound of running bootsteps on concrete. Moira winced as both of Addie's eyebrows lifted and Cleo covered her mouth in wide-eyed shock.

"Does he talk like that all the time?" Addie asked mildly.

Moira shrugged. "Depends. Like I said, bad timing."

"Well, all you have to do is give me the scissors and we'll leave you to your business."

Moira shook her head and crossed her arms. "Sorry. Not happening."

Cleo tugged on Addie's sleeve. "You said we were going to dinner as a family. You promised."

The elder sister brushed Cleo's hand away. "Not now."

"And you promised not to fight."

"I promised to *try,*" Addie said in exasperation. "Moira's not making that easy."

"No, I'm not. Now excuse me." With that she strode directly at her sisters and bulled between them.

"Rude!" Cleo snapped. "You could have asked."

"I'm a bit pinched for time," Moira shot back as she tossed her shoes onto the roof of the car and beat on the side of the muscular-looking station wagon with her fist. "Yo! Gunner! Wake the hell up!"

"Gunner?" Addie asked as she stepped away from the car. She gave the darkened windows a sidelong glance. "There's someone in there?"

Moira, busy patting down her pockets, nodded. "You could call him that. Damn it! I think I left my

keys in my purse." She reached out to smack the tailgate with her open hand. "Gunner! Up and at 'em!
He's gonna need shells!"

The tailgate popped open without warning, almost
clipping Moira and the curious Cleo both in the chin.

"Put a sock in it, blondie," said a sullen, gravelly
voice from within. A web belt bandolier filled with
crimson shotgun shells shot out into Moira's waiting
hands. "Your boyfriend's gonna be fine." With that
the tailgate slammed shut again.

"Rude!" Cleo shouted back before turning back to
Moira. "Who the hell was that?"

"Like Addie said, it's *somebody*," Moira replied
with a sigh. "And *rude* is just his way. You get used
to it . . . sort of." Cleo turned a doubtful expression
on the tailgate while Moira spun back toward the
ramp. Before she got two steps away, though, a vise-
like hand clamped on her left bicep.

"The scissors," Addie said in a soft, cold voice,
"Now."

Moira shook off her sister's grasp and spun to face
her. "What part of *no* don't you understand, sis? You
never use the damn things anymore, for pity's sake.
Why are you so hot to have them back?"

"They're my responsibility."

"Your symbol of power, more like. Just get used to
sharing for a while!"

Addie's hand drew back and a spinning ball of purple lightning snapped to life beneath her fingertips.
Moira shouldered the bandolier and crossed her arms,
bringing a flickering wall of translucent cerulean to
life between the two.

"No fighting!" Cleo shouted at the pair, followed
immediately by a panicked shout from up the ramp.

"Moira! Shells!"

A faint smile crossed Addie's lips as she slowly lowered her hand. "Your master calls."

Moira straightened. "Get your vocabulary right," she said sweetly. "The correct term is *lover*."

Nelson let the SPAS dangle on the shoulder rig so he could dig into his coat pocket for the car keys as he ran down the ramp. The thumping distraction was ill-timed. By the time he became aware of the tense little scene near his car, he had already lost any reasonable opportunity to run back toward the ghouls.

"Oh," he stammered as three pairs of stressed eyes turned toward him. "Cleo. Addie. Hi. Um, this is a really bad time." No doubt Addie's stare would have frozen him solid if she had retained any significant power in his world.

"So I've been told," she practically growled. Cleo's expression, on the other hand, turned from misery to heartfelt relief. She darted around Moira and sprinted forward to grab him in a fierce hug.

"Nel! Make them stop! They're fighting over those damned scissors!"

"Again?" he snapped as tried to pry Cleo off. "This really isn't the time or place for that!" Glancing down at her face, he spied a sparkle of silver in her right nostril. "Is that a nose stud?"

"You're not going to give me crap about that right now, are you? This is serious! I told Addie not to fight, but she won't listen to me. She never listens to me!"

"They're not sanitary, you know? Besides, aren't you allergic to silver?"

"It's nickel!"

An angry hissing echoed down the ramp from the upper level.

"Oh, crap," Nelson muttered as he finally got Cleo loose. He pushed her toward Addie and Moira and reached under his duster to grab a canister off his web harness. "You guys will want to get behind the car, cover your ears, and open your mouths." Moira grabbed a sister in each hand and dragged them behind the Dodge. Seeing that she had things well in hand, he turned back to the ramp and pulled the pin on the flash-bang grenade.

"God," he prayed as he let the paddle spring free, "please let these bastards be really, really stupid." With that he hurled the smoking green cylinder up the ramp toward the gathering cloud of ghouls. Before the bomb had even cleared the ramp, Nelson was on the move. He ran back to the car and rolled across the hood, landing with a bone-jarring *thud* behind the front wheel just as the grenade detonated.

The blast shook free dust and flaked concrete from above them, coating everyone with a fine grit. Fortunately, they were far enough away that none of the vaporized silver nitrate, iron filings, or saltwater reached any of his fae charges.

Getting up on his hands and knees, he took quick stock of the little group. Addie and Cleo both looked a bit like surprised owls, wide-eyed and dusted with white. Glancing up, he felt a little thrill of pride when he saw that Moira was already back on her stride, systematically dusting off her hair, peasant blouse, and jeans while wearing an expression of vague irritation.

"You're really something, you know that?" he told her, the warmth he felt washing away his earlier frustration. Her irritated expression disappeared into a private smile.

"Dancing. I'm serious now."

"Bath first?"

"Kinky. I like it."

"If you two are done verbally feeling each other up," Addie broke in, "I think your new friends are regrouping."

Nelson let out another string of his grandfather's choicest words. Catching sight of Cleo's shocked expression, instinct kicked in and he just managed to jerk backward out of range of Addie's open-handed swing.

"What the hell?" he snapped at her.

"Watch your foul mouth, you heathen! There's a child present!"

"Heathen? Look who's talking, you refugee from a Greek—" Moira's wildly waving arms and vigorous head shaking caught his attention. Gritting his teeth, Nelson choked his temper back under control. Best not to tempt Fate . . . any of them.

He stood up with a jerk and pulled his keys out of his pocket. "Fine," he said in a flat voice before pressing the unlock button on his key fob. Reaching between Moira and Addie, he opened the back door. "Get in."

"What?" Addie huffed in affronted shock.

"Get in. The damn. Car. We're leaving."

The hissing was starting to gather up the ramp again as Addie and Cleo scrambled into the backseat. An odd echo caught Nelson's ear and he turned his head down the lower ramp to sort it out. There, a second ball of darkness was gathering just outside of a puddle of sunlight near the exit tollbooth.

"Moira," he said softly when he took the bandolier off her shoulder.

"Hmm?" she answered as she gave him a warm kiss on the cheek. He held up the keys in front of her nose.

"You're going to have to drive."

"Ooh!" She snatched the keys from his hand with a gleeful expression on her face. "I finally get to drive the hemi!"

Nelson focused on trying to keep an encouraging smile on his face while his stomach was busy crawling into his boots. Somehow, despite Moira's gleeful chuckling and rush to adjust the driver's seat, he suspected that it came off forced.

Oh, my aching insurance premium, he mourned silently.

Six liters of Detroit's best iron grumbled to life next to him. Before the engine could even settle into a smooth idle, Moira opened the throttle up twice in quick succession, revving the motor to an ear-splitting howl each time.

"At least give it a couple of seconds to get the oil pressure up!" he snapped while dashing around the front to get to the passenger door.

"Yeah, yeah," she shouted, adding a flippant hand wave. "Listen, studly, get in, sit down, shut up, and hang on. I am *so* up for this!"

The moment his butt hit the passenger seat, Moira shifted into reverse and floored the accelerator. The tail of the Magnum spun back and to the left, almost flinging Nelson out onto the concrete. She stabbed the brakes, bringing the abbreviated power slide to a door-slamming halt that left the nose of the car pointed up the ramp.

"She calls this driving?" Addie wailed from the backseat as she struggled off the floorboard in front of Cleo and back onto her seat.

"That was cool!" chimed in the securely seat-belted Cleo. "Do a doughnut next!"

"Don't encourage her!" Nelson snapped as he pulled shells from the bandolier loops and stuffed them into the SPAS. "Drop the passenger window, Moira!"

The movement of the Magnum had drawn the attention of the ghouls. Their massed darkness was already flowing down the ramp toward the momentarily stationary car. Nelson could only assume that the second ball of darkness below was flowing upward toward them as well. He disconnected the SPAS from his shoulder rig, jacked a fresh round into the chamber, and shoved the gun through the passenger window opening.

"Go!" he yelled to Moira, then pulled the trigger. The SPAS jumped in his hand and a ballistic path opened in the dark wall ahead. He jerked back into his seat, fully expecting a V-8 roar and a sudden surge of acceleration.

Instead, he heard Moira saying, "Hi, Timothy! What's up?"

His head ratcheted left, inexorably drawn to stare at Moira, slack-jawed, as she finished fitting her wireless earset, her BlackBerry carefully slotted in the center console.

"Well, I told you that the prices would do that. Why can't you ever just do what I say the first time?" She looked at Nelson with a raised eyebrow, *What?* expression.

He bunched his shoulders and gestured out the front window, his brows pulled together in his best

Remember this? expression. Moira rolled her eyes and dropped her hand to the gearshift, pulling the lever into drive with a click.

Business, she mouthed, her eyes flashing dangerously.

Nelson drew the index and middle finger of his right hand across his throat then pointed back out the windshield where the ghouls were closing the gap in their ranks.

So? she mouthed. With that, she floored the accelerator. The engine roared through his open window. Smoke clouded the air to the sides and behind as the Magnum broke completely free and spun up to speed. Tires squealing, the car surged forward up the ramp, Moira smoothly cranking the steering wheel left to offset the drift of the tail.

"Look, Timothy," she shouted over the mechanical cacophony, driving the Magnum practically sideways up the ramp toward the swirling mass of ghouls, "it's a simple option-out deal. If you can't handle a little variation in the details then I'll find someone who can."

"Moira!" shrieked Addie as the side of the car began to blow through the diaphanous substance of the ghouls. Vague faces with sharp teeth and disembodied clawed hands slammed into the windows then splashed into smoking goo. The hissing that had previously characterized their gathering foes changed to a howling wail of confusion and horror.

"Gross!" Despite her disgusted pronouncement, Cleo was watching the ghoul-smashing show through the window with obvious glee.

"We left the Beyond to get away from creatures like this!" Addie snapped back at her while clawing her way across the seat toward her little sister.

Moira feathered the throttle just a tad, allowing the tires to hook back up with the concrete. The Magnum straightened out and surged forward, bouncing Addie off the seat back then onto the floorboard with an outraged squeak.

For a moment, the ghoul-splatting continued on the windshield. Then a white face twisted with anger passed before them and Moira was spinning the steering wheel right to avoid the onrushing wall of the parking garage.

"Where to?" she shouted. "No, not you, Timothy!"

Nelson jerked his thumb up. "Head for the roof!"

"Was that her?"

"I think so, yeah. We need some room, so get us topside."

"Her who?" Addie asked from between the front seats.

"Best guess is she used to be Carmen Voistra," Nelson told her as he slipped another shell out of the bandolier. "Bit of a local legend."

Another corner loomed and Moira put the Magnum into an abbreviated power slide. As she cranked the steering wheel, a clunking noise came from the roof above Addie and Cleo.

"Gunner!" Moira howled. "My shoes!"

The tailgate lifted even before Moira had finished. A dark shape swung out from under the cargo cover to land on the roof with a thump as Moira straightened the Magnum out for its charge up the final ramp to the rooftop lot. Then the process reversed itself as the shape returned and slammed the tailgate shut again.

"Did you get them?"

"Yeah, yeah," came Gunner's rumbling reply. "Try to keep your head screwed on next time, toots."

The shoes appeared between the two front seats next to Nelson's head, dangling by the heel straps from a jet-black clawed hand.

"Yo, N-man," Gunner chuckled, "your custom silver paint job's hosed . . . again."

"Gee. Great news. Thanks," Nelson said as he turned to take the shoes. At that moment, he caught sight of Addie's horrified, blood-drained expression. She took in a deep breath and he knew without a doubt what was coming next. "Oh, crap."

"Imp!" Addie screamed at the top of her lungs, thus kicking off a World Fae Federation cage match in Nelson's backseat.

If Gunner had just tossed the shoes up front, he probably could have gotten away clean with only minor hearing loss. However, in his enthusiasm to tweak Nelson about the damage to the Magnum's finish, he had inadvertently exposed his stocking-capped, knobbly head out from under the cargo tonneau. A born scrapper, Addie took advantage of not being restrained by a seat belt to curl up on her back and start kicking the living bejeezus out of the imp's head and shoulder with her black patent leather pumps. Not to be outdone in either panic or reaction time by her elder sister, Cleo let out a battle scream of terror that ululated in time with the overhead blows of her clenched hands smacking the imp in the face.

"Ahh!" the two demi-goddesses shrieked in unison, over and over again, at ear-splitting volume.

"Help!" howled Gunner. "Get 'em off of me! Get off! Oof!"

"No magic in the car! Ixnay on the agicmay!" Nelson yelled when he caught a flicker of purple coming from Addie's fingertips.

"No, Timothy, we're not having an orgy!" Moira snarled, "And you most certainly may *not* bring your boyfriend to join in!"

All things considered, Nelson could have just let the three fae in the backseat duke it out until the car had at least stopped. Even as he twisted around to restrain Cleo's fists of doom, he had a vague suspicion that he should stay out of reach and let things come to a natural balance. The moment he got hold of Cleo's wrist on the upswing, though, the entire situation spiraled out of his control.

With the bludgeoning to his head at least temporarily restrained, Gunner took advantage of the change in action to use his free hand to grab one of Addie's ankles. The elder sister screeched in outrage and twisted to throw her arms around the headrest of the driver's seat . . . and Moira's throat.

"Get it off! Don't let it eat me!"

Gurgle! Moira would have said more, but air is generally required for conversation and Addie had just cornered the market on her younger sister's personal supply. Nelson heard the engine roar and knew his girlfriend had stiffened up against the accelerator while trying to escape Addie's choke hold.

"Lady, you're too damned stringy to eat! Just quit kicking me!"

"Addie! Let go!" Nelson shouted as he tried to pull her arms away from Moira's throat. "She's driving!"

Nelson believed that in every knock-down, drag-out, fur-ball fight there came a point where a single moment of clarity could change things for the better or the worse . . . or maybe just point out how incredibly stupid all the participants really were for forgetting certain key facts. That instant of epiphany for this particular scrap came when the Magnum launched full throttle off the top of the roof ramp and, for a fleeting second, everyone involved felt the unmistakable stomach lurch of ballistic weightlessness, thus simultaneously remembering that they were on the top floor of a five-story parking building.

Four separate voices and one choked gasp combined into a single howling chorus of panic.

The screaming stopped when the Magnum slammed back down on the rooftop parking lot. The front left tire hit first, slewing the vehicle sideways into a spin as the other bits of its suspension made contact. During their brief moment of flight, Moira had somehow managed to get her foot off the gas and onto the brake, so the sound of squealing rubber and the smells of hot iron and friction pads suffused everything inside the car. Nelson, Gunner, and Addie bounced around the interior like Ping-Pong balls in a washing machine as the dynamics of the spins had their way with them. Features of the roof lot flashed by, repeating themselves once, twice, three times before the big Dodge rocked to a final groaning halt mere inches from the far retaining wall. The rumble of the V-8 coughed to a stop with the click of a key.

Nelson counted five heartbeats of silence before the mutters and moaning began. At that point, he was willing to concede that they had, in fact, cheated death. Since he had somehow ended up facedown on the front passenger seat floorboard, he used his right hand to open the door before rolling out onto the pavement in a relieved heap.

"Timothy," he heard Moira wheeze from inside the car, "now is not a good time. Just deal with it." There was a soft beep and then the earset sailed out Nelson's door and clattered across the concrete. He pulled himself up on the rocker panel and gave a disheveled Moira an ironic grin.

"Rough day at the office?" Her answering glare only made her that much cuter in his eyes.

"Oh, shut up."

Chuckling, Nelson pushed himself off the ground as the door behind him swung open. Cleo staggered out, took two steps, and then collapsed onto her hands and knees.

"You okay, kiddo?" When she looked up at him, Nelson got the distinct impression that the green of her complexion and the purple of her dye job clashed.

"If I wasn't me," she told him miserably, "I'd puke."

"Hang in there, Cleo. At least the ride is over." He turned to pound on the roof of the car. "Yo, Gunner! You still with us or did you take an express back to hell?"

"I'm good, Nel," came an entirely too cheerful gravelly chuckle. "Real good, in fact. Soft landing you might say."

That doesn't bode well, said a little voice in the back of Nelson's mind right before a low feminine moan transformed into a squeal of outrage.

"Get your face off my chest, you pervert!"

"Oh, honey," Gunner said in what, for him at least, passed for a seductive voice, "for an old broad, you've got one hell of a rack. I think I'm in love."

"Are you moving your hips?" Addie shrieked. "Get off right now!"

"Gunner," sighed Nelson, "quit scre . . . messing around. Get your polished black ass in the back and get me a claymore."

"Killjoy," muttered the imp. Still, Nelson could hear him moving to get in the back, followed by a relieved female sigh. Seconds later, Addie's door popped open as the elder sister escaped into the late afternoon sun. She stood up, straightened her skirt, brushed a stray strand of hair out of her eyes, and then shuddered violently. With that, a bit of her composure returned and she was able to turn and glare at Nelson.

"I. Need. A. Bath."

He pulled a stick of gum from his inner coat pocket, peeled the paper off, and popped it in his mouth.

"Join the club. You can have it after Moira and I are done." He banged on the roof again. "Hurry it up, Gunner. You're burning daylight!"

The tailgate popped open and a familiar black arm deposited an obviously homemade square box by the side of the car. "Yeah, yeah. There it is. Like letting me have a bit of fun would have mattered."

Nelson closed Cleo's door and walked back to pick up the box. "You never know," he said calmly toward the still open tailgate. "Not too much longer until the shadows of these buildings get long enough. I think we're about to be hip deep in soul eaters. Hey, don't those guys report back to your old boss?"

The tailgate slammed shut and Nelson couldn't help but chuckle. For a political refugee from hell, Gunner had all the self-preservation instinct of a lemming unless you pointed things out to him. Gigging the imp was yet another of the little joys that made his day complete.

"Nel?" came Cleo's tremulous voice. He looked up and saw her standing several feet away with a none-too-sure expression on her face.

"Yeah?"

"Something doesn't feel right about this."

"She's right," Addie chimed in from the front of the car. "This isn't some random tear in the fabric between worlds."

Nelson sighed as he hooked up the "clacker" switch to the wires leading from his homemade anti-fae claymore mine. "I know."

"And I know, too," Moira chimed in from the driver's side of the car. "That's why you asked me to come with you today, isn't it?"

He grabbed hold of the handle on top of the box and stood up, turning to look at her. The concern in her eyes touched him to his very core. Despite the fact they bickered and shot sarcastic little jabs at each other every day, he knew that she loved him every bit as much as he loved her.

"Why do we fight so much?" he asked her.

"Balance," she answered without hesitation. "Otherwise we'd form a singularity and black holes are bad for tourism."

"Touching little love scenes aside," Addie broke in, "what's causing this?"

Nelson shook his head to clear his thoughts and began walking back toward the ramp. "I think we've got a binding going on."

"Eh?" Cleo asked in surprise. "You mean some human cut a deal?"

"Looks like it," Nelson said as he started counting paces. When he reached twenty-five, he set the box down on the concrete, turning the side with the words THIS SIDE TOWARD SPOOKS in the direction of the ramp. He then began walking back toward the car, spooling wire off the back of the box as he went.

"This Carmen Voistra wasn't a very nice person,"

he told Cleo and Addie as he walked back. "In fact, she was pretty damned near the devil incarnate."

"Hey!" came a muffled protest from the interior of the Magnum.

"Relatively speaking. No offense, Gunner."

A haughty sniff echoed out of the car. "None taken."

Nelson chuckled as he opened his door. He looked up at Addie. "You'll want to be either inside the car or behind a door. Your choice." He turned his head to look at Cleo. "You too, squirt.

"Anyway, during the course of a rather colorful criminal career, she managed to acquire quite a collection of enemies, most of whom shared her more . . . peculiar tastes in violence and revenge. They caught up with her in an alley right next to this parking garage."

He sat down on the edge of the passenger seat and looked up at the buildings surrounding them as the shadows lengthened in the waning daylight. "The cops found twelve dead men and women clustered around a systematically dismembered female corpse that had been raped and abused multiple times before it was carved up. The twelve surrounding bodies showed no discernable cause of death." He paused to blow a bubble with his gum and pop it.

"I think Carmen reached through the veil while she was being tortured and made a deal with a dark fae boss of some kind. She became a gate in exchange for revenge against her enemies."

"That's not good, Nel," Cleo said. "She'll be tied to his power."

"Yup. Plus she's using that ball of ghouls like a shield. We're going to have to strip them away before we can get at her."

The shadows that had been creeping across the roof moved closer and closer to the ramp entrance line like the shadowed arms of night reaching to open a door. A familiar hissing sound started to grow from the darkness of the ramp.

"Showtime," Nelson said as he stood up. He looked back across at Moira. "You ready honey?" She winked and blew him a kiss.

"Piece of cake."

The shadows closed on the entrance at last and the black cloud that defined Voistra's shield of spirits flowed up and out of the ramp. Nelson watched the white dashed lines disappear beneath the boiling mass faster and faster as they approached the claymore. Finally, he dropped behind the door and lifted the clacker.

"Fire in the hole!" he shouted and smacked the switch three times out of habit. The mine detonated with a muffled thump and thousands of fragments of rock salt mixed with silver and iron shot into the black cloud. The concussion rocked the car and set his ears ringing but, by the time he got up, Moira was already on the move.

A wind crossed the roof and drove the lingering smoke sideways along the parking lot as Moira dashed forward. She reached behind her back with her right hand and shifted through the veil between the worlds to where she hid the sheathed scissors of Fate.

She could see Voistra clearly now. Nelson's bomb had cleared away the swirling cloud of ghouls the bitch had called to defend herself. Beyond that, Moira could see the twined silver threads that bound both Voistra and her unknown fae sponsor in their deadly pact.

"Gotcha!" she cried as she pulled the scissors from

the Beyond into the Now of Nelson's world. With her left hand she twisted and bound the threads in her fingers and pulled them tight. The ethereal fibers hummed and strained against her grasp as she swung the bronze shears into play. The look of surprise and horror that replaced the rage on Voistra's face brought a grim laugh to her lips.

"My sisters and I may not hold sway in the world of men anymore but you're not from around here now, are you?"

With that she snipped both threads with a single cut.

A pair of agonized shrieks rattled across the rooftop, one from a disembodied human soul, the other from a far more distant fae throat. Neither, however, would play any part in either world ever again.

"Give Uncle Hades my regards, you pissants!" she called after them.

After favoring the now-clear ramp with one final desultory glance, she turned around to saunter back to the car, the bulky archaic scissors bouncing jauntily on her right shoulder. Nelson grinned at her as she neared the car and Moira could not help but return his smile.

"You're really something, you know?" he called to her as she approached.

She walked up to his door and kissed him hard on the lips, holding his head with her free hand for good measure. After much tongue wrestling, they broke apart with a gasp.

"I have to be to keep up with you." She nipped his nose lightly then chewed her stolen gum twice before blowing a bubble.

"Gross!" Cleo exclaimed from behind her own car door. "You two can be so *childish*!" Moira waggled her eyebrows at her younger sister.

"If you don't like it then don't watch." Leaving Cleo spluttering in indignation, she turned back to Nelson with a grin. "Bath, then dancing?"

He jerked his head over his shoulder to indicate her flustered little sister and the just-emerging Addie. "What about these two?"

"Let them get their own dates."

"I'm available," came a gravelly voice from inside the car, "and I love a good ménage à trois."

Ignoring the twin shrieks of outrage that rose to meet Gunner's suggestion, Nelson smiled and reached out to pull Moira into another kiss. When she leaned forward to accept it, she felt a pinch between her breasts when the car door pressed against the jeweled ampoule that dangled from a necklace beneath her shirt.

Ah yes, she thought as she opened her lips to Nelson's, dear Aphrodite's tears. *I think I'll only use two drops tonight. Three* was *a little much last time.*

A RAT'S TALE

Barbara Nickless

Walking the path to the shifting field on the surface of Denar is like stuffing yourself inside a
nail-lined barrel and then rolling around in it. The
wind will peel off any unprotected skin and turn your
lungs inside out.

Even in pressure suits it's not pleasant.

I followed Darro and Fahler down the tube to the
changing room. Johannes, the new guy, trailed after
me. He'd shown up at the rec room an hour ago, the
size of an elephant with the voice of a mouse.

"I'm your new teammate," he'd announced, "here
to help protect the future for everyone."

He said it like he meant it.

We all laughed.

"Guarding the Past to Save the Future," the recruit-
ment brochure said. We called it Sooner hunting. As
in, the tourists would sooner die than let us drag them
back to Earth.

The pressure doors dialed shut behind us as we
stepped onto the surface. Around us rose the gray-black
rock of Denar, tinged crimson as the planet rolled toward
its sun. Our shadows streaked across the landscape.

Johannes hesitated, letting the wind buffet him, looking for all the worlds like he was a tourist admiring the scenery. This guy was going to be trouble. Why do they send me the optimists and the losers? I tapped my radio.

"Jo—let's go."

His gaze rested unsteadily on my face. "Sure, Nathalie."

"It's Gratz," I snapped.

We huddled together on the shifting field and took out our black boxes. We needed only one box to shift. But in case something freaky happened, like one of us being sucked into the wrong wormhole, we all carried our own. Denar sits at a space-time nexus, where shifting is efficient and precise. But the nexus is a maelstrom more warped than I am. We knew Denar's coordinates better than we knew our mother's faces.

Those of us who had mothers.

My shifter box fed our destination's four-dimensional coordinates to the other boxes.

"Jo, you done this before?" I asked.

The giant of a man shook his head.

"You'll probably puke," Darro said. "And when you land, your eyeballs might be growing out of your toes. Don't let it bother you."

"Shut up, Darro. Jo, hold on to Fahler and don't let go of her. Fahler, make sure he's got the right coordinates on screen." I lifted my shifter. "We're going to the lovely vacation world of Rocaste, for those of you who care."

I opened my shifter and was sucked into a nightmare that lasted forever.

And for no time at all.

That's the nature of plummeting into a time-well.

The shifter grabs the time-well, then shoves you along the time axis and simultaneously compresses space. It does weird things to your body while it's at it. Sometimes you really do come out with all your toes and fingers in the wrong places.

Sometimes you come out dead.

We thumped down.

Johannes didn't throw up, from what I could see inside his helmet.

Our Sooners, a couple named George and Carrie Nace, sat twenty meters in front of us, dressed in coats and hiking boots, warming their hands over a campfire. Tall pines soared around us. Yellow-white morning sunlight filtered through gray-green needles. I couldn't smell or feel the wind, but I knew just what it would be like. I'd sampled the sims of long-ago Earth, so like the Rocaste of this time-well. A Rocaste that didn't exist in our space-time. For only a minute, I imagined living here for the length of my natural life and understood the temptation the Sooners faced.

George and Carrie stood.

"Damn," Carrie whispered. Still young, still beautiful. Rocaste was world enough for someone like her, if only she'd had the time. There was never enough time.

George kicked at the fire. "We had two weeks." In his wire-framed glasses and brown sweater he looked like a college professor.

Transmitters, courtesy of World Time-Well Association and hidden from Carrie and George in their implanted shifter-boxes, carried their voices into our skulls.

None of the tourists ever caught on that we monitored their timelines in case they decided to become Sooners and shift illegally. Every time a tourist tried to run, he risked emerging from the well before he went in. Maybe before he was born. No one had ever proved that the laws of physics provided chronology protection. WTA had people calculating time lines and tracking the shifters. Whenever there was a ripple, the trackers sent us in to keep it from happening.

We knew whenever the tourists went.

"It wasn't enough time," Carrie said.

"It was all we could afford." George must have been wondering why we had shown up. He hadn't done anything wrong. Not yet.

"I'm not going back to Earth." Carrie's voice broke on a sob. "Nothing is worth *that*!"

"But they'd find us," George said. "When could we go where they couldn't find us?"

We were advancing without getting too close, proffering bottles of water and smiling. Poor George didn't have a chance. Carrie had already convinced him to flee a million times over, across every permutation of the time line. The trackers had spotted it and sent us back three minutes before the Naces jumped.

"Darro, do your thing," I said. We were still ten meters away.

Darro drew his gun. "Stop right there, folks." His voice was flat, bored. "Come with us."

Fahler and I pulled our weapons. Fahler smiled inside her helmet.

Carrie shrieked and reached behind her ear for the shifter controls.

Darro blew her arm off just above the elbow.

George lunged for Carrie. Maybe to protect her. Maybe to keep her with him. With her other hand, Carrie clawed for the shifter.

Fahler shot them both.

Good-bye, George. Good-bye, Carrie. Their time line lay flat.

There was a noise behind me. I looked around.

Johannes was throwing up in his helmet.

Hours later, in the heart of the guards' barracks on Denar, there came a tap on my door. I grunted.

"It's Johannes. May I come in?"

I rolled over and snapped off the snuff-porn. "Sure."

Johannes ducked as he entered the room. I offered him a chair and a glass of vodka. He took the seat but shook his shaggy head at the vodka. I poured myself a drink and studied his face.

"Fahler says you wouldn't go with her. You should give her a chance. I've heard she knows some moves—"

"Nobody told me I might have to kill people on this job, Gratz."

I resettled on my bunk. I could feel the hum of the generators through the mattress.

"It's not exactly a well-advertised point. 'Join the Time Guards and Kill Sooners.' Wouldn't go over well back on Earth."

"I think I can bring them back."

"Huh?"

"I'm good with people. I could talk them out of running."

"Yeah? Well." I drank my vodka. After five years it no longer burned going down. "The good folks of WTA don't care about that."

"WTA has a tough guy image. But that's probably not what they really feel."

"What planet are you from, Johannes? Nobody gives a damn about Sooners."

"Just let me do the talking before you shoot."

I stood to get some ice for my drink.

I believed in the fundamental stupidity of people.
I'd heard every breathless cry about the nobility of
man. But mostly I'd noticed that if you feed them,
give them something to screw, and stick a VR box in
front of them, they cluck like chickens in a henhouse.
The Sooners were smart enough to try to get out of
the coop, and for that I could almost admire them.
But they weren't smart enough to escape a rat like me.

Still, Darro had been my point man for three years,
and he hadn't convinced a single Sooner not to run.
What could it hurt to give Johannes a chance?

"Okay. You can talk. But we know precisely when
they're going to shift. You either convince them before then or we blow them away. That's the job. Any
longer than that, and we mess with the future."

"It's not enough time. We could shift in a minute
or two earlier."

I frowned. "Nobody likes blowing people up. But
it's my job to make sure those people don't alter the
time line. They'll drop me in vacuum if I fail. You
know we're restricted to the time slot we're given."

I'd talked to the time-physicists, and I knew we had
a little more time to play with. But I was curious to
see how much Johannes knew.

"I've read the journals," he said. "We have an additional three minutes before the time disturbance is
large enough that we can't resynch the Sooners to flat
time. And that's just with the shallower wells. We usually have more time than that."

Johannes leaned forward. The cheap plastic table
creaked under his weight. His eyes were a startlingly
light shade of gray, somber and hopeful. Given the
way things happened around here, in a few months
only Johannes's sorrow would still be showing.

But that hope had me hooked.

"Go on," I said.

"Let's go in a little early, and if I don't talk them out of it, you can do what you have to do, right when their time is up. I'm not asking you to risk anything. Just give me a chance."

"Aw, hell. Okay. Three tries." I raised my glass. "Congratulations. You're my new point man."

My reward was a billion-watt smile.

"Get out of here."

The next call was a family of five.

I hate it when kids are involved.

"Hello!" Johannes called in his high voice, yelling across twenty meters of emerald sand. A sapphire ocean hissed on our right. "We're here to talk you out of running."

So now the Sooners knew we spied on them. Hell.

"I don't know what you're talking about," the father said in the cautious tone of the would-be innocent. "We're just getting ready to return to Alpha Base."

Johannes shook his head and, against all regulations, removed his helmet. His blond hair fell past his shoulders. In the silvery sunlight his suit reflected diamond points on the sand. He walked forward.

"It's not so bad on Earth, is it? You've got your job. A nice apartment. Your kids should have a chance to grow up. Is this where you really want it to end, Mr. Wakeman?"

"Jerry?" The wife hugged the youngest of the children. A baby, really.

"It's okay, Sue," Jerry said. "Mister, we're shifting back to base. Just like we're supposed to."

"You've got two minutes, Jo," I said.

He took a few more steps until he was only seven meters from the family. I had to fight the urge to drag him back. If one of the family shifted, they'd take pieces of Johannes with them.

Fahler snarled a curse.

"Think of your kids, Mr. Wakeman," Johannes said. "You can't get away with this. We'll find you. We always do. We have eternity to look for you. I know Earth isn't the best, man. I've been there. But you want your kids to grow up, don't you?"

"Jerry." Mrs. Wakeman started to cry.

"I—" The father was at a loss. He studied Johannes, and I imagined him seeing that same look of sorrow and hope in those gray eyes. "I—I don't know what you mean."

"Trust me," Johannes said. "You can trust me."

"Sixty seconds," I hissed.

"Listen to me. I'm one of you. You can't make it. These worlds, these vacation planets, they aren't for the likes of us. We're of Earth. Earth is our home, our fate. We don't belong anywhere else." His voice was both lullaby and command. His words vibrated at some sweet level, and I think he could have talked the angels down from heaven. "Take care of your family, Mr. Wakeman. Return home."

The father made a decision. I could see it in the way his shoulders fell and his face lost all hope.

I heard the voice of one of the trackers on Denar in my ear. "They're shifting back to Alpha," she said before it happened.

Johannes backed out of range just in time.

That night we celebrated. Word had gotten out that we'd saved a family, and we were heroes.

"You did great," I said to Johannes when he joined me at the bar. I slapped him on the back. It was like hitting an oak tree. "Why don't you have a drink? You deserve one."

"I already feel good." He smiled at me and the bartender and the mirror of people swirling by.

"Jesus, you got a nice smile."

He smiled again.

I pulled back a little. I didn't want to be a member of the Johannes fan club. Friendships aren't healthy here. You can't afford to trip up and worry about someone else. Besides, I knew he couldn't be perfect. He was a guard. We all had that special *something*, that edge of darkness, to earn us this kind of crap job.

"What the hell got you here, Jo? Darro's here because he's got the empathy of a cockroach. Fahler killed her own parents. You don't strike me as guard material."

The lights twinkled off the bottles behind the bar. A sail of laughter drifted past.

"We all have our secrets, Gratz."

I tossed down my vodka and waved my hand for another.

"You're a spy, right?" I said after the bartender had deposited my drink on the counter and moved away.

"You could call me a revolutionary."

I glanced around. The room echoed with voices. The bartender was at the other end, watching a drone wash the glasses. No one even looked our way. "Very funny. But don't say that around here. Some people might not know you're joking."

He lifted his big frame from the stool. "Righto, Gratz. I was just fooling."

I watched him leave. The guards cheered and clapped him on the back as he passed.

I drank an extra vodka for him.

After three more no-kill runs, other guards started coming to Johannes for advice. A month after his arrival, he organized classes in the rec room on Wednesday nights. The number of deaths fell. We grew friendlier with each other. A few relationships became permanent. The owner of the pharmacy complained that his drug sales were down.

Don't ask me to explain it. I didn't think these guards could love anyone. But they loved Johannes. Fahler might have been one of the few who didn't fall for him. Fahler's self-esteem came from the notches on her bedpost, and—near as I could tell—Johannes was the only straight male guard who didn't sleep with her. But if she resented him, she never let on.

I saw a lot of Johannes because, crazy son of a bitch, he liked me.

"What makes you so angry?" he asked me one day.

We were in my room, drinking. Vodka for me. Water for Johannes.

I spun my glass on the table. "I grew up in an Earth slum before WTA took me away at the tender age of thirteen. All us slum kids are angry and paranoid. We can't help it. When the recruiters came through, Jesus, we used to watch the sims of vacation worlds and dream about getting out."

"Is that why you're here? You wanted to see the worlds?"

I barked a laugh. "Get real, Jo. Everyone is here cause the other choice was a life doped up behind bars. It's not like we're *enjoying* those worlds."

He closed his eyes and opened them again. In the dim light, his gray eyes looked almost black. "What did you do?"

I thought about it awhile. You didn't have to commit a crime to become guard material. You just had to have a Psycho-An that showed you were capable of violence. I could have lied to Johannes. I was surprised when I didn't.

"I was a whore. One of my johns tried to slit my throat. I turned the tables." I'd never confessed to anyone. I jammed my hands on my hips and batted my eyes. "It just played havoc with my Psycho-An."

"Did you get help?"

"For the murder or the whoring?"

"Either."

"Sure. Trained psychiatrists came down once a week to make sure all the child prostitutes were happily adjusted."

"I grew up on a farm. A converted asteroid." There was wistfulness in his voice.

"Gee, I never would have guessed. You probably harvested the fields by yourself and carried injured cows back to the barn where you healed them by laying your hands on them."

"You're joking," he said with that smile. "But you're right."

I don't know how much longer our no-kill record might have stood if Fahler hadn't talked. Maybe until we were all able to retire to the far side of Denar, rich and a bit less guilty than we would have been if Johannes hadn't come into our lives. My team hadn't killed anyone since I made Johannes the point man.

But one night at dinner, Fahler said, "They're killing them, you know."

Darro looked up. "What are you talking about?"

We were off duty, but Darro wasn't using many stupors these days. His words weren't even slurred.

"The Sooners. WTA kills them after they go back to base."

Fahler watched Johannes from the corner of her eye. The giant had frozen with a bite of food halfway to his mouth. His face turned ashen.

"Shut the hell up, Fahler," I said. "You don't know what you're talking about."

"Why would they kill them?" Darro asked.

Johannes dropped his fork. It hit the edge of the table and ricocheted to the floor.

I slammed the table with both palms. "Shut up, both of you. They're not killing anyone."

"Anyone who tries to run is obviously trouble, part of the criminal element," Fahler went on. "WTA can't take the chance they might try to run again, wind up in the past where they could wipe out the Association. So they gas 'em. Really, gassing is worse than if they let us shoot them. At least that's fast." She folded her hands on the table and arched a brow at Johannes. "They do the kids first."

I slapped her, hard, across the face.

She fell back in her seat, a trickle of blood running from her nose.

She licked at the blood with a pink tongue. "The truth hurts, Gratz."

Johannes dragged me back to my room and made me swallow some stupor pills, washed down with vodka. Then he took off my boots and put me in bed. I think he kissed me on the forehead, like my mother used to do. I felt better. Like one of his cattle, I supposed.

I woke in darkness.

Sleep had burned the fuzzy edges in my brain. I thought about Sooners and Johannes, and finally I sat up and went over to the computer.

A farm boy who healed cows didn't wind up on Denar. It was time to learn the truth. I was taking a risk if they caught me, but I could always say that as Johannes' team led, I felt justified in checking his Psycho-An. Never mind how I got the passwords.

WTA, operating as the Democracy of Aligned Worlds, kept psychoanalysis sheets on everyone, starting at birth. Psycho-Ans we called them. The tests were subtle, and most people weren't even aware of them. WTA monitored you until you were thirteen, then they encouraged you to move where they wanted you. If you were smart, you took their advice.

Well, maybe I was drunker than I thought, and I punched the wrong combinations. Or maybe—and I think this is right—Johannes wasn't all he claimed to be. There was no Psycho-An on Johannes. There was no DOB certificate. There wasn't even a goddamn driver's license.

I hit more keys. I found Fahler and Darro. I found my mother and my dead brother. And I found my own Psycho-An and spent a couple of minutes staring at my picture, wondering if I was really that ugly.

But, according to the computer, Johannes didn't exist.

This didn't even fit into the realm of the theoretically possible. WTA did a psychoanalysis on *everyone*. Who the hell was he?

I spent half an hour chewing on all the possibilities before coming up blank and stumbling back to bed.

I dreamed that Johannes carried me to a place far

from Denar and time-wells and guards. I struggled in his arms, because I'd always walked on my own. But I was glad—glad that I was leaving. As a bright yellow sun set behind Johannes' massive shoulder, I wept into his shirt.

He shook me awake. The vodka and drugs had worn off, and I felt like crap. I was too hungover to get up.

"Screw this headache," I said when my eyes focused. He sat on the chair. "It's true, Nath."

"What's true?" I struggled to sit up. Lights ricocheted off the insides of my eyelids.

"I checked with a couple of sources. They kill the people as soon as they return to base. Fahler was right."

"You don't know crap."

I got up and poured a drink.

Johannes put his face in his hands, and after a while I realized he was crying.

"Hey," I said, as gently as I could through the hangover. "Maybe it's for the best. If they ran, they could really mess things up."

He looked at me. "I'm going, Gratz."

I got a chill. "What?"

"I'm going to run. I can't do this anymore. I'd rather die."

"You *will* die, if you run. You think you're the first guard to get this idea? WTA's tracked them all down, and we've killed them."

"I thought I was here to save the Sooners," he went on as if he hadn't heard me. "But now I know it's something else, something bigger. It's time for me to run. I'm here to prove it can be done."

"It *can't* be done."

"They won't know where I've gone, or when. They don't have a transmitter on me."

"Why the hell not?"

"Friends in the right places, Gratz."

"That's why you're not in the computer."

"The revolution is bigger than anyone realizes. WTA is so intent on protecting the past, they forgot to look ahead. We've responded to their plans before they know what their plans are."

"They'll find you. They'll see the ripple when you shift, and they'll hunt you down." I paused. "And what if you do succeed? You'll cause a paradox."

There. The worst kind of crime.

Johannes smiled. My heart thumped.

"I *am* a paradox, Nathalie," he said.

I gaped at him. "You're saying you're from the future?"

He took my small, cold hand in his large one. "Do you think it's possible?"

I looked away. "What do you want me to do?"

We took the elevator shaft in the hurricane-eye quiet of night. I helped Johannes into his suit. He smelled of sweat and endorphins. He hugged me before he put on his helmet.

"Come with me," he said.

"Sorry. I don't want to die."

"Good-bye, Gratz." He started toward the door.

"Johannes?"

He turned back. He looked supernaturally large in the dim blue light of the suiting room.

I walked forward until his shadow swallowed mine. "Please don't let me find you."

"I don't think it can be helped." He snapped his helmet. "When you find me, Gratz, kill me."

"What?"

"For the future."

I stayed in the suiting room long after he left, wishing I'd had the guts to go with him. But Johannes was born larger than life. I was born small and hungry, a rat in a maze.

Johannes managed to avoid us. He *was* smarter than he looked, after all. He took to stealing some of the Sooners before we got to them. We heard he'd organized a base deep in a time-well. He and the revolutionaries had blown up some space stations and Alpha One. David against Goliath.

Fahler, Darro and I had a new guy, Winger, and he'd worked out pretty well. We were back to killing all the Sooners who ran. Darro took stupor pills, Winger drank more than I did, and Fahler still shacked up every chance she got.

Me, well, I was still a rat. Devious, sneaky, skulking for scraps. There are some things you can't escape.

Everyone was surprised to see Johannes.

He'd shifted in to help the Sooner, and he must have miscalculated. I caught a flash of the Sooner's long, dark hair and wide eyes before he stepped in front of her.

"Well, well," Fahler said. "If it ain't our old friend."

Darro lifted his gun. "Johannes. What the hell?"

"This the great Johannes?" Winger grinned.

Curiosity must have gotten to the Sooner. She peeked around Johannes's shoulder.

Fahler got her with a single shot through the eye and then aimed at Johannes.

I pulled my gun and pointed it at Fahler. "Hold your fire."

"We got orders," Darro said.

"To bring him in alive."

"Screw that," Winger said. He chambered a round.

I whirled and fired, a single round through his heart. Fahler aimed at me, but I was faster. I shot her and—when his shot ricocheted off my helmet—Darro as well.

I forgot about Johannes as I stared at my dead companions.

He moved up beside me. "Nath," he said, reaching for me.

I ducked away. I was covered with blood.

He hadn't aged nearly as much as I. Of course not. He'd been hiding in time-wells, living on borrowed time.

But I loved him for being what he was. For escaping.

"Get out of here," I said. "I'll blame you for their deaths and say I barely got out with my life."

"They won't believe you."

"They will."

"The time lines are written, Nat. But I landed in the only one where you didn't kill me. You were supposed to kill me."

"And I suppose I was supposed to kill them, too?"

He looked at the bodies. "It was self-defense."

"So what? Get out of here."

He grabbed my gun and jumped away from me. For a second, I thought he was going to shoot me. But he touched the barrel to his chin.

"I'm sorry, Nath. We need a martyr. I'm more useful to my people dead."

"You can't die. They need you. *I* need you. How can you help anyone if you're dead?"

"Read about Joan of Arc sometime." He smiled, but it was sad. "Get out of the maze, Nath Rat."

He blew his head off.

*   *   *

After Johannes died, I lied at the inquest and then retired to the far side of Denar. From time to time, guards came to me, asking questions about time-wells, needing advice. The ones who were serious, I helped escape.

Ten years after everyone thought I killed Johannes, the revolutionaries toppled WTA. A week after that, they came for me.

They're going to execute me for the murder of their leader. The mob has demanded it, and their martyr can't be a suicide. My own words framed me for his death and now all of history will curse me. Jo knew this, and though he loved me, he loved them more.

But even a rat can look over the edge of the maze and see the world beyond, maybe become part of that world. I knew what my fate would be when the rebels won, but I'm okay with dying. I'm even okay with being reviled for the rest of time.

Like Jo, I came to love those he tried to save.

For a while, I was more than a rat.

THE BONES OF MAMMOTH MALONE

Esther M. Friesner

The name's Malone; Mammoth Malone. You got
questions? I got answers. You got problems? I got
solutions. I keep them in my bones.

It was a cold day out on the tundra. It's *always* a
cold day out on the tundra. If I had any sense I'd
move the hell *off* the $%@*& tundra, but where else
is there, these days? It's *all* tundra, baby, except where
it's ice, and Mammoth Malone doesn't do glaciers. I'd
just poured myself a double shot of breakfast when
she came into my yurt like she owned the place.

She looked like trouble. Most broads do, but not until
after they take their coats off. Until then, they look like
most guys. This one was different: It takes a lot of
woman to fill out a blargh-skin coat like that, and believe
me, she filled it out like the blargh never did. (I don't
know what they used to call blarghs back in the times
before the Big Chill hit and hit hard, but these days we
call 'em like we see 'em. A big, shaggy, horned, nasty-
tempered beast looks you in the eye, snorts so hard your
grandkids are covered in nose-goo, and says "Blargh,"
that's what you call him. Saves time chipping through
the ice to reach an encyclopedia.)

"Mr. Malone, I need help," she said. No intro, no hi, how are you, how're they hanging (Like icicles, sweetheart!), just slapped her cards down on the table, straight out. I liked that in a broad.

I thumbed back the hood of my parka and said, "That's my business, sister: helping people. I'm just one big freakin', frostbitten heap of altruism. Keep talking."

"Would you mind if I sat down?" she asked.

I glanced around the yurt. It was a mess: piles of storage boxes, blargh hides, a giant rack of reindeer antlers, and over by the firepit a heap of bones from about a dozen different kinds of animals. I could even I.D. some of them—like the reindeer—by their names P.B.C. (Pre-Big Chill). I was proud of that.

"Sister," I said, "if you can find somewhere to sit in this dump that won't freeze your *farfegnügen* to the ground, help yourself."

She gave me a smile that went through me like a polar bear's claw. "Not exactly a gentleman, are you, Mr. Malone?"

"This 'gentleman' thing of which you speak, what's that? Can you eat it? Can you sell it? Can you—"

"Never mind." I expected her to drag one of my storage boxes up to the desk, but instead she sashayed over to the big rack of reindeer antlers, tossed a blargh hide over them, and made herself a pretty impressive chair. Pleased with herself, she patted the bony armrests and said, "Anyone ever tell you that you've got a nice rack, Mr. Malone?"

"You didn't come here just to tell me what I already know, did you, angel?" I said. "Because if you did, this is going to be the easiest job I've had in a long, long time."

She stopped smiling. "I'll get to the point then, shall I?" She peeled off her mittens and reached into the pouch at her waist, pulling out something small and furry and squeaky. She tossed it onto my desk and the two of us watched it scamper around in bewildered circles for a while. Then it seemed to get its bearings. It stopped, looked around, saw the edge of my desk, and tore off at blinding speed. There was no mistaking what it was or what it had in mind, if you like to think that a lemming *has* a mind to start with.

A lemming. Of all the desks in all the yurts across all the tundra, why did she have to bring that rodent into mine? Little buggers creep me out, for some reason. Never trust anything small enough to run up your pants' leg and rearrange your outlook, that's what I always say. I reached for the bottle. Kumiss isn't the answer to everything, but sometimes it lets you ignore the question.

Before I could yank the stopper, the lemming had zipped across the desk all the way to the very edge and there . . . he stopped. No legendary leap into the void, no minor splat when he hit the floor, no comical bounce-on-impact, nothing. Not even a glance at the precipice and the rodent equivalent of a *What the **** was I thinking?* look on his face; he just *stopped*.

"Well," I said, taking a long swig straight from the bottle. "That's different."

"I'll say it is." She took a deep breath. "Mr. Malone, my name is Randi Vixen, hereditary freelance zoologist. Ever since the Big Chill, my tribe has made it our business to keep an eye on the world's fauna."

"And don't think we're not grateful," I told her. That was true: I still remembered my grandpa telling us kids the stories *his* grandpa used to tell about how it was when the Big Chill first hit and took hold. The ice sheets cometh, er, came, and came fast. Scientists couldn't explain it. Some blamed fluoride in the water, others the latest crooked elections, but as far as coming up with anything that was truly *helpful,* no dice. While civilization took a tumble down the cosmic crevasse, people everywhere were waking up to the realization that the salad bar was closed and that their continued survival depended on how many of their fellow species were catchable and edible. (I never did understand what a salad bar was, but every time I asked the old man for an explanation, he forgot where he was in his story and had to start over from the beginning. It was either stop asking questions or have *both* of us die of old age before the story was over. I made my choice.)

The freelance zoologist tribe took on the responsibility of policing the rest of us, making sure no one got greedy and hunted a particularly slow/stupid/tasty species into extinction (and out of the global pantry). They also looked out for the animals on a more direct level, keeping tabs on their birthrate, migratory patterns, and behavior, any one of which could do a number on continued human well-being.

When something weird cropped up in the animal kingdom, the freelance zoologists always took it seriously. They were a proud tribe who guarded their status jealously. They moved secretly among us ordinary Joe Floes, watching from the shadows, troubleshooting, averting crises. Sometimes we didn't even know there'd *been* a crisis averted; we only heard rumors. That suited them just fine: They didn't like outsiders.

Which kind of made Miss Vixen's visit all the more intriguing.

"Mr. Malone, I won't lie to you," she said. (I knew

what that meant: She was going to lie like a wolfskin rug.) "My tribe doesn't know I'm here. We're never supposed to get help from Outlanders."

"Then why'd you do it, dollface?" I asked. "Why come to see me? Rodents aren't my specialty, unless you count my ex-wife's lawyer. Sure, I can ask the bones, but they're mostly good for coughing up the will of the gods, savvy? You got a question that needs a yes/no answer or starts with who, what, where, or when, and I can make a shinbone sing pretty. But questions that start with *why* . . . no can do, sweetheart."

She glared at me. "You're not exactly a sympathetic character, Mr. Malone," she said.

"Sympathy doesn't put any blubber in the bank account, princess. Anyway, what's the big deal if this lemming's acting weird? It's not like you should go jump off a cliff just because *he* won't."

Her pretty little eyebrows drew together until she was wearing a scowl fit to stop a charging blargh in its tracks. "I'm sorry if I didn't make myself clear before, Mr. Malone," she said, her voice hoarse and strained. "It's not just *this* lemming. It's all of them. For some reason, the entire species is becoming more . . . cautious. They still take part in the mass migrations for which they are famed, but when they come to the edge of a precipice, or anything even vaguely resembling a precipice, they stop. All of them."

"Well, excuse me, sister, but I find that a little tough to swallow," I said. "If you're talking a bunch of lemmings on the move and the little squeakers up front reach the edge of a cliff and stop, the furballs behind them—way, *way* behind them—can't see the drop-off.

They've got no reason to stop, and if they don't, they're gonna shove the ones ahead of them until you get the domino effect. The front lemmings aren't jumping, but they're sure as hell gonna get *pushed*."

Miss Vixen's scowl softened to a look that as good as said *You poor, dumb, ignorant bastard,* only in a nice way. "You'd think that, wouldn't you?" she said sadly. "You'd *like* to think that. *I'd* like to think that. But it's not true. When I say that the lemmings all stop when they reach the edge of a cliff, that's exactly what I mean. They *all* stop. It's as if the herd was being guided by a single mind, a single will."

I rubbed my chin in thought. "Okay, now *that's* bizarre, I'll admit it. But I still don't get why you're coming to *me* about this."

She pursed her luscious lips and let out a sigh that calved my glacier. "Are you at all familiar with the hierarchy of the freelance zoologist tribe?"

"If it's like other tribes, you're probably split up into clans, and the clans are divvied into kinship units, right?"

She nodded. "Well, my clan's totem beast is the lemming." Then she burst into tears.

I'm a tough guy. In this racket, you've got to be tough. Sometimes you get a client who doesn't like what the bones tell him, so he decides maybe he'll take out his disappointment on *your* bones. Or try. I can take a spear to the gut, a club to the noggin, and a bowl of bad dolphin au gratin to the belly, but I just can't take a weepy dame.

"Here, sister," I said, handing her the lemming. She was so broken up, she dabbed it at her eyes, blew her nose in its fur, and tossed it into the wastebasket without noticing anything out of the ordinary. As for the

beast, it took what she dished out without the smallest
squeak or squirm until after it hit the wastebasket.
Then it climbed to the rim, glowered at us, and made
low, chittering sounds that sounded somehow threat-
ening. I'd never looked closely at a lemming before—
like I said, they creep me out—but in the short time
I'd shared yurt space with this one I'd noticed that it
had worn a blank, mindless expression right up until
the instant it hit the wastebasket. Now, in used-
handkerchief mode, there was actually a gleam of
awareness in its eye; angry awareness.

Definitely weird, I thought. But before I could get
what it all meant, Miss Vixen was talking again, and
I was distracted from the hostile rodent.

"I'm sorry to be such a weakling, Mr. Malone,"
she began.

"Call me Mammoth," I said. "And you're no weakling; you're just upset. Can't say I blame you. Bad
enough for a freelance zoologist when *any* animal goes
nuts on your watch, but your clan's totem beast? *Big*
trouble. Major consequences, and I don't mean just to
the ecosphere. This makes it *personal.* Am I wrong?"

She smiled gratefully. She had a pair of killer dim-
ples to match her pair of killer . . . eyes. "You're a
sympathetic person after all, Mr. . . . Mammoth. And
you're quite right, this phenomenon does have personal repercussions for me. Very deep, very real ones.
You see, among the hereditary freelance zoology
tribe, there is a great prophecy that says—"

Oh, murder. Prophecies. A *great* prophecy yet. If I
had a walrus's *oosik* (hey, look it up!) for every great
prophecy that's loused up someone's life, I'd be up to
my eyeballs in pinniped dingdongs.

"Hold it right there, sister." I raised one hand, silencing the delectable Miss Vixen. "Let me take a stab at this 'great prophecy' of yours: If the lemmings start acting wacky, your clan has to set things right by making a huge sacrifice to fix things. Well?"

She didn't respond. I presumed her silence meant she agreed with me, so I forged on: "And I bet I can tell you who made that 'great prophecy,' while I'm at it. Someone from the tribe of hereditary *seers*; the tribe that the rest of you have to buy off— I mean, *thank* for making nice-nice between gods and mortals."

This time Miss Vixen did react: She looked horrified. "How can you say such blasphemous things?"

"Easy, dollface: I *am* a seer, remember?"

"Of course. That's why I came to you. But the way you're talking, it's as if—"

"—I've divorced myself from the rest of the tribe? Bingo. No hater like a self-hater, as my dear old dead grandpa used to say, right before he walloped my skinny behind for doubting the chief of the bone-readers' clan. Yeah, our clan-chief, good ol' Marmot Eddie, now *there* was a bone-reader's bone-reader. Man, he could tell you your fate from the cracks in an anchovy's rib! Funny thing, though—it seemed like every time he tossed a femur in the fire, the cracks all came up telling us that it was time to give him the rrrrowr's share of dinner, or the prettiest maiden within sniffing distance to be his bedmate. Like my sister, Lutefiskina. Trouble was, when she said she'd rather die than embrace the fate Marmot Eddie swore was in the bones for her, she wasn't kidding. Hey, someday you really ought to get a load of the view from Lutefiskina's Leap, Miss Vixen. Spectacular."

"Just because *you* had some bad experiences with

your fellow bone-readers does not mean that all who interact with the gods are corrupt," she said stiffly. Her face was pale. Something in my story had touched a nerve. Either that, or she'd shifted her weight unwisely in the makeshift chair and one of the prongs on the reindeer rack under her rump was getting personal.

"Maybe not, but I bet *you'd* like that to be true," I said. "I've got you figured out, angel. You come to my yurt, you show me your rodent, you start telling me about this 'great prophecy,' but you don't need to tell me that whatever it prophesies is curdling your chai. *That's* as obvious as a pile of rrrrowr droppings. Yeah, you're upset, unhappy, but you're *here*. Why? Because we both know that one thing in this crazy world that trumps prophecy is a last-minute reprieve from the gods themselves."

Her eyes weren't just dry by now, they were hard and cold as polar pebbles. "You're a very astute man," she said, her mouth tight and small.

"What I am, angel, is a *seer*. It's our business to know things. Things like how the *real* money isn't in passing along the will of the gods as it comes to us, hot off the bones, but in making a few little editorial changes along the way."

She frowned, puzzled. "What's 'editorial'?"

I shrugged. "Obsolete word from P.B.C.; got it from Grandpa. He said it referred to a legendary monster that changed whatever it touched past all hope of recognition. But isn't that what *you're* after? A bought-off seer to editorify the 'great prophecy' for you? Easy enough: My people work solo. When little Bobby Bone-reader hands down the verdict from on high, folks *have* to take his word for it that he's telling like it is. Who's gonna tell 'em that he's crooked and there's no way the bones say what he claims they do?

"But why am I telling *you* all about shady shinbone shysters, angel? That's why you're here. It's not about the leapless lemmings, it's to buy a bone-reading that'll save your own sweet skin from that 'great prophecy' fallout."

"*Mister* Malone, I don't think I care for your tone." Her voice made the temperature inside my yurt drop a good ten degrees. "You're partly correct: The great prophecy states that if our clan's totem beast should ever behave in a way that goes against all natural law, it is a sign that the Great Winter is upon us and we must—"

"Whoa, whoa, whoa!" My hands went up in surrender. "You people have a *great* prophecy about the *Great* Winter coming? Baby, has anyone in your clan bothered to stick his nose out the doorflap in the past umpty-ump years? If you're waiting for the Great Winter, what do you folks call the meat-locker we're living in right now? The *Pretty Good* Winter?"

My would-be client stood up and looked down her nose at me. "Is that all you can do, Mr. Malone? Doubt? Question? Blaspheme? Sneer at things you don't understand?"

"No, sweetcakes," I replied, pulling open the top drawer of my desk. "I can do this, too."

Before she could say another word, I reached into the open drawer and pulled out a little brass saucer, a cube of charcoal, a flint, and a piece of steel. Two quick strikes and the charcoal was blazing. Smoke filled the yurt, making the adorable-if-snippy Miss Vixen cough. (There were even a few backup barks from the lemming still holding on to the lip of the wastebasket.) By the time she'd wiped her stinging eyes, I'd opened yet another desk drawer and plucked out a tiny bone that I dropped onto the miniature brazier. Sparks flew while I muttered the proper incantations. At the very instant that I fell silent, there was a sound like the crackle of chain lightning; the flames and smoke rising from the bronze saucer froze, then were sucked back down into the ashes of the charcoal square and vanished in a heartbeat.

Taking my second-best pair of chopsticks from the dirty yak-butter tea mug on the desk, I picked out the bone and turned it this way and that, studying it. Miss Vixen watched, fascinated. After a time, I spoke:

"Who's Harvey?" I asked.

Miss Vixen's eyes rolled back in her head and she collapsed in a heap. I got her onto a pile of skins before she froze to the floor. I rubbed her wrists, patted her face, and held the remains of an ancient sardine sandwich under her nose, trying to revive her. Her eyelids fluttered, and the first words out of her mouth were: "How—how did you know about Harvey?"

"The bones talk, I listen. It's what I do. And I never talk *for* them, got it? Not at any price. So if you're still hoping the get me to play along with whatever you've got in mind—"

"No." She bowed her head. "I'm sorry, Mammoth. You were right, I did come here hoping to convince you to return home with me, fake a bone-reading, and tell my people something that would make them drop all thought of the great prophecy and—and what I'll have to do if we want to stave off the Great Winter. I've been wrong, trying to fight my fate. What will be, must be. There's no escape. I should just be a good girl and yield to my destiny."

"A good girl?" I repeated. "Don't you mean a good princess . . . princess?"

Her eyes flew wide open. "How did you . . ." Then she glanced at the burned bone, still pinched between my chopsticks. *"Ohhhh!"* came the dawn.

"Want to know what else this little splinter has to tell me?" I asked. She nodded. "That you and my poor sister Lutefiskina have a lot more in common than I ever wanted to know."

The holt of the lemming clan was hidden away in a narrow gorge where natural hot springs gave the people a little taste of temperate paradise lost. Even though Randi and I had muckponies to ride, the place was so far removed from any other human settlement that by the time we reached it we were on a first-name, fifty-third mukluk-knocking basis, if you get my drift, and I'm not talking snow. If the rest of the women of her tribe were even *half* as hot as Randi, the men of *my* tribe wouldn't need fires to put a few cracks into the ol' bones.

Yeah, I said that to her, too, after about our fifth go-round. I even backed it up by giving her my crowd-pleasing boyish grin. She gave it back in the palm of her hand, smacking it smartly across my cheek. But that didn't stop her from coming back for helpings six-through-fifty-three of that famous Malone ohbabyoh-baby magic. Let's just say that there's more than one reason they call me *Mammoth,* sweetheart.

As we rode into the lemming clan holt, every door-flap was thrown back as Randi's clan emerged to check us out. I didn't know how well she got along with her kin, but even if she was voted Most Likely to Give Everyone Gingivitis, I expected *some* words of welcome, at least.

What she got was silence and surly stares. From the way everyone was glaring at her, you'd think she'd come home with a big basket of Mad Blargh Disease for the kiddies. She ignored the battery of belligerent looks and rode on, sitting proud and tall in the saddle, until she reined in her muckpony in front of one particular yurt. A plump, silver-haired woman stood in front of the doorflap, arms folded, face stern. I didn't need any bones to catch wise to the family resemblance: Mama Vixen wasn't real pleased with little Randi, or I was a penguin's uncle.

"Young woman, do you have any idea of the anxiety you've been putting your clan through?" she snapped. "The wedding is supposed to take place tomorrow, or the great prophecy won't be fulfilled and the Great Winter will descend on all the land! Where have you *been*?"

"Out," said Randi. I could've hugged her for having that kind of backbone in facing down one formidable-looking old lady. I could've done more to her than that, but not in front of Mama.

Mama Vixen's eyes slewed from her sassy daughter to me. "And *what* did you bring back with you?" she demanded. "For the last time, no, you may *not* have a pet yeti, I don't care if you do promise to feed it and walk it and pet it and squeeze it and call it George."

I moved fast, before Randi could reply. Slinging one leg over my muckpony's back, I dropped easily to the ground and flashed the same mini-bone-reading kit I'd used back at the yurt. (I had it packed in one of the leather pouches at my belt for the trip. You never know when you're going to need to ask a mouse-skull for directions to the nearest tavern.) By the time Mama Vixen said *George,* I had a charcoal square on fire and a bone dropping into the flames.

The thunderous sound a good bone makes when it gives up its secrets is a real attention-grabber, and the plume of black smoke that spouts, then drops back and disappears isn't too shabby either. When the air was clear, I had Mama Vixen and every other soul in the lemming clan holt standing in a spellbound circle around me—at a safe distance.

"People of the lemmings!" I declared, holding the bronze saucer high above my head with two hands. (*Damn,* that sucker was hot!) "I am Mammoth Malone of the bone-reader clan, a son of the tribe of seers! I come to you with the word of the gods! Hear me now, before you make the worst mistake of your lives, in the name of your great prophecy!"

"Who dares invoke the great prophecy of the lemming clan?" The voice that rang out over the heads of Randi's clanfolk was so loud and ugly it would've made a blargh wet itself. It blared from a hulking, wrinkled, balding, saggy old guy who came plowing through the crowd like he owned the place.

"Chief Harvey!" Mama Vixen gasped. Well, whaddaya know? He *did* own the place! Or at least he ruled it. The whole clan whirled away from me and bowed to him so low, so fast, that suddenly I was staring at nothing but . . . butt.

I sized up the lemming clan chief. He towered over me by at least three hand-spans. The waves of stink coming off him made me want to find a beached whale carcass and do deep-breathing exercises just to clear my head, fighting reek with reek. He may've been old, but he still had the remains of some pretty impressive muscles roping his body. Too bad said muscles had gotten into a tug-o'-war with gravity. (By the way, gravity was winning.) At least he hadn't gone for Old-Guy-Who's-Losing-His-Hair's Stupid Trick #1, a.k.a.

The Comb-Over. No, he went for O.G.W.L.H.H. Stupid Trick #2 instead: The Pity Ponytail. He might've been a looker in his heyday, but hey! Not *this* day.

By the time Harvey reached me, everyone had stopped bowing. A low buzz ran through the massed clanfolk, a buzz he swatted into oblivion with one frosty glance. Then he turned to me.

"Outlander, why are you here?" he demanded. "I could kill you where you stand."

"Tsk. And I thought you'd be happy to see me, big guy," I drawled. "I bring you *good* news: The Great Winter's been called off on account of lemmings on the playing field. Or should I say *no* lemmings?"

Chief Harvey's getting-higher-by-the-falling-follicle brow creased into the mother of all scowls. "You *dare* to take the name of the sacred rodent upon your blasphemous lips, Outlander scum?"

"Hey, just doing my job," I replied, holding out the bronze saucer. "I've been told all about what's going on here, how the lemmings aren't acting normal. How your 'great prophecy' says that when that happens, it is the fate of the princess of the lemming clan to wed the chief of the lemming clan, and if she denies that fate, the Great Winter will come." I nodded to where Randi still sat astride her muckpony. "Now I'm not even going to bother figuring out how come you people have a clan princess *without* having a king and queen, but I will tell you this: Those lemmings are *not* acting weird on account of any prophecy, great or small. I know: I asked the bones and the bones don't lie. The lemmings are all higgledy-piggledy because someone's been tampering with th—AK!"

Chief Harvey's huge paw shot out, clenched itself around my windpipe, and cut me off in mid-wiseguy.

The bronze saucer and the burned bone in it went tumbling across the tundra. Slowly he lifted me until I just brushed the ground with the tips of my mukluks. A cruel smile curled his lipless mouth.

"Now when I put you down again, Outlander—*if* I choose to put you back down instead of snapping your neck like a dry grass stalk—you will speak to me with *respect*. And then I'm going to snap your neck anyway. Got it?"

I tried to nod, but it was damned hard to do with that meathook collaring my throat. His smile got a little wider and he let me drop. I hunched on the ground, coughing and trying to get my eyes to focus again.

The lemming clan chief chuckled, then looked at Randi. "Does this pitiful specimen belong to you, my dear?" he asked. "I hope you didn't pay him *too* much. You should've asked me for a recommendation: I know where you can get corrupt bone-readers cheap. Which they are."

"I didn't pay him *anything*." Randi leaped lightly off her muckpony and knelt beside me, holding me tenderly to her bosom. I didn't know if she really had protective feelings for me or if she was only trying to piss off Chief Harvey, and I didn't much care: I was just enjoying the view. "And he's *not* corrupt. He can prove it."

"Yeah," I croaked, getting back on my feet with Randi's help. "Unlike some people I could mention." I thrust my hand into my belt pouch and yanked out a small, brown, wriggling beast that chittered angrily at the massed clan. "Does *this* look familiar?" I cried, holding the lemming high above my head.

The clan gave a shared gasp of horror and outrage.

"The Outlander has touched the holy rodent!" someone called out. "He must die!"

"Or at the very least, apologize," someone else added.

Before the mob could act, Randi snatched the lemming from my hands and confronted her outraged kinfolk. "You fools, don't you know our own lore? No Outlander may lay hands upon the holy rodents except those gifted by the gods! This man is a bonereader, a seer. No one is closer to the gods than he!"

"That remains to be seen," Chief Harvey said dryly. "My dear Princess Randi, it seems that when you told me you would rather die sooner than marry me, you weren't just whistling Dixie—whatever *that* means. The gods are benevolent, but they are also notoriously cranky. Hence, the penalty for blasphemy is death, lest the all-merciful ones take umbrage. To aid and abet one who utters blasphemy is to share his guilt and his punishment. Are you willing to take that risk?"

"Mammoth Malone is not a false seer!" Randi replied hotly. "His powers are true; I'll stake my life on it."

"You just did."

Some time later, I found myself standing in the center of the lemming clan holt with a huge brazier to my right and a table to my left. On top of the table was a basket and in that basket were a baker's dozen of prime lemmings.

At my feet were the bones I'd brought along with me. They came from a bull blargh and their spiritual power was in direct proportion to the physical power the beast had enjoyed in life. While the lemming clan watched, I recited the proper incantations, held a blargh thigh-bone high, and called out, "O gods, as we strip the changing flesh from the solid bone, strip away the shadows of deception from the substance of fact! Behold, against their nature, the lemmings no longer plunge into the depths. What's up with that? Speak to us! Give us a sign to show that what I read in the fire-born cracks in this bone is the truth! And make it a good one, okay? I'll owe you one."

I threw the bone into the fire and everyone witnessed the usual routine of *snap-crackle-BOOM-whoosh*. As soon as the smoke vanished and the flames went out, I removed the bone and studied the cracks that fire had made. It was just as I'd suspected.

"People of the lemming clan!" I cried. "The gods reveal that someone has been tampering with your rodents. I'm not one to name names, but if you check out Chief Harvey's yurt, you'll find a *very* interesting stash of herbal mind-control potions and kind of a girly atomizer. They're hidden under a pile of *Hot Clan Princess Action* scrolls."

"Lies!" the clan chief thundered. "I'll slay any man or woman who dares cross my yurt's threshold running this fool's errand!" He gestured dramatically in my direction, a foot-long knife suddenly in his hand. "If what you say is truly from the gods, I demand that you prove it here and now!"

"Hey, no sweat," I said calmly. "Not in this weather. Behold!" I picked up the basket full of lemmings and dumped it onto the tabletop. The little creatures scurried around in a panic, then formed up ranks and headed right for the edge. The lemming clan held its collective breath, watching, waiting, and—

The lemmings reached the table's edge and stopped dead.

"You see?" Chief Harvey bared his teeth in a triumphant grin. "It is even as the great prophecy says! The fate of the world is—"

I picked up one of the frozen lemmings and blew my nose on the critter's back, hard. Then I set it down again. The lemming blinked, looked around in bewilderment, then focused on the table's edge and with a joyous cry of a rodent embracing its destiny, raced forward and did a swan dive into the void. Before he hit the ground and took off for the horizon I managed to grab his fellow lemmings by twos and give them the same treatment. One rather slimy snort to the fur and they all went through the same wake-up call routine. As the last of them made the leap, the clansfolk cheered.

Chief Harvey did not. "That proves nothing," he growled. "Except that you are one of the most unbelievably disgusting seers I've ever met."

"Flatterer." I winked at him. I reached into my biggest belt pouch and pulled out one more lemming. It was the same one that Randi had brought to my yurt, the one she'd used as an improvised hankie, the one I'd toted all the way back here. I was getting kind of attached to the little guy, all the more so since I'd read the bones one more time before we'd left my yurt and they'd confirmed my theory: That to make the great prophecy serve his own ends, Chief Harvey had somehow contrived to dope as many of the local lemmings as possible with his mind-control spray, but that the effects of that potion were shattered by a big enough shock to the rodents' system. Having someone blow his nose on you? Yeah, I'd be shocked, too.

I talked fast, bringing the lemming clan up to speed. Before I could finish, a couple of enterprising young clansmen came running up, their arms full of waterskins. While their chief had been distracted, they'd been busy boys.

"We found these in Chief Harvey's yurt, just where the bone-reader said we would!" one of them exclaimed. Harvey let out an enraged roar and lunged for him, knife held high, but a bunch of his kin used sheer numbers to overpower, disarm, and immobilize him.

Arms pinioned by half a dozen angry clansmen, the lemming chief could only growl, "So you found a couple of waterskins in my yurt. So what? I get thirsty."

"For this?" I snatched one of the waterskins and squirted a little of the contents into Mrs. Vixen's face, then commanded, "You're a chicken!" When Randi's mother began to cluck, Chief Harvey scoffed, claiming I'd bought the old doll off. What'd he want? *Eggs?* I had to give seven more lemming clan tribesfolk the same treatment and get a whole flock going before I proved my point.

"What're they going to do with him?" I asked Randi as we watched the men of the lemming clan drag their former chief away.

Her eyes could've given chill lessons to a glacier. "He sleeps with the narwhals," she said somberly. Then she giggled, because it's impossible to say the word *narwhal,* even as part of a death sentence, and keep a straight face.

I watched until Chief Harvey was hauled out of sight. I felt kind of sorry for him, but the feeling faded fast when I reminded myself how far he'd been willing to go to satisfy his own desires. It was a big, wide, frozen-solid world out there and it'd be a better one for having one fewer ruthless, self-serving *oosik*-heads in it. I turned my back and left him to the narwhals.

Heh. *Narwhals.*

I stopped snickering in time to see Randi smile at me. Then I heard her give the command to her kin to go forth, find all the lemmings affected by Chief Harvey's evil plot, and free their minds in the only way possible.

"Ewwwwww!" the lemming clan replied as one. Some of Randi's clanmates touched their noses and sniffled self-consciously, yet in spite of their reluctance, they knew that if they ever hoped to get things back to normal, they had no choice but to find, catch, and sneeze on every lemming they could find.

Yeah, *ewwwwww,* but what did they expect? Like my grandpa always said: Fate's nothing to sneeze at.

It's not.

DEATH AND TAXES

Kristine Kathryn Rusch

Sixteen years and half a continent away from the great American Midwest, Patrick saw Keri. She was running out of the market across the street from his favorite coastal café, a bottle of wine in her hand.

At first he thought it couldn't be her. Her long brown hair caught the sun, reflecting it in golden highlights. She was slender, and the blue sundress she wore hung off her as if she hadn't grown into it yet.

Perpetually twenty. That was what he thought as he sipped his mocha and returned to *The Wall Street Journal*. Keri would always be twenty and coltish, not quite grown into her body.

He smiled at himself, at his romantic nature. Proof, perhaps, that he had loved her because he saw her in every gangly twenty-year-old with the promise of great beauty.

Then a car horn made him look up. The woman was standing in the middle of the street, staring at him, cars stopped all around her. The bottle of wine had shattered at her feet.

His gaze met hers.

She hadn't changed.

And there was a look of abject horror on her face.

Sixteen years and half a continent away, he'd been twenty-five, callous, and certain of his own future. The son of a prominent lawyer, he'd become a lawyer too—not with the thought of practicing law, but with the thought of creating it. He studied politics like it was a religion, and decided that he had to be in the seat of government. So, with his newly minted certificate from the bar, he headed downstate thinking the capital would welcome him.

Instead, he learned that any state capital had its share of locally grown lawyers. With his pedigree, the partners at the large local firms said, he could get a job anywhere. The following question—why here?—had an underlying meaning: what's wrong with you? How come you haven't gone to your father's firm?

He couldn't very well say he had come because he thought getting into politics would be easier here. It wasn't. He didn't know anyone, and the art of politics was the managing of connections.

Eventually, he got a job as a junior staff lawyer at the Fair Housing Coalition, a job he saw as beneath him both financially and politically. Yes, yes, he believed everyone should have a home and everyone should be treated fairly, but most of the people he saw were too dumb to realize that a lease agreement was a legal document and that their behavior had put them in trouble with their landlord and the local laws.

He could have, he later supposed, joined the inter-office coalition that was working to change some of the more egregious landlord-tenant laws, but his heart wasn't in it. Instead, he gravitated to the local university, spending his time in the student union, drinking with people who reminded him of his friends back home, talking philosophy and planning to change the world, one little decision at a time.

That was how he learned about the professors Simmons and their interdisciplinary study—financed by any number of government agencies and private corporations—and extended, theoretically, over decades.

The study only made it through the first five months of its existence.

It caused two deaths, and derailed any hopes he had of politics—at least out front. Only fast-talking and the excellent attorneys of his father's firm had saved Patrick from being disbarred.

By then, he didn't care. He'd already met and lost Keri.

And had his belief in everything shattered.

He grabbed his mocha as he headed out of the café. Interesting, he would later think, that he'd left his PDA and his newspaper, but took his beverage.

It was a clear sign that he wasn't thinking, just re-acting, running through the closely set tables to the double doors, pushing them open and hurrying into the street.

A VW bug swerved past him, and the driver shouted an obscenity. A sedan, following, leaned on its horn.

But he didn't move. He stared at the broken bottle, the red wine running like blood down the empty sidewalk.

Keri was gone—as if she had never been.

The professors Simmons were not related. There were four of them, all in different disciplines. They met at a large university faculty gathering where everyone had been asked to clump alphabetically. Their common last names, their common ages, and their uncommon interests held them together a lot longer than the meeting had.

Professor Abigail Simmons taught philosophy. She had two seminars in which she tortured undergraduates, forcing them to challenge the realities in the world around them. She also taught three graduate seminars to the same twenty grad students, the courageous few who thought majoring in philosophy was a good idea, no matter how badly it ruined them for the job market. She had grown frightened for her own job, discovering that publishing occasional articles in philosophical and religious journals wasn't enough to impress her dean. Apparently, she had to do some sort of breakthrough research to justify her salary. But, she would argue, breakthrough research and philosophy were by definition incompatible, something her dean believed she—of all people—could overcome.

Professor Roderick Simmons taught political science. He was the right-wing guru of the poli-sci department, the man that local media always called to give a reliable—and seemingly balanced—view of local elections. Roderick Simmons specialized in political systems and, in addition to his well-received books, he spent a lot of time away from campus, consulting with various groups, many of them tied to the Republican Party. He was tenured and secure, which made him perfect for this joint project.

Professor Marilyn Simmons was a biologist. Her teaching work involved occasional lectures to overcrowded 101 classes (with the day-to-day work done by teaching assistants) and supervising the research of sleep-deprived graduate students. Her seat at the university had funding from outside grants; she was a star professor who felt her own area of expertise had grown a bit stale. She was looking for a new challenge, one that would improve her prestige even more, and this, she felt, was it.

Professor Nash Simmons was the youngest and the most professionally insecure of the group. Even his specialty reflected his insecurities: His professorial bio said that he focused on cognitive analysis and behavioral theories—a lot of words, he liked to joke, that meant he had no idea what he was doing. He did whatever it was that he did from the behavioral science department, where he taught upper level psychology classes and graduate seminars about the brain. He supervised almost no graduate students and his thesis, a trailblazing work on cognitive theory that had been published to great acclaim, was now several years old. He had to produce something new, and in the way of all who were acclaimed when they were too young, he felt that the something new had to be trailblazing as well.

Patrick had no idea how the multidisciplinary study went from cocktail party talk to grant-writing to grant-winning, but by the time he had encountered Simmons-N, as Nash Simmons had been designated by those involved in the work, the study was looking for willing bodies. That Patrick wasn't a student and had an understanding of the body politic made him an unusual choice.

That he was willing to step into the real world in the name of science made him even more unusual.

But it was his willingness to apply experimental

techniques to that real world that made him the most
desirable candidate the professors Simmons had found.

Patrick walked into the market. It smelled of garlic
and fish overlaid with the faint scent of roses from a
display near the door. The place was dark compared
to the street and cramped, which instantly made him
uncomfortable. He preferred the large chain grocery
store at the end of town, where the lights were bright
and the products were displayed according to dictates
of some corporate official in another state.

As his eyes adjusted, he saw six different aisles
heading toward the seafood department along the
back wall. The seventh aisle, which started behind the
cashier, carried wines, beers, and hard liquor. Ciga-
rettes were stacked high, where no one could get them
without help from the staff.

He waited in line, noting that everyone ahead of
him had fresh produce and canned products with the
words *healthy* or *organic* or *natural* on the label. He
shuddered, hating the pretense, remembering when he
used to do the same thing just to fit in with his university friends.

When he made it to the front of the line, he reached
into the back pocket of his jeans and pulled out his
badge. Most people in this small town knew their sheriff, but he was cautious for the handful that didn't.

"The woman who just left," he said. "The one with
the wine. Can I see the copy you made of her license?"

The clerk flushed and for a moment, he thought the
gambit wouldn't work. Keri still looked twenty; she
should have been carded. Oregon law stated that anyone who looked thirty-five and younger had to show
identification to buy liquor.

But the clerk nodded and called for a manager, who took Patrick to the back office where he could look at the fuzzy identification that had been scanned into the computer system.

Kerissa Simon, the I.D. said, the last name dangerously close to Simmons—so close that it made his head hurt.

"Any idea where she's staying?" he asked, knowing the store didn't need a record of that, but often took it to avoid problems later on.

He got the name of a roadside motel, cheap but comfortable, and somehow it didn't surprise him, just like her appearance in his refuge hadn't surprised him.

Although it should have.

The meeting room was an old lecture hall in one of the campus's earliest buildings. The building was now used primarily for offices, but this room had clearly been too big to give to just any professor.

Radiators ran along the walls beneath the single-paned windows, and despite the constant heat blowing into the room, there was still a draft. Patrick sat near the door in a wooden desk chair that was at least eighty years older than he was. Some of the names carved into the desk's surface had been there so long that their edges had worn smooth.

He traced them, feeling out of place among the students, knowing he looked out of place in the suit his father had purchased for him before his first moot court appearance. Patrick had taken off the tie and stuffed it into his briefcase, but the fact that he had a briefcase instead of a backpack and a suit coat instead of a sweater already showed that he wasn't One of Them.

A few stared, and a couple kept glancing at him like they expected him to get up front and talk about the various studies.

He had had some preliminary meetings with the professors Simmons and the assisting graduate students; he assumed these other participants had as well. Now, though, they were getting together for their first official meeting. They would have four such meetings before splitting into various subsets, four meetings in which the professors Simmons would lay out the purpose of the studies as best they could, without tainting the results.

The professors stood in the hallway, heads bent, conferring, while a graduate student with a clipboard checked off the names of each attendee. Finally, a young woman, snowflakes melting on her hair and collar, stopped near the graduate student, gesturing an apology as she gave her name. Then she slipped inside the room, and took the only remaining chair, right next to Patrick.

"The snowstorm they predicted came, huh?" he asked.

She leaned away from him and finger-combed the moisture from her brown hair. Then she peeled off her coat, meticulously hanging it on the back of her seat.

"The roads are a mess," she said. "I had to park six blocks away."

He was in one of the private lots, courtesy of the Fair Housing Council. He hadn't really noticed the snow until he started climbing the hill. Then he worried about the swiftness of the storm, knowing that the sidewalks could get buried during the few short hours of the meeting.

"I'm Patrick," he said as she sat down across from him.

"Keri." She stuck her mohair scarf inside her coat sleeve, then smiled at him. "You need the money, too?"

No, he wanted to say but didn't, *I just need the company.* He knew this study paid the highest of any conducted on campus, and he thought he knew why. The interdisciplinary approach allowed for even more grant money than usual, and the professors decided to use that money to pay the subjects extra, so that they'd stick for the duration rather than leave when the semester ended.

"Money's always nice," he said, which was as much of a dodge as he wanted to give her. He wasn't sure why he felt this odd need for honesty. She was a bit thin for his taste—all elbows and knees and sharp angles. She was also at least five years younger than he was, an undergraduate when he'd been out of school for a year now.

She smiled at him, then pulled an older laptop from her backpack. The laptop barely fit on the desk. Several other participants had laptops or AlphaSmarts or PDAs with keyboards.

He hadn't even thought of taking notes, which suddenly showed him how far he had come from the student mentality. He leaned to the right, opened his briefcase, and pulled out both a legal pad and his BlackBerry, not sure which would work best in this situation.

Then the door opened one more time, and the professors Simmons came in. Their appearance was as varied as their disciplines. Simmons-A was short and dumpy, her curly hair a mixture of gray and grayer. Simmons-R wore a suit as expensive as Patrick's. His black hair had a precision cut, and his hands looked

manicured. Simmons-M was slender and wore her long
red hair in some sort of upswept 'do that looked like
it took time and three other people to create.
Simmons-N had the prerequisite professorial ponytail
and wispy goatee. His glasses fell to the edge of his
nose, making him seem even more absentminded than
he probably was.

Patrick's stomach turned. Studies, waivers, payment
by the hour, altering his behavior because he had
agreed to do so, not because he wanted to do so.

Was he that lonely? Was he that lost?

He glanced around the room, at the stressed, pimply
faces around him, and realized he probably was.

The motel had been built in the late 1950s, when
this coastal community had been known as the Dis-
neyland of the Pacific Northwest. Once there'd been
a theme park (although in those days, they'd called it
something else) on the outskirts of town. Only a few
remnants remained—a red and white store downtown
that made its own candy; a go-cart park across from
a restaurant once known as (and still referred to by
locals as) the Pixie Kitchen; and a five-story resort
hotel built in the Cape Cod style where presidents had
stayed but which had become, in the intervening years,
an old-folks' home.

This motel, unoriginally called the Beach-Goer, still
advertised that it had television and clean, comfortable
rooms. It stood on a bluff overlooking the ocean,
prime real estate that the elderly owners refused to
sell to all sorts of development firms.

The main entrance was off a narrow drive that
barely fit today's SUVs; he had no idea how the large
automobiles of forty years ago had negotiated the
same road.

He drove a truck van combination with an engine modified for high speeds. The county owned the vehicle, and if he ever lost a local election, he would have to give the thing back. Sometimes he thought he might miss it—in the back was all sorts of life-saving equipment mixed with weaponry—but mostly he saw it as a burden of his job, one of many he hadn't understood when he learned that his checkered past mattered less to the people here than it probably should have.

He parked just outside the entrance, making sure that the official decals were facing away from the street, so as not to interfere with any walk-in business. Then he went inside.

The desk clerk was a local gal who played bingo at the casino every Wednesday night. He didn't know her name, but they'd seen each other around. It was hard to miss the other locals in a town of seven thousand.

She smiled at him with recognition. He didn't have to flash his badge. He just asked for Keri Simons's room, and the clerk gave him a room key.

He weighed it in his hand as he walked along the concrete sidewalk. The key was a kind of power: if she wasn't there, he could wait inside her room, surprise her, let her know who was really in charge.

That he even had the thought surprised and appalled him at the same time. He had never thought of control in connection to Keri before.

But the study itself, the reason they met, was all about control.

And hubris.

And the belief that somehow, humankind had the power to alter its own destiny.

* * *

"For thousands of years, mankind has felt it has a destiny." Simmons-A stood in front of the long wooden desk beneath the chalkboard. She had taken a piece of chalk before beginning her welcoming remarks, almost as if the chalk provided a kind of comfort. All during her talk, she kept the piece in her palm, alternately rolling it and clenching her fingers around it.

Patrick found himself watching the chalk instead of her face, partly because she reminded him of every professor he'd ever disliked, and he wasn't exactly sure why.

"Not just a species destiny," Simmons-A was saying, "but individual destinies as well. We can turn to almost any early document based on the oral tradition and find evidence. Genesis tells us that God created Man in His own image, and just that sentence alone implies that God had a purpose for Man, a purpose that Woman screwed up, of course."

The group laughed, but it sounded dutiful. Patrick made himself smile, even though he hadn't felt like it, but Keri crossed her arms.

"Mythology gives us story after story of people confronting their destinies, from the Christ story to the Greek story of Oedipus."

Patrick shifted in his chair. He didn't need the history lesson if that was what it could be called. He just wanted to get on with the actual business of the study, whatever it would be.

"Fighting destiny is one of the greatest themes mankind has." Simmons-A tossed the chalk into the air and caught it. "Look at Joseph Campbell's *The Hero's Journey*. Look at our own fiction from popular tales of Harry Potter to *Star Wars*. Even romance fiction flirts with destiny. Romance hints that every person on earth has a soul mate—someone they're destined to be with. If we take the time to find that person— or if we recognize that person (apparently some of us do not)—then, the theory goes, we shall live happily ever after."

Keri bit her lower lip. Patrick didn't know when he started looking at her instead of Simmons-A.

"From time immemorial," Simmons-A said, "mankind has tried to fight its destiny, whatever that destiny might be. Few are born with that proverbial silver spoon in their mouths. Even fewer accept that spoon with grace. If you do not believe me, look at the remaining royal families of the world. Such tales we hear of debauchery and rebellion."

A few people smiled, but most stirred, just like Patrick had.

"What has this to do with us?" Simmons-A asked. "Simple."

She then gave a capsule summary of the faculty meeting, the conversation the professors Simmons had in lieu of listening to faculty debate.

"The only thing that the four of us could agree on that evening," she said with a smile that transformed her face from sour and discouraged to slightly pretty, "was that Benjamin Franklin was right: in this world, nothing is certain but death and taxes."

"And being born," someone said from the front row.

She looked at him in surprise. He had broken her rhythm. Simmons-M, the biologist, came forward at that moment, rescuing her colleague.

"We can't change that," she said. "We've all been born and we've survived. So once we're here, all we can be certain of are death and taxes."

She had a powerful voice with a touch of music to

it. She also had a great deal of charisma, and Patrick found himself wishing that she had been in charge of the opening speech instead of Simmons-A.

But Simmons-M knew her place, at least in this beginning. She made a little bow to Simmons-A and returned to the cluster of Simmonses near the blackboard.

"Precisely," Simmons-A said, attempting to recover. "Death and taxes. We argued about that flip remark for weeks. And somehow, we went from a philosophical discussion of certainties and uncertainties in this world to what we're calling a multidisciplinary study. According to our grants, we're attempting to see if humankind can change its known destiny. But between us—"

And she grinned again, looking over her shoulder at her colleagues like a schoolgirl. Only Simmons-N smiled back.

"—we decided to have a race. We have four things to prove. That we do indeed have destinies. That we can change them. That human-made systems—in this case, taxes—can be changed. That biological systems—in this case, death—can be changed."

Then she stepped back with a little nod, and Simmons-R came forward. Patrick slouched. He'd never realized until this moment how much Simmons-R reminded him of his father.

"You'd think," Simmons-R boomed and half the room sat up as if they'd dozed off and been rudely awakened, "that human systems would be the easiest to change. But I have my doubts. In a cursory search of governmental systems throughout human history, I cannot readily find an example of a society without taxation. Once again, let me turn to the Bible. The Egyptians . . ."

And as he discussed the levies that the Egyptians placed on their subjects, the taxes that built the Roman roads, the demands the medieval Japanese put on families, he made an eloquent, if familiar, point.

Patrick assumed the point probably wasn't as familiar to the undergraduates—few people in the room besides the professors Simmons were as overeducated as he was. He glanced at Keri. This time her gaze caught his, and she smiled.

He felt twelve again, and actually had to resist the urge to write a note on his legal pad and pass it to her. So far, she hadn't typed anything into her laptop, and he'd only written down "Death and Taxes" as if it were the topic sentence of an essay exam.

In fact, he never wrote anything else down that night. The remainder of the evening was a jumble of lecture—Simmons-M discussing the necessity of death, not just on an individual scale, but on a worldwide one (species death; death of ecosystems; the eventual death of the planet itself), and the arrogance of humankind to think it can alter death, even on a small scale; and Simmons-N referring to behavioral studies that suggest humankind's perceptions of the world have led humans to misunderstand it—and an increasingly shared but silent intimacy with Keri, who seemed to find the whole thing as pretentious and amusing as Patrick did.

"One of the things that we're going to examine," Simmons-N said in his nasal voice, "is whether time actually exists or is just a matter of perception. Because if it is a matter of perception, then nothing around us is real—or everything is real, from the primordial soup that the earth once was to this moment to the heat death of the universe, all happening at once."

Simmons-A smiled through that entire speech, as if she agreed. Indeed, it seemed to Patrick that she would have been better off saying it than the cognitive and behavioral scientist.

Patrick said that later to Keri, at an all-night coffee shop just off the main drag. They'd ducked inside on their way back to their cars—or, more accurately, on the way back to hers; he'd passed his blocks before, but hadn't told her, enjoying her company enough to hazard the ice pellets and heavy wind that the storm had become.

They found a booth in a warm corner away from the door, where they spent the next few hours laughing about the pretension, about the silly race between the disciplines *(which implied,* Patrick said, *that they would all succeed in areas of study where no one had succeeded before),* about the ironic coincidence that led the professors Simmons to each other in the first place.

Sometime during the evening, Keri postulated that the winner of the entire thing might end up being the philosopher, who had somehow gotten a group of diverse people together to reexamine their beliefs in a way that seemed as irrational as the most screwball religious cult.

Patrick had laughed at that remark. And it was his own laughter that he thought of most often when he thought of Keri. Not of those nights at his apartment, not of the horrible last day. Just the laughter.

And the professors' fight against a complacency that he didn't then understand.

He understood it now, even felt it on days when the sunlight hit the ocean, and his small town was bathed in a clear, almost unworldly light. He would tell himself, as he looked at that beauty, that he had done the best with what he had.

But there was always an itchy restlessness underneath— a what-if chorus that continued to sing: What if he had gone to his father's law firm first? What if he hadn't been interested in politics? What if he had never met Keri?

What if, what if, what if.

He played the scenarios in his mind as if he were a screenwriter finishing a script for a time-travel movie. What if . . .

He didn't know. He would never know.

He only knew that if the ancient Greeks had written his life story, the what-ifs didn't matter. Destiny was destiny. The Greeks always showed that no matter what changes mere mortals tried to make, destiny would win out.

Somehow, the Greek version seemed to tell him, he would meet Keri anyway, she would die, and everyone would be sued. Careers would end. Lives would be ruined. Simmons-N would commit suicide all over again.

And Patrick would end up here, carrying a little sheriff's badge in an unimportant town on the Oregon coast, living alone, and wishing none of it had ever happened.

He paused before knocking on the door to her room. Only now, with a key in hand, and the memories fresh, did he realize how silly he was being.

Keri Andreeson was dead. He'd seen her corpse. They all had. They had clustered around it in the biology lab, her mouth slack, her tongue protruding ever so slightly, her eyes bulging, and her skin an unnatural clay color, and they had stared.

No one had said a word. He wasn't sure, even then, if anyone completely understood how much her death would change everything.

He wasn't sure he understood even now.

He swallowed against a dry throat. Was standing here a sign of a growing insanity? The fact that he was willing to believe that some girl—coincidentally named Keri (spelling the same)—whose driver's license claimed she was twenty-two and from Illinois (Keri had been from North Dakota, complete with a melodic Fargo accent)—the fact that he was willing to believe she was the same person as the girl whose body he'd seen, the fact that he was willing to believe she was alive, and looked the same, and was terrified of him—showed just how far he had fallen intellectually, how little he believed in reality anymore, how much he hoped for miracles.

Which made him no better than the people who had placed their faith in those studies.

Or put their faith in anything, for that matter. For what was faith, but a belief in the impossible? An irrational belief in something unbelievable.

He clutched the key in his fist, tempted to open the door and scare the girl, whoever she was. Who would she report her fear to? The sheriff?

He felt a bitter smile cross his lips. Then he turned away.

Better to leave the past in the past. Better to leave destiny or fate—or the lack thereof—to the philosophers and the professors and the dreamers.

Better to return to the realities of traffic accidents and one murder a year and a lonely house on a cliff face overlooking the ocean, a house with a television as large as his bookshelves, a place where he went when he couldn't stand reality anymore.

He had just stepped into the parking lot when he heard a lock turn and a door open behind him.

And before he had time to think—or maybe he lied about that: maybe he did have time to think and he chose this—he turned, and stared Keri Simons—Keri Andreeson—in the face.

They'd become lovers even though the professors Simmons had cautioned against fraternizing. That alone might have skewed the study—or one of the studies—had any of them been completed. But the thing had barely gotten off the ground when it all ended. Patrick had just received his work orders from Simmons-R the week before, work orders that included an overall personal plan that extended for five years.

The breadth of the study surprised him, even then.

Patrick was to ally himself with a local political group—any political group would do, so long as it worked on the grass-roots level—and slowly ease them to a new vision: that taxation was a scourge, that government needed fiscal responsibility, and that required budget-tightening, reduced spending, and no new taxes. Over time, the no-new-taxes pledge would become a no-tax pledge, depending on how high up the political ladder he could climb, how much power he could attain, and how many followers he could convert to his—actually, Simmons-R's—way of thinking.

Patrick, in his naïveté, had thought it possible. Much as he believed politics was the art of compromise, he also knew it lived in the realm of argument. A charismatic man with the right argument could change the playing field—make compromise happen on the one-yard line instead of the fifty-yard line, and yet convince everyone that they had attained a middle ground.

He'd actually see it happen, years later. The political center moved farther and farther right as he moved farther and farther west. When he finally stopped long enough to look at what America had become while he'd tried to outrun his past, he found himself wondering if some of Simmons-R's other subjects hadn't continued with the experiment, working their way up the political ranks until they reached the national level, influencing everyone from senators to the president himself.

Then Patrick would shake that feeling off—surely he would recognize someone from the bad old days, right?—and he would remind himself that taxes still existed, that the United States went through cycles of heavy taxation followed by cycles of light taxation, but never, in its two-hundred-plus-year history had the United States ever gone without taxing someone for something.

.He found that vaguely reassuring, just like he found the obituary columns reassuring. People continued dying. Humankind kept fulfilling their destinies, one grave at a time.

She was twenty. That was the first thought which reached his brain as he stared at her, framed in that cheap wooden doorway, sunlight peaking over the building's eaves and the shush-shush of the ocean beyond.

In no way could this woman be in her mid-thirties, stretched by time and loss and years on the run.

She put both hands on the doorframe as if bracing herself or blocking his entrance or simply holding herself up. She was as thin as ever, coltish, all angles and lines, a girl who had not yet fulfilled her physical potential, whatever that might be.

"Can I help you?" she asked in a voice he wasn't sure he remembered.

He flushed. She had seen him pause in front of her door, maybe even seen his hand raise slightly, his fist clench the key. She'd certainly seen his indecision, and, ultimately, his retreat.

"You bought a bottle of wine today," he said, finally choosing an official approach.

"Is that illegal?" She tilted her head slightly as if she were interested in the answer. The movement was familiar. Keri used to do it when she was flirting.

His heart literally contracted. He'd only felt that squeezed sensation once before, when he saw her on the cot in the lab, her arm dangling to one side, the IV still taped into it but listing, as if it had died with her.

It took a physical effort to bring himself to the present.

"No," he said. "Buying wine isn't illegal. Neither is dropping it. But you could have picked up the glass."

"Is this town so poor that it has sends someone out to get its littering fees?" Then he heard it: the Scandinavian music behind the Fargo accent. The accent existed in the up-and-down cadence of the words as much as the long-vowel pronunciation.

She had cured the long vowels, but not the melodious intent behind them.

"I'm not here to collect any fees," he said, "even though I am the county sheriff."

"I would have thought that a man who read *The Wall Street Journal* had higher ambitions."

She had seen him then, drinking his mocha and reading his paper, taking his afternoon break and pretending he was someone else.

If she had seen him, then that look of horror had been real.

And if that look of horror had been real, did that mean she had recognized him?

And if she had recognized him, did that mean she was Keri Andreeson masquerading as Keri Simons?

"I did have higher ambitions once." He felt odd discussing them with a woman he thought dead in the parking lot of a cheap motel. "I left the café to talk with you, but you'd already vanished."

"Vanished." She smiled. That smile belonged to a woman, not a girl. It was learned. It held a wisp of sadness as well as a touch of irony. And through it all, her eyes hadn't changed. "Leaving broken glass behind."

He should have brought a bottle of wine. He saw that now. It would have eased the moment, given it some symmetry. But he wasn't that kind of thinker.

Or maybe he was—a man who knew better than to tempt fate.

"We got it cleaned up," he said as if he had something to do with it.

She nodded. She didn't ask who he was. She just studied him in the odd light filtering over the building.

Finally, he had to become the supplicant, even though he didn't want to. "Is there somewhere we can talk?"

She shrugged a single shoulder, her hands remaining in place. "This is fine."

It wasn't fine. Even though the motel was sheltered by the trees, there were other doors, other windows, other rooms where people might be. They might listen. The desk clerk might be listening, and later she'd mention the odd conversation to her friend in the bingo hall, telling them how strange the sheriff seemed on that sun-dappled afternoon.

"It's not very private," he said.

"I don't see other cars," she said, as if she'd expected his objection.

He sighed, and walked back toward her. She locked her arms, and he had the sense she had done that instead of flinching. Why would she be afraid of him? If they hadn't met, then it was something about her. If they had, then she was afraid he'd recognize her. He'd know that she hadn't died, that people had gone to jail for no reason.

But she had died. He had touched her waxy skin. He had cried for her.

He'd loved her.

He hadn't thought of any way to approach this conversation, and now he felt tongue-tied. Did he ask her if she'd known a Keri Andreeson? Wouldn't someone who had changed her name deny it? Or should he ask if she had gone to the university? Or simply ask what brought her here, to the literal end of the earth?

Finally, he settled on, "Have we met before?"

Her mouth opened as if she planned to answer him, then closed as if she thought better of it. "You mean besides now."

He nodded, not willing to play any more word games.

"Outside the market, you looked at me like I frightened you," he said, then wished he hadn't.

"That's why you ran outside?" she asked, her voice rising. "That's why you tracked me down?"

"I was already thinking you looked familiar," he said, letting the implication hang that yes, he had sought her out because he wanted to find out what terrified her.

"A lot of people say that." She gave another one-shoulder shrug. "I have one of those faces."

But not one of those bodies. Not in combination. But he didn't dare say anything like that lest she think it improper. Not that she would have any recourse here, in this small town, where he normally was the recourse.

"Still," he said. "Something you saw frightened you."

She studied him for a moment. "I don't think we have met," she said, answering the earlier question. "You seem like a man a woman would remember."

He felt his breath catch. The other Keri had described him that way. When he had asked her why she had gone with him that first night, she had said she would have regretted not going. He had asked why. She had smiled. *Because,* she said, *you're the kind of man a woman would remember.*

The echo bothered him. Everything about this meeting bothered him.

"You came to see me because you thought I was frightened," she said.

"I came because I wanted to find out if you're the woman I remembered," he said, noting the echo in his own language.

"Am I?" she asked.

He swallowed, his throat still dry. The movement was painful.

"No," he said after a moment. "I don't think you are."

* * *

She died testing the equipment. That was the official story. She was lying on the cot, taking a bit of fluid in the IV, seeing if the heart monitors worked, when somehow, she went into cardiac arrest.

Experiments on human beings, whether in government-funded labs or university trials, were forbidden in the United States. Tests could be performed—trial runs of pharmaceuticals, for example, or psychological batteries—all with waivers, properly signed, and the risks carefully laid out.

For the death study, administered by Simmons-M with help from Simmons-N, the risks hadn't been properly laid out. The implication—never proven—was that the participants would be brought to the brink of death and brought back. At the brink of death they would attempt to prolong life, through perception changes or medications or some other procedure.

But unlike the tax part of the study, none of this was written down. They didn't dare, although the grant for this part of the study had been explicit enough to bring the two professors Simmons to criminal court and drag the university into a system-wide scandal. Simmons-R got brought in when it became clear he had lobbied the institution that issued the grant money, but Simmons-A remained untouched.

Simmons-A had only her grant proposal to delineate her involvement, and her participants were going to examine the philosophical underpinnings of both death and taxes, with a touch of psychological attribution.

She claimed betrayal by the other Simmonses, and

that was how she parlayed her involvement into best-selling nonfiction books, while the other professors spent years in court.

Arguing over Keri's death. Accident? Possibly. The administering nurse was really a nursing grad student, not through her pharmacological classes. Perhaps she had put a sedative into the IV in error, or grabbed the wrong IV in error. But there was too much verbal testimony otherwise.

Too many indicators that the Simmons Three, as the press had started to call them, had become arrogant enough to believe they could conquer death. Simmons-N's suicide, shortly after he had been let out of jail on bond, led to jokes in the local media—that the Simmonses were again trying to prove they could conquer the state, if not death itself.

There was no sympathy.

Not even from Patrick.

He had stayed for the trials, even though his father told him not to. He had stayed, even though he (and the other tax participants) were classified as non-involved.

No one discovered his relationship with Keri, and he didn't confess it.

He watched as Simmons-M's brilliant career dissolved, as Simmons-R went from being an authority to being a blowhard, as the two of them sat across from a jury and waited for judgment.

What's your destiny now? The reporters would ask as the two of them and their lawyers hurried out of the courtroom every night.

Their destiny, it turned out, was a plea bargain. Negligent homicide for Simmons-M. Conspiracy for Simmons-R. A few years' time in a minimum security prison, followed by community service.

None of this brought Keri back.

Simmons-A didn't even attend the trials. When Patrick went to see her, after the trial, she grew rude and frightened when he said he wanted to discuss the study. But he didn't leave.

Did you really want to change destinies? he asked.

I told them it couldn't be done, she said. *It's the one thing philosophers agree on. That in life, some things cannot be changed.*

He almost fell for it. Then he realized that she was wrong. The Hindu system was based on knowledge— reincarnation as learning, improving, changing, growing—and, by implication, changing destiny. Not accepting it as the Christians taught. Not bowing to its inevitability, like the Greeks.

But he didn't challenge her. He no longer had the energy.

He couldn't change his destiny. But he could change his life.

So he headed west.

Where, he thought as he got into his truck, he had become a man who drowned in taxes. They created his job, provided his ride, paid his salary. In an odd, and completely unplanned way, taxes were his destiny.

Just as death would be someday.

He started to pull away, and then he stopped.

None of that explained Keri, her look of fright, her resemblance to the other Keri, the one he thought he had loved.

He couldn't leave. Not yet.

He rested his head on the steering wheel and sighed. Then he got out of the truck one final time.

He rehearsed what he was going to say as he crossed the parking lot.

Do you believe in destiny? he'd ask. *Do you believe in soul mates? In love that doesn't die?*

He didn't know what he'd do if she said yes.

But he was willing to find out.

FATE DOGS

Robert A. Hoyt

He was a somber gentleman, of the sort who might be a CEO, and as it happened that afternoon, he was manning one of the many roach coaches in New York on my lunch break. He had in his hands a copy of the *Times* but for some reason the picture on the front page wasn't quite visible.

As I walked by, he lifted his head, and in the practiced voice of a street salesman said, "Fate in a bun, sir?"

I paused in mid-step, and turned to look at him.

"What?"

"Fate in a bun, sir. I can add mustard if you like. No extra charge."

I looked up at his sign, which sure enough said, clear as day, FATE, in big bold letters, printed on gaudy yellow and red stripes.

The man behind the cart, clean-cut and wearing an expensive designer suit, was as out of place as a cabbie speaking Oxford English. Part of the act?

I had to admit, it was original. After a moment I reached discretely for my wallet.

"What the heck. I admire the gimmick. How much

for a 'fate'?" I asked, a crisp five-dollar bill between my fingers.

"Five dollars even will get you a Business Fate, sir. Would you like anything with that?" His expression didn't seem to contain even a hint of irony. I guessed it was for the believability.

"Do you have any relish?"

"Always, sir." And he reached behind the mysterious semi-counter that all of the hot dog vendors have on their cart.

A couple of moments later, he handed me a steaming hot dog. At least I imagined it was a hot dog, although I couldn't really tell through the steam.

"And, as ever, all of our fates our guaranteed, or your money back," he said, while carefully filing my bill away in a cash register that I didn't remember seeing before.

I decided that it would be prudent not to attempt to interfere with his business approach, and took a bite of my hot dog.

For a second, I didn't taste anything. There was a sort of faint, watered-down impression of a sensation, as if I were remembering eating a hot dog before.

And then, through the mists of my mind, came things that I had only half heard.

The grain company that my boss was about to drop all of the stock on due to a twenty-point decrease in the last few days. The market analysis that I glanced over briefly on the subject.

And the twelve years of market investment experience coming into sharp focus between the two.

A sweet taste flooded my mouth, like dollar bills dipped in honey.

Success.

Laboring with the weight of my sudden realization on my shoulders, I wolfed down the remainder of the hot dog, taking off in a running sprint for my office.

The lobby of the building was empty, as it always was at lunch hour. The air felt heavy with the scent of fresh coffee in twelve stories of offices, and the faint muffled tone of groundbreaking meetings being held in the remote reaches of the building.

Briefly, I paused by the elevator. But the instructions in my mind burned like a red-hot poker inserted into my forehead, and I couldn't wait.

Half crazed, I charged through the door to the stairs, and pushed my legs to their limits as I ran the seven flights separating me and my office.

I burst out into the silent reception area, and frantically greeted the secretary.

She was a stunning blonde named Sophie, who had surprisingly not developed a junkyard dog personality in so many years of playing mother hen for a little over a hundred disgruntled employees.

She was beyond beautiful to me, but then if I had to tell the truth, I was in love with her. Unfortunately, I knew she was out of my league.

"Sophes, will you buzz me in please? I forgot something on the computer." My voice wavered a little. She smiled.

I would have smiled, too, but it was all I could do not to rip down the door. I had to get to my computer.

She took my keycard and buzzed me in.

The screen saver lazily taunted me, a glaringly colored bouncy ball striking the edges of the screen and bouncing through the middle again. I moved the mouse, and with a speed that I had never had before, struck keys in rapid succession, first bringing up the stock reports, and then the information for buying the stocks.

The stock was running at a lowly twelve dollars a share.

I paused as I decided where to find crazy investors. Finally, I bought a large block of stock from my own account, but not before I called up a few friendly clients who liked taking risks.

As my own little gift to her, I sent Sophie an e-mail with my hot tip.

With a final sort of fortitude, I pressed the enter key to accept the transaction.

Three days later, the grain company announced a major breakthrough in genetic engineering. At the press conference, the representative revealed that their long awaited zero-carb flour called Puff was finally developed, tested, and slated for rapid approval. With luck, it would be hitting the shelves within the year.

The representatives from the FDA, for once, agreed.

The ticker price skyrocketed. In less than a week, the company was running strong high seventies, and was expected to continue to increase.

In the meantime, the adrenaline rush of investing my life savings on a whim had caught up with me. I even considered confessing to the boss.

And I did, when the timing was correct.

I hadn't had time to eat lunch for a while, and I hadn't gotten another fate dog since the first. But when the ticker price on the grain company went through the ceiling, I did tell my boss about my little personal venture.

There was a silence that lasted about two minutes, as he seemed to ponder the situation in a serious manner. Finally, he looked up, put his fingers around the cigar that wreathed his face in smoke, and said "You took a risk . . . you followed your gut. And it seems one of your tip buddies told a friend at one of our biggest clients, so they're mighty happy with us, too. Far be it for me to criticize one of the few workers around here with balls."

I thought I had just barely survived, until a week later a promotion came through. I was suddenly a whole new level of business broker, and my paycheck rescued my bleeding savings account from the incident.

Even Sophie pulled out a tidy little sum, her somewhat shy smile as I walked past in the mornings an ever-present reward.

And the more that I considered this unimaginable and unforeseeable run of good luck, the more trouble I had with telling myself it was all a coincidence.

But the extra wad of money in my wallet wasn't enough to justify it as true for my subconscious. And the more I thought, the more I realized that only one thing would satisfy my curiosity on the subject.

I had to get another fate dog.

So when my lunch period came around that Thursday, I used the elevator, and walked out on the street to find the vendor.

I laughed at myself when I saw him in the same place he had been then. I was almost afraid that he would have left.

As I walked up, he carefully put down his newspaper, folding it down the middle, and without yet having made eye contact said, "Fate in a bun, sir?"

"Yes," my mouth said, before my brain could attend to the matter. Wrestling for control, I added, "But could you tell me the menu first?"

"Business for five, Gambling and Dispute for ten, twenty for Love, and, of course, our famous fifty-dollar Chance, sir. Chance covers what the others don't." he said dryly. His businessman's tone could have fit in without a single turned head at a board meeting. "Difficult to get prepared, though, sir. That's why it's more expensive."

I thought about it for a second. In the end, Chance seemed the most likely prospect. But something about his tone put me off the idea. I wasn't really sure what he meant, but it didn't seem entirely pleasant. As for Dispute, that was something that the newly rich do well to avoid.

But if Chance and Dispute were out, then the most likely one would be . . .

"Gambling. I'll have a Gambling dog, please."

Once again, the same complicated technique with reaching behind the counter, and a steaming bun whose contents were just barely obscured emerged.

I stared down at it. For a second I felt somewhat apprehensive.

"No, it's just a silly urge. A lucky strike. Nothing to be afraid of," I told myself.

I rammed the hot dog in my mouth quickly, before I could think of a rebuttal and let my good sense get in the way.

Once more, the watered-down hot dog taste, like eating something extremely far away. And then, without warning, I knew more than I had ever realized about the world around me.

I could taste the things around me happening, and

I knew at once where the money was being made and lost.

"No!" This was in my best Telling-a-Dog-It's-Done-Something-Wrong voice, and aloud, which fortunately didn't make me stand out from all the street crazies around.

But I had to interject some willpower.

Too little, too late. My legs were off on their own. Like a deranged maverick, I cut through the crowd of lunchtime commuters.

I would have felt some sort of fatigue, I suppose, after the first mile, if I had paid attention, but I was more concerned with this urge to keep going.

Finally, my legs drew me to a halt in front of a local gambler's haven. It was a grand and exceptionally notorious establishment in my circles, hidden behind a grubby iron door in a back alley, ignored by police who didn't want to get certain people angry.

My legs took me through the front door. The floor of the gambling den bristled in my senses. And then, I saw the roulette table.

I couldn't hold myself back. I ran past the bouncer, who vouched for me to the boss with a nod, and entered the game with ten thousand dollars.

The wheel spun hypnotically and the whirl drew me in. A man standing next to me took me for a tourist, snickering under his breath.

He didn't expect my money to last too long.

But my brain screamed at me. Red 32.

With no choice but to obey, I placed all of my cash on Red 32. The wheel whirled, the little white ball clicking along rhythmically.

Time slowed down for a moment as the ball came to a stop balanced between two numbers, finally landing on Red 32 with a little plunk that took up the majority of my consciousness.

Three spins later, a couple of men came up to me and ominously requested that I retire for the evening. I knew better than to say no.

I cashed out, getting a standard tin suitcase to hold my phenomenal winnings—less my original stake, which I pocketed for ready cash—hailed a cab, and took it home.

But as I stepped out of the cab I heard a click behind my head.

My thoughts cleared as only a cocked hammer on a powerful handgun can make them.

"And now, sir, if you would be so kind as to hand over the suitcase, then I believe that we can both call it a night," the barrel pressed into my neck.

I tried to calculate my chances in my head, and realized that my ability to gauge odds had deserted me, like my heightened ability to sense the air around me.

"Very interesting," I said, to no one in particular, as I handed the suitcase to the man who had come up behind me. "Disappears under high duress."

By this time, my cab driver had taken the opportunity to get far away from us both.

"Much obliged. And now, as I can see I have made you uneasy, I shall be glad to repay you by helping you sleep."

A gun handle clocked me like a cavalry charge, and I fell to the ground.

The early morning sun shone on my face. I was in the suit that I had been wearing the day before, slumped over on my front doorstep.

The quick run over my senses acknowledged that I had the sort of deep-seated headache that seeps into your brain and permeates every single nerve with pain.

I looked at my watch, which luckily I still had.

But then again, in my state, I didn't look the sort of person who would own a watch anyway.

My spine went as straight as a rod. I was an hour late for work.

Not even bothering to dress in fresh clothes, I stood up, and felt in my inside pocket. A sheaf containing ten thousand dollars—less last night's cab fare—came to hand.

I hailed a taxi. Ten minutes later, I was standing in the reception lobby of the ninth floor, where my promotion had booted me.

Of course, it looked like the same lobby as the seventh, and more importantly, Sophie was at her desk.

She looked at me in surprise, "Are you all right? You look horrible." She seemed genuinely concerned.

"Fine, fine. Could you just check me in, Sophes, and hold my calls for a while? My head hurts a little. Nothing more."

A little meaning horribly, I added to myself.

"Normally, I would. But the boss asked to see you as soon as you came in. You didn't check back in yesterday."

Damn. I had forgotten to come back to work in my starstruck haze.

I would lay even money now that the boss was not about to offer me a CEO position. If I was lucky, he might offer me references after he fired me.

I should be so hopeful.

"Good luck." She said, as she buzzed the private elevator with the button under the desk.

My humiliation was complete. I would be fired after showing up to the office and attempting to get the girl that I loved—I supposed it was high time I admitted it—to check me in, immediately after I disappeared randomly . . . all the while looking like a bum.

Gambling fate. Lovely.

I stepped into the elevator. The doors shut with a ding and it began to whir along quietly, passing floor after floor.

Finally, the moment to face the music came. The elevator doors opened, revealing the boss, looking stern behind the thick, smelly cigar smoke.

"Take a seat," he said, hand gesturing toward the leather guest chair.

I did so, the red carpet thick like molasses under my feet.

"I hear that you disappeared yesterday. Care to elaborate?" he asked, with a sort of trap taunting me in his voice. You could almost hear a sort of half-hearted chuckle in his question, as if he were enjoying a fine irony at my expense.

I considered telling him about the fate dogs, and the inexplicable urge to go and gamble impossibly large amounts of money, and the whole shebang.

And then I asked myself why I felt it necessary to get into therapy, and the loony bin, when I was already getting fired.

"I ran into a client," I said, my mind spinning an elaborate yarn. His eyebrows rose.

"Who?"

"I don't remember. We went out for drinks, and then I came back around. But a man mugged me, and clocked me on the head, so I don't feel so well, as you may imagine."

A complicated alibi needed more memory than I had.

He stared at me for a moment.

"I see," he said, and then after a minute asked, "Can I get you a drink?"

Why was he toying with me?

"No, thank you."

"I didn't think so." He shook his head and leaned forward. The desk creaked under his weight.

"How about you just tell the truth, kid? You met some blonde piece who you helped invest, and you have a hangover from drinking enough alcohol to stock an infirmary. I was young once, too."

He got up, poured himself a gin, and downed it in a single shot.

"Look, just don't let it happen again. We can't have you disappearing in the middle of an important deal. Now go on. Use the executive gym and get yourself cleaned up."

I couldn't believe it. I walked over to the door of the elevator. It made a little ding, and opened. The boss stopped me by the door.

"Remember, kid, I have hopes for you. Do me and yourself a favor and don't piss it away."

I just nodded.

After the ride down, I was greeted with Sophie's face. She was waiting expectantly.

"Which way to the hotshot's gym, Sophes? I need to freshen up a little."

I handed her my access card, and she swiped it for mods with a smile I hoped was because I had not been fired.

"Down the hall and to the left. Congratulations on surviving!" she called to me as an afterthought.

I just smiled halfheartedly, and headed for the shower.

For a day or two, I was too scared to think about the hot dog stand.

But hope springs eternal.

The more I thought about it, the more I fell for Sophie. I even occasionally toyed with the idea that she might feel the same way about me.

And if there was anything that might give me the fortitude to charm her, I had to try it. And then I thought of the Love option the man had mentioned.

It was insanity, I knew. I was throwing good money after bad, I knew.

But . . . I knew I would regret it if I never tried.

I waited carefully, biding my time until Friday came.

That way, if something went wrong, then at least it wouldn't interfere with work. I wasn't taking any chances. I waited until the day ended to find the hot dog vendor, sitting in the usual place.

"May I ask you something?" I asked the man in the booth, and waiting only long enough for him to glance up at me, plowed ahead "I know that this is a crazy question, but will a 'Love' make me able to charm a girl whom I already love?"

He stared at me blankly. "Yes," he replied flatly, without thought.

I forked over a twenty-dollar bill.

"One Love, please. Mind you, remember the ketchup." I was half deranged with precautions.

Seconds later, I held in my hand a Love dog. I didn't even think about it. There was no argument, I just ate it.

And even as I bit into it, I realized that I had only

asked if I would be *able* to charm her. And it struck me very hard that I likely wouldn't *want* to.

However, I could already feel the beginning of the craziest night of my life pressing itself into my mind.

I knew where to go, and I knew what to do for the night.

My first stop was a local nightclub.

Almost involuntarily, I greased the doorman with a hundred-dollar bill, and slipped through the door.

I was there for half an hour. In that time I got two drinks and two girls who had had far too many drinks.

I don't recall their names.

I don't even recall offhand whose place we went to.

Two hours later, I woke up in the bed of whomever's place we had gone to, in between the two girls.

I resisted the urge to peek beneath the covers, even though I knew that if they were in the same state I was in, I would regret that for the rest of my life.

I got dressed hurriedly, took a quiet shower, and left the apartment with the other two still sleeping.

It was early in the morning. The majority of the city was undoubtedly still asleep.

I walked beneath the city lamps, the early morning chill clearing my head. It was a quiet part of the city, and there were no people on the streets.

Well, so much for saving myself for marriage. Or, somewhat more urgently, just facing Sophie. The worst part was that I remembered everything because I kept thinking about Sophie. I had had a night that other men only dreamed of, and I had actually hated every minute of it.

Congratulations, I said to myself. *You have officially gone crazy.*

But who cared? I had pretty much blown it anyway.

My last chance to get Sophie was gone. I had used the fate dogs, and they had reacted perfectly.

But not the right "Perfect" for my purposes.

I was ready to cry. I saw worst-case scenarios rain down, each one with her finding out in more and more uncomfortable ways.

It would take a miracle.

The man said Chance dogs handled "everything else."

"Forget it," I said aloud. "It isn't going to happen."

I wasn't worried about looking insane. There was no one around, and besides, I might well be insane anyway.

But that prying little voice that had gotten me into this situation in the first place persisted.

And little by little, I broke down, until I found myself standing on the street where the vendor normally was, in spite of my better judgment.

For a moment, I peered into the night. I told myself that I wouldn't see him.

For a second I believed it. But I knew what I wanted.

And then, even in the fog of the predawn glow, I could see the gaudy yellow and red stripes.

They wrapped around me like a blanket, and I took a step foreword.

I would just buy a Chance dog, and then I could have Sophie.

That was how the world worked, I knew it.

I walked forward, and came to a stop in front of the vendor.

He looked up in anticipation. The air grew heavy and thick, as if he were simply waiting for me to give a request that he already knew.

Even in the city that never sleeps, there is a lag in pedestrian traffic at five in the morning on this street.

But looking around, I suddenly realized that I was standing alone on an empty street. Not even a car in the road.

"Can I help you?" he said. His slate gray eyes fixed cold and unfeeling on mine.

My skin crawled.

It didn't feel right.

It wasn't right. But I needed to do it. It was my only chance with Sophie.

But that wasn't right, either. Even I knew that.

Even before, we had always talked. We knew each other. Maybe I could have a chance anyway.

A chance at a little more than a one-night stand. That was really what I had been after, even if I hadn't admitted it.

I felt my hand go to the money in my pocket.

I was about to spend fifty dollars. I was about to lose control of my decisions again.

Could I really afford that?

I paused. The tiny little itch in my mind suddenly had a megaphone, and was screaming in my ear, in none too diplomatic terms.

I never really could control the fates these dogs gave me, and telling myself I could was madness. I knew in my heart that another fate dog would just make me lose control again.

And at the same instant I realized that none of them could possibly act as I would. It was like becoming someone else, someone who loved other people, knew other things.

Wanted other things.

And none of them were Sophie.

Finally, defiantly, I seized the reins of my own willpower.

I stared the man at the stall in the eyes.

"Good morning," I said, with a slightly ironic smile on my lips, and walked away.

The man in the stall went back to reading his paper. The sun peeked over the horizon, showering the streets with gold.

After all, if I still had a chance, then I wanted to make the most of it.

I thought about where she lived.

It wasn't a long walk, really.

"Besides," I chuckled to myself, "I feel lucky."

THE MAN WITH ONE BRIGHT EYE

Jay Lake

This is a story about the Lord Douglas-Ouyang, who was born to a life ordained by the group-mothers of the worlds. This is a story about how the Lord Douglas-Ouyang met the Queen of Roads and defeated her knife golem. This is a story about how the Lord Douglas-Ouyang vanished beyond the rainbow wall. Most of all, this is a story about how the Lord Douglas-Ouyang cheated fate.

Now, like life itself, the story begins.

"He is born," proclaimed group-mother Anna-Chao to her colleagues arrayed in council at the Bright Oval. Her hair streamed on a time-wind, blown back so far no one save a Kroniate adept could have seen the other end. Some said she had lost—or perhaps hidden away—her favorite lovers in the years-long amber tresses. Whatever the fate of her hair, and those who might have climbed it down the well of entropy, her eyes were firmly in the present. Blazing with chips of congohelium, in point of fact, so that her gaze cast shadows.

The other group-mothers bowed their heads in vary-

ing combinations of ill-suppressed resentment and
ophthalmic self-preservation. None objected.

Anna-Chao reached a few hours into the past and
unswaddled a sleeping baby from an eddy in her hair.
The child was not much bigger than the palms of her
two hands but he was fat in that way that babies are.
His pate was bald, lacking even the ordinary fuzz
clouding an infant's scalp. Some of the group-mothers
noticed he had no knot upon his belly, just smooth
skin from groin to nipple, but they had forgone their
right of objection.

"I give him vision," Anna-Chao said. She used her
left pinkie to hook her left eye out of her head, then
popped the same eye from the sleeping child. He woke
with a pained screech, but Anna-Chao slid her blazing
orb of congohelium into the baby's socket, and he
settled down again. His natural eye, pathetic, bloody
thing that it was, she tucked back into her hair. "He
shall be the Lord Douglas-Ouyang."

"Homage to the group, homage to the worlds, homage to the Lord Douglas-Ouyang," the group-mothers
intoned. One by one they came to kiss the child, then
filed out of the Bright Oval to scuttle off for coffee
or sex or some other diversion, and to gossip over
how Anna-Chao was passing ever farther out of phase
with the realities of life.

The little Lord Douglas-Ouyang was seven before
he understood that not everything he saw was real. Or
even imaginary. His one bright eye frightened other
children, though its tendency to occasionally set fires
brought them giggling back to him again. (He learned
to stay away from the bracken of his forest home
when the weather was dry.) With that eye he saw seas

of honey-colored hair, the fate of men, and sometimes what was going to be served for dessert later in the week. With his other eye, colored the gleaming blue of a spring sky, he saw the usual things of childhood: hammock bowers, teachers clanking and chuffing up their morning head of steam, Improbables springing out of traps in the soil to go about their odd business.

Both eyes saw rainbows, of course.

He was still bald, though wrapped in a dignity that no amount of hair might have given him.

Maristella was the child the little Lord Douglas-Ouyang was closest to. She had eyes the color of their crèche-forest, hair the hue of rhododendron bark, and could run faster than any of them. The little lord and Maristella often slept in the same hammock. "You will be a hero," she said, cradling him close and stroking his scalp. "Just like Vuang." She whispered stories of champions from ages past: Vuang of course, as well as Rose-Kolodny, Churchill, Piotr the Great, Alaric— the list ran on and on.

Douglas-Ouyang knew that she was right. His one bright eye saw futures of gleaming swords and chanting crowds and honors given on tall reviewing stands. "Please," he asked her. "What must I do to be a proper hero?"

"Be like the great ones out of time."

So, fighting with sticks among the deep green, the Lord Douglas-Ouyang made it his business to be like the great ones out of time.

When the Lord Douglas-Ouyang was fourteen, liveried men came and took him away from his weapon and his women. He was dancing naked and armed on the edge of a cliff, his hairless body gleaming with

olive oil. Far below his feet a frothing fall flickered
with winged salmon making their way up the gravity
gradient. His three lovers of that week, Althea,
Naomi, and Merope, sat at the edge of the grove,
legs tucked beneath them, their pert breasts in no way
distracting the lord from his sword dance.

Three men arrived without warning through a door
of air, which instantiated to reveal gleaming lights in
darkness beyond. They were tall, broad-chested, with
the heads of dogs above their scarlet collars with the
silver piping. One snarled at the girls, who fled
screaming into the flicker-leaved aspens beyond the
lord's dancing ground. The other two moved to seize
the Lord Douglas-Ouyang.

The lord stepped into their attack and pierced the
shoulder of one, a proper hit. The man did not yelp,
but simply ran Douglas-Ouyang down, snatched away
his foil, and broke his arm in the three places.

His fellow lashed restraints to the lord's feet.

"That was *not* sporting," Douglas-Ouyang yelled as
they dragged him to the door of air.

"You will trouble me no more today," growled the
one he'd wounded. "If you do not fight to win, why
fight at all?"

Indeed, he thought, but he kept his bright eye shut,
for he wanted to know who had sent him this attack
more than he wanted to burn away the faces of these
miserable miscreants.

In darkness reeking of machines and stale air, the
Lord Douglas-Ouyang's captors dropped him before
six women seated in an arc. He could smell their sex
upon them, and hear their breaths quickening as they
looked him over.

"You are much changed since we saw you last,"
one said.

Douglas-Ouyang knew by the catch in her voice that she felt desire for him. He rolled onto his left hip, favoring his broken arm and allowing them to gaze upon the beauty of his youth. Let them be distracted— he knew who these women were now. His mother's friends.

"Greetings, group-mothers." His bright eye saw them in a different place, filled with light and water, being harangued by Anna-Chao. "You are most brave to lay hands on me so."

"We have already destroyed the dogs." A different voice this, but also eager. Distracted as well, judging from the cadences. "No one else will mark this moment."

"Save me," said the Lord Douglas-Ouyang. "I do not expect my memory to lapse in the foreseeable future."

"A threat?" This, from a third.

"I do not threaten." Douglas-Ouyang kept his voice mild. "I merely remember."

"Enough," said the first. "You were made for a purpose. This is why you are the Lord Douglas-Ouyang, and not merely a man in your own right. The time has come to prepare you for the next stage of that fate."

He opened his bright eye and gazed upon them with the fire of congohelium. Though none of the group-mothers had forgotten what gift Anna-Chao had bestowed upon her son, they had not realized his control of the forces behind the door of his eyelid.

The Lord Douglas-Ouyang moved his gaze from group-mother to group-mother. Each shrieked or moaned, covered her face, cowered in her robes. Their chairs were not thrones, merely folding metal seats. The great machines behind them showed in the bright-

ness as nothing more than racks lined with broken
automata, some still struggling weakly or mouthing
forgotten speech.

And they were dumpy, pale, flowing with flesh.
Nothing like his sweet girls back in the forest, who
were lithe as fawns, able to wrap themselves round
him and each other like grapevines.

He shrugged off his bonds with the power of his
bright eye, healing his arm in the same moment. Then
he stood, and walked close to each seat in turn. His
nakedness swung before the group mothers as the
Lord Douglas-Ouyang stared each down, then
moved on.

"No one tells me what I will or will not be. No one
tells me what I am capable of." He let them see, and
scent him, before bounding off naked into the darkness, away from his fate and toward whatever chance
might bring him next.

When the Lord Douglas-Ouyang was twenty-one,
he went traveling among the worlds of man. The Second Great Road ran through all of the major cities of
all the worlds, and many of the minor ones. To use
that storied highway one was generally required to
travel in the company of a Kroniate adept, or else
purchase a ticket on one of the δ-coaches, great silver
and copper Faraday cages powered by force-grown
whale muscles immersed in nutrient tubes. Kroniates
were scarce and rarely for hire, while the δ-coaches
were the bane of ethicists everywhere; they also possessed a distressing tendency to leave their passengers
with unscratchable itches deep inside their backs and
buttocks.

Because of the congohelium embedded in his bright

eye, the Lord Douglas-Ouyang had found he could simply walk the Second Great Road. So he adventured, dressed in the simple azure robes of a *na*-paladin. Some cities taxed his weapons, others set men to bar his way or fight him. All bowed before him when the lord grew bored with struggle and presented his parentage.

There came a day when the sky above the lord's head had just segued from a pale violet to a creamy mauve. The Second Great Road had been surrounded by the spare windworn rocks near the desert city of Port Desire. In that moment the highway made transit into the redrock highlands above the ancient pleasure domes of Eura-mél-Khos, where even the very air is perfumed with the scent of youth in ecstasy. The Lord Douglas-Ouyang smiled to see Eura-mél-Khos—many travelers never reached those fabled precincts, and he had a mind to sample such delights as "three virgins in wine."

The creature that rose from the fractured pavers before him was a nightmare out of darkest legend. It was all metal, with a thousand edges, bundled blades and whipcord saws and glittering scalpels, a whirling serrated disk for its cyclopean eye, and a mouth made of needles flexing open and shut.

"Who are you?" the Lord Douglas-Ouyang asked, drawing his chromed yatagan with the circuits printed on the blade. (He had taken up the yatagan which his mother had prepared for him when the foil proved too predictable, not to mention easily broken.)

"He is mine," said a woman behind him.

The Lord Douglas-Ouyang turned to see the most beautiful woman in all the worlds. She was of moderate height, with a good set of hips beneath the fall of an orange robe, hair stubbled short and brown. But she carried within herself a soul-stealing beauty that nearly drew him down.

The lord cut a charm through the air with his yatagan, the circuits glowing as the blade whipped. Her glamour faded some, though his body still strained with desire.

"All men are yours, lady," Douglas-Ouyang said with a clumsy attempt at gallantry.

"Most do not draw blades in homage." Her voice was mild, but still she nodded past her shoulder. "Kill him for me."

The Lord Douglas-Ouyang did not know whether she spoke to him or to the creature of blade and edge, but he supposed it did not matter. In either case, the command was the same. This was the first great battle on his hero's journey. He moved even before she was done speaking, his *na*-paladin's robes hardening into ballistic fabric as the yatagan began singing a death song in three voices—the whistle of a microscopically sharp edge, the hiss of cloven air, and the hum of ancient circuits brought fully to life.

He was made and born to be the greatest fighter of his age. He was blessed by a parentage both magical and mighty. He carried a weapon which gods would have squabbled over. Still the Lord Douglas-Ouyang could do little better than stand his ground against a creature that had more blades than a sunflower has seeds, and that spread them wide as a fisherman's net. Every twisting block the lord made was surrounded by a cage of steel. Each canny, curving stroke met a counter that seemed to have been woven from his own thoughts. Every low thrust was caught with a lower parry and a dozen replies in the same moment.

They fought till sweat stood in the lord's eyes. They fought till the edges of his azure robes were lacy with cuts, while sparks striking off his opponent had set the roadside grass to smoldering. They fought till the shadows walked from one side of the highway to the other. The most beautiful woman in all the worlds watched with lips pursed and eyes glittering.

Finally, as the lord's arms tired and his blade began to waver, she called, "Halt."

He and his opponent both stopped in the same breath.

"My lady," the Lord Douglas-Ouyang said. He lowered the tip of his blade and surreptitiously took a moment's rest.

"No one has ever stood before my knife golem so long." She walked around him, inspecting him. "You are that child, are you not? Of the renegade Anna-Chao."

"Yes, she is my mother," he said, thinking of years-long hair the color of honey. "And no renegade at all."

"The perfect man. Well, I am the perfect woman." The smile was far more disturbing than perfected. "You may address me as 'your majesty.' I am the Queen of Roads. Bend a knee, sir."

The Lord Douglas-Ouyang had bent a knee to no one in his life, not even the group-mothers. He would not start now. Instead he turned back to the knife golem and hurled the yatagan high into the air, trusting its circuits to know what to do next. He stepped close into the blades, trusting his *na*-paladin's robes to accept their edges and turn their hurts. He opened his one bright eye and stared close into the whirling disk of the knife golem's eye.

The congohelium's translight flared off the spinning metal and fractured into more colors than the world could know, blinding both the knife golem and the Queen of Roads. The yatagan dropped from the sky right between the bent blades of the golem's head, shattering the engraved metal chem within.

The Lord Douglas-Ouyang snatched free his trusted blade and ran for the next transit of the Second Great Road, forgoing the pleasure domes of Eura-mél-Khos and its wine-soaked virgins. Even as he plunged into the wet night beyond, he wondered what the Queen of Roads had intended for him.

At the age of twenty-eight, the Lord Douglas-Ouyang was finally ready to become a man. He had found his way back to the high castle of the group-mothers, above the Sea of Indolence. There he studied the law and the sciences and the arts. He killed a free man, and raised a slave to life. Word would come from time to time of the rampages of the Queen of Roads, but even the great Kroniate proctors could not seem to catch her at her crimes.

He sat with Anna-Chao on a terrace overlooking the worldforest that stretched east and south from the quiet shores of the sea. Her hair reached some hours into the past here before being folded by a mouse-bodied servitor who was doing maintenance.

"I have come to understand more of you, Mother," the Lord Douglas-Ouyang said. "You command secrets within secrets, but you are not too subtle."

"Not at all," said Anna-Chao. "Others make what they will."

"You made *me*."

"That is what parents do."

They both watched the doghawks bark and quarrel

above the trees awhile, and enjoyed the breeze scented with lemons. Finally, the Lord Douglas-Ouyang spoke again. "I do not understand one thing."

"Only one? You are to be congratulated."

He refused to be diverted. "I do not understand why you made me."

She sucked air through her teeth a moment, in his experience a sure sign she was about to lie. "I reach backward through time to the uttermost years, when men cowered from the tiger-haunted night in their primitive zeppelins and mud huts, praying to some lost god through vacuum tubes. But I only reach forward as far as I can see, and I am tethered by the present." One hand slipped up to pat her hair. "You as my child, my son, are also my spear cast forward through the years to come. It is your fate to carry my fate with you. Ever it has been so with parents and children."

The Lord Douglas-Ouyang stood and went to the railing of the terrace, leaning on the low limestone with his back to his mother. "In earlier years, I would have rejected your weird out of hand. 'Say what you will,' I might have told you, 'but my fate is my own.' I know better since I met the Queen of Roads, who commanded me with words. I am not my own." He turned back to his mother. "But when I step through the Chalcedony Gate and become a man, then I will be my own."

She opened her one bright eye, twin to his, and seared him with the light of her regard, until the Lord Douglas-Ouyang saw only rainbows inside the translight of congohelium. He could not counter her attack, not his own mother's, so instead he let himself tumble backward over the railing. Unfortunately, he fell into the rainbow wall within the translight.

The Queen of Roads waited there for him.

"You killed my knife golem," she said from atop a surge of bright maroon. "You owe me a servant, or servitude."

Once more her words possessed him, but the Lord Douglas-Ouyang had not wasted his studies. He closed his ears with snatches torn from yellow and smiled at her. "I owe you nothing," he said, "but I will give to you freely nonetheless."

Blind to her voice, he could not hear her response, but the lord took her by the hand. "Walk with me awhile," he shouted, knowing his words to be over-loud from his temporary deafness.

Her own beauty did not suffice to armor the Queen of Roads from Douglas-Ouyang's charms, and so she followed him.

A hairless man with a strange gleam in one eye and a woman with plain but extraordinarily beautiful features stepped out of a door of air onto a corner of an ordinary street. He looked about thirty-five, she a little older. Both had a strange pallor to their skin.

No one noticed. Not in this city of pale stone and black roads and gray skies.

"Here," he said. "We will never need to go back. Or forward either."

She tapped the side of his head. He pulled something bright yellow from his ear, that vanished amid a belch of diesel exhaust from a passing bus. "Sorry."

"What about her?"

Anna-Chao, the Lord Douglas-Ouyang knew she meant. He reached back into nowhere and retrieved his gleaming yatagan, circuits bright with the heat of metal thought. "I can cut her hair with this, should it reach across the hours and years."

They both looked around. Honey-colored tendrils would stand out in this place better than fresh blood on wedding sheets. She shrugged and picked a direction. He followed, the two of them shedding unnoticed rainbows as they went, until both were gray as the people around them.

No one even noticed the sword.

Now, like life itself, the story ends.

Not with death, or the grand agony of families and generations. Someone else was found to work the will of the group-mothers in the name of fate. Someone else patrolled the Second Great Road with a mystic weapon. Someone else fit what was needed, for someone else always does.

But the man with one bright eye and the oddly beautiful woman had their time together. When he was done with his life, he sent the sword back to his mother's latest hero, to tempt fate once more.

A TAPESTRY OF SOULS

Paul Crilley

We fought a war against God today.

When I remember the events of this terrible afternoon, two images will stand out from all the others, stark against my mind like the black branches of a tree against a gray winter sky. The first was a brief glimpse I had of the Goddess, caught through a gap in the screaming hordes. She was felling seraphs with glances from her terrible, beautiful eyes, sending them plummeting to the ground with their wings ablaze, leaving trails of greasy smoke as they fell.

The other image . . . well, the other is the reason for all of this.

You see, it is my fault, this war. I bear the burden, but I feel no guilt.

For it was love that led me here, and love is pure, is it not?

She came to our village one summer's afternoon when I was twelve. I sat in the shade of the stables watching the horses flick their tails lazily against the heat, their sides quivering with irritation at the flies. My father was working in the forge across the street.

I could hear the pounding of hammer on metal, its usually loud echo muted in the stifling air. The heat was a massive hand pressing everything down, dulling everything with its weight. I felt a twinge of guilt. How hot must it be in the forge? I was supposed to be helping him, but again I had managed to escape the work. It was not that I shied from any kind of hard labor; it was just that I did not want to learn the craft of smithing. We had argued, like we always did, and I had stormed out feeling frustrated and angry, because he asked the question he always asked me when we fought: What did I want to do with my life then? I didn't know, but he couldn't understand that. He was a practical man, my father.

I had just resolved to head home and fetch him a tankard of ale by way of apology when I saw the air above the crest of the hill outside the village begin to shimmer.

I wiped the sweat from my eyes and peered hard, thinking it nothing more than the heat waves rising from the ground.

But then I watched as the shimmer drew closer, floating slowly above the ground.

A voice shouted suddenly behind me. Stef, whose turn it was to make sure the talismans around the village were still intact, stood in the middle of the dusty street staring over my shoulder. He shouted again and ran off. I could not tell whether it was fear or excitement. Possibly both. I stood up and sprinted after him.

The town square was filling rapidly by the time I arrived, panting and sweating and nursing a stitch in my side that was like a needle point under my ribs. A discordant clashing of noise crashed around the

square, people jostling and shoving each other as they
vied for positions they thought would be the most ad-
vantageous. I hung back, uncomfortable, not understanding the barely suppressed violence I seemed to
sense in people who were normally the best of friends.
Others my age were huddling in the doorways of the
buildings surrounding the square. I saw my friend
Kian being pushed through the mob by his red-faced
mother.

Other things, images and sounds, assailed my senses
until I felt myself suffocating beneath their weight:
Kian's mother slapping Mrs. Kenndir, raking her
cheek with ragged nails when she failed to move out
of the way. Sela's father raising his arms in the air as
he tried to calm people down. A feeling of building
pressure, like the air before a thunderstorm.

My ears popped. I felt myself falling, my vision
blurred behind a sudden veil of tears I did not
understand.

Then someone propped me up. I wiped my eyes
and saw my father smiling down at me, his eyes excited. He ruffled my hair, his way of saying sorry. Then
he cradled his hands together and boosted me up onto
one of the empty ale barrels that the oldsters used as
gaming tables outside the tavern.

"They notice everyone, young one. No need to get
crushed with the fools."

Then silence fell, utter and complete. I looked up
and saw everyone staring behind me. She was coming
toward us, no longer a vague presence in the air, but
a woman, the most wondrous woman I had ever seen,
and floating four feet above the ground. I squinted at
her and saw that the shimmering I had seen earlier
formed the shape of half-seen wings, extending ten

feet to either side of her body. She drew abreast of me. Her long black hair floated in the air behind her, drifting in silent, undulating eddies. A strand touched my face, a spark of energy. I must have cried out, for she turned to me and smiled. Her hand came up. She stroked my face, wiping my forgotten tears away.

My life changed in that instant.

I stared at her in awe. "I love you," I said simply, so low that even my father directly below me could not hear. But she did. Her smile widened. Her deep brown eyes looked into mine.

"Thank you," she said. Her lips did not move as she spoke, though I heard her words clear as the clang of metal on a winter's morning. "I love you, too."

Her hand lingered for a moment, and then left my face. She turned her eyes forward and drifted higher into the air, over the heads of those watching me jealously.

My heart felt empty. I wanted to cry out for her to return, to put her hand back on my face and leave it there forever. I wanted to look into her eyes again, for I was sure there was something hidden there, some unknown truth that I would discover could I but stare long enough.

I watched her all afternoon. My father told me she was a messenger from the Goddess who lived in a thousand-foot tower somewhere to the north of us. She carried petitions and grievances back with her so that all could be judged fairly. He said the tower was made from the frozen tears the Goddess wept when her lover deserted her and brought night to the world, the time when evil walks and good must hide.

He also told me of a man who thought himself powerful enough to rule over a section of countryside in

his own name instead of that of the Goddess. Her
anger was terrible, and she rained fire down upon the
man and his subjects as a lesson to all.

I shivered in the cooling afternoon, my earlier sweat
now clammy on my body. My father left to close up
the forge and stoke the fire so it would not die. I
watched her face as each person stepped up to speak
to her. I don't think it was my vanity, but I did not
see her smile at any of them the way she smiled at me.

There were few people left now. She would be leaving soon. My heart ached, my stomach clenching un-
pleasantly at the thought. I was scared I would never
see her again.

Twilight faded into night as I made my way up the
road outside the village. I walked for half an hour
until I came to a large tree growing by the side of the
road. I was relying on my hope that she would carry
on through the village and follow the road northward.

I sat down with my back to the tree's rough bark,
staring up at the stars and listening to the insects chir-
ruping in the bushes. I stroked the feathered talisman
I had taken from our home. It was a strange feeling
to be out at night. I'd heard stories of the horrors that
scoured the land every time the Goddess went to sleep
and her Betrayer awoke, but the fear I expected did
not come. I think it was the fact that I felt safe with
her close by rather than any benefits the talisman
might bring. It was as if she held the evil back, that
while I thought of her I could not be harmed.

A cool breeze brushed my cheek and I thought
again of her touch caressing my face. I closed my eyes
and settled in to wait, but it was not long before something made me sit up again.

I peered out from behind the tree and saw her drifting slowly up the road. I stepped out from my place of concealment and waited as she drew closer.

She stopped in front of me, her wings more clearly visible now as they picked up silver highlights from the stars. They vibrated gently in the air.

I performed a clumsy bow, then saw the leaves and grass that stuck to my leggings as I did so. I flushed and tried to brush them away. I could see a small (beautiful!) frown of puzzlement etching her forehead.

"What are you doing so far from the village?" she asked, and again her mouth did not move.

"I . . . I came to see you. One last time. Before you go. You see . . . I really do love you. I didn't just say that."

She stared at me for some time. She drifted to the ground, then bent her knees so that she was kneeling before me. Horrified, I tried to get her to stand up, then realized that I shouldn't even be touching her. I snatched my hands back.

"Please!" I said. "You mustn't kneel before me. Please stand up. Please!"

"Hush," she whispered, and put a finger to my lips. Startled, I looked at her again and saw a single tear slipping from the corner of her eye, white and glowing like mother-of-pearl in the moonlight. Instinctively, I reached out and wiped it away with my finger. It rested there awhile, still glowing, then it slowly faded to nothingness.

She reached out and hugged me. I hesitated, then hugged her back, feeling my own tears flowing onto her chest.

We stayed like that for a long time, the stars winking at us, the moon moving gently in the Heavens.

Finally, she pushed me gently away.

"I must go," she said. "Keep you compassion, Crispin. It serves you and others well."

"I . . . I will," I said, watching as she lifted gently off the ground. "Good-bye."

She smiled. "Good-bye, my little love."

I followed her, of course. I'm not sure why. I think I had some foolish notion of watching over her, protecting her on her journey. I felt somehow that *this* was what I was meant to be doing. I didn't know what *this* was, just that it meant something to me in a way that hitting bits of metal into tools and weapons never could. I waited until the moon on her wings was no more than a distant glimmer, then set off in her wake. I think she knew I was following, for she set a pace that I could easily follow. She even stopped after a few hours to rest. I crept up the road and hid behind a bush. She floated in the air above a field off to the side of the road, to all intents and purposes asleep. I tried to stay awake but my body refused. Soon I was asleep and soaring through the stars with this mysterious beauty I had so gravely and naively fallen in love with.

I awoke with a start.

The sky was gray in the predawn, my clothes soaking wet with dew. My heart pounded erratically in my chest, my breath coming in short gasps. Something had startled me. A noise heard in sleep but forgotten upon waking.

A scream of pain erupted suddenly behind me. I shot upright and scrabbled around the bush. There I froze, crying out in horror.

She was twisting in midair, her limbs flicking spasmodically, bending in ways they were not meant to bend. Her face was clenched in a hideous mask of pain. I ran to her.

"No!" Her eyes found mine. "Flee, Crispin. He has found me. Go!"

"I will not!" I screamed, not understanding her words. I tried to reach up to her but she was too high. Her limbs twisted unnaturally, like someone was trying to push and pull them out of joint. I heard a horrible cracking sound like dogs crunching on meat bones.

"What's happening?" I shouted, tears streaming from my eyes.

Her eyes had closed. She opened them again. We stared *into* each other.

Then I saw the life fade from her eyes, as if a piece of gauze had been pulled across her vision.

I stroked her hair. I knelt by her body for hours, waiting, willing her to wake up. My mind would not accept that she was gone. I stared at her chest, watching for the rise and fall that breath would bring.

I would convince myself that there was movement, the smallest inhalation of air, and I would wait expectantly for her to open her eyes again.

She didn't, though, and I finally realized that she never would.

I picked her up. She was as light as a bird. I looked, once, back toward the village. Then I turned my back on it and headed up the road in the opposite direction. It seemed the right thing to do.

To take her home.

I stayed far from the roads, walking through the forests when I could and avoiding villages. I knew how to fend for myself. All the children in our village took turns going out on hunts with the elders. We were shown how to make traps and forage for food.

She did not decompose. After a couple of days in the summer heat I was dreading what it would be like carrying her body back to the Goddess. But her skin remained marble smooth.

I would lay her down each night we stopped, fold her arms over her chest, and watch her by the light of the stars and moon. I still found it hard to believe she was dead. I think deep down I was hoping the Goddess would bring her back to life, that she would open her eyes and I would see her smile once again.

My father told me the Goddess's tower was a week's ride to the north. It took me almost four weeks. Days of bathing in streams and hiding at the sound of hoofbeats or voices. I grew to know every angle of her face. The lines around her mouth where she smiled. The small mole just below her lip. She was the last thing on my mind when I slept and the first thing when I awoke.

A few days before I reached the tower I woke up to find a small girl watching me. She looked a few years younger than I, and stared at me with an expression of puzzlement.

"I was trying to decide if you were like the lady. But you're not."

"No," I said, rising into a sitting position.

"What's wrong with her?"

"She's dead."

The girl frowned. "How?" she asked.

"I don't know. I'm taking her back to the Goddess."

"Maybe she'll think you did it."

"Why would she think that?"

The girl shrugged. I stood up.

"Are you going now?" the girl asked.

"I am. And you should be getting back to your family."

"They're gone."

I paused. I noticed for the first time how disheveled the girl looked. Her hair appeared knotty and uncombed. "What do you mean gone?"

"Just gone. Some people came to our farm and took them away. I've been following them," she added proudly.

I frowned, not understanding. "What, you mean they took your family against their will?"

She looked down at the ground. "I'm not sure."

"Well, were they struggling?" I asked, exasperated.

"I don't know!" the girl screamed, then abruptly burst into tears.

"Oh, here, look, I'm sorry." I hesitated, not knowing what to do. I couldn't leave her alone. "You can come with me," I said, after some thought. "The first village we come to we'll ask about your family, yes? It's probably all just a mistake."

"Do you think so?" she asked, sniffing.

"Sure. Come, let's go. What's your name?"

"Sara," she said.

We reached the tower before we reached a village. I had been staring at it for a long time before I realized what I was looking at. An afternoon storm that had been building all day, sucking every drop of moisture from my body, had broken. Purple bruised clouds spat lightning and rain. Thunder bellowed, like the cracking of dry wood. We stood on the edge of a copse of trees looking out onto miles of grassland, the shin-high grass swaying and flicking violently in the warm wind. I noticed that the falling rain formed a glistening shape far off in the distance. It took a while for my brain to realize I was looking at the home of the Goddess. I had finally arrived.

I shifted her weight in my arms, then looked down at Sara.

"This is it," I said. I felt curiously deflated. I wasn't sure why. I had reached my goal. I had brought her home. Maybe that was the reason. I was handing her over. I would never see her again.

"I want to walk with you," Sara said.

I glanced down at her.

"We can look for a village after. You said."

I smiled. "Yes, I did. Let's go then."

We walked into the refreshing rain, the warm wind soothing our cheeks, the wet grass dragging over our legs.

We reached the tower as nightfall descended. As we slowly drew closer I had looked for some means of gaining entrance, but I could find none. It seemed we would be forced to walk its circumference until we came to some way inside.

"I'll take her now," said a woman's voice.

I looked around and saw only Sara standing beside me.

"I thank you for bringing her home to me," said Sara. At least, the voice came from her mouth, but the voice was not hers. "Even though her soul is lost we can still say good-bye. Good-byes are important." She reached out her arms. I looked down at the body I had carried for the past month. When I looked up again, Sara had gone. In her place stood the Goddess. She was tall and pale and had bright red hair. Black feathered wings jutted from her back and rose gracefully above her. I fell to my knees and gently laid the body before her feet.

"Come, Crispin, rise. Have we not become friends over the past days?"

I looked up at what I thought was the humor I heard in her voice. "All that time . . ."

"It was I." She picked up the body, staring at the smooth features. "So . . . it has come to this," she said softly. "Things will change, young Crispin. He darkens the weave with his actions. Bad times are coming."

"What do you mean?"

"He has done this. He attacks my servants, seeking to possess them. This one fought him. In a way she won."

"I don't understand."

"He has her soul, Crispin. He wanted her body, to add to his army. She fought him off, but he has her soul."

"What will he do with it?"

"Imprison it. Toy with it. Torture it. Whatever is his whim. He has gone mad, I fear. He seeks to destroy the Tapestry."

"Will there be war?"

She looked at me with a strange expression on her face. "Maybe. When he gathers enough strength."

"Why do you not strike first, before he can gather his strength?"

"You are young, Crispin," she said. "In time you will see that if I did that, I would be no better than him. Worse, because I know better."

She turned to the tower, carrying the body.

"Goddess," I called. She turned back to me.

"What was her name?" I asked.

"Ser'ashen."

I returned to my village, ignoring the looks from those I passed. Obviously, my parents were furious. They demanded to know where I had been, but I couldn't find it in myself to tell them. I felt terrible about deceiving them. I think they'd thought me dead, taken on the road by some creature or another.

The days and months passed, and they eventually stopped asking. I wandered listlessly through the village, avoiding my father in the mornings when he set off to the forge, barely speaking to him when he returned. Something had been taken from me with Ser'ashen's death. A part of me had gone with her, so that I could no longer muster up enthusiasm for anything. My life stretched ahead of me, lonely and frightening. It was as if I had glimpsed a possibility of what could be, that my life might have some meaning, but then it was yanked away again, leaving me worse off than before, because now I knew there was something better out there.

I dreamed of her every night.

The rumors increased over the next few years. Of demonlike creatures attacking villages and towns in the middle of the night, then even during the day. They were crossing over into the Goddess's time, slaughtering man, woman, and child.

I traveled to the tower once a year, on the anniversary of her death. I never saw the Goddess again, but I didn't mind. I did it for her, for Ser'ashen.

I lost my childhood because of that fateful day. People my own age seemed ludicrously childish and irritating. I think they found me pompous and boring, too serious to partake in their experiences.

One cold afternoon in winter none of that would come to matter. I was sitting with my back against my father's forge, reveling in the warmth and staring into the cold gray sky. Dusk was approaching. I seemed to recall my mother saying that today was the shortest day of the year. Wood smoke, for me the very smell of winter, drifted from the roofs of all the houses and huts, the peaceful scent mingling into the sharpness in the air.

The attack came suddenly. One second I was living in a mundane world wondering whether I should return home for some hot soup to warm my bones, the next I was staring into a street suddenly filled with bestial screaming and hordes of nightmarish creatures.

I felt a hand tug at my shoulder and jerked frantically away. It was only my father. He took a quick look up and down the street and then yanked me into the forge. He ran to the back wall and pulled two old blades from his reject bin. He wrapped cloth around the hilt end and handed me one. I looked up at him, expecting to see the fear that was washing through my body in great shivering spasms, but there was no fear there. Only determination, and anger. Lots of anger.

"There's no way around this, son. Kill or be killed. Those things out there, they're not taking prisoners. Understand?"

I nodded.

"The talismans must have failed. We have to get through to your mother. She needs us now." He hefted the blade in his hand, testing its balance. He breathed in deeply, let the air out through his nostrils. "You ready?"

No.

"Yes," I whispered.

He bent down and hugged me. There was no time for extra words. Later, you always wished you'd said things, things that you know will be remembered long after the moment they are uttered, but in real life there's not always the chance.

My father opened the door. The cold air flurried in and touched my face. I shivered, imagining it was Death himself caressing my cheek. Then we were out in the street, running toward home, and everything became confused.

I saw my father slice and hack his way through a group of the hollering creatures. My mother had told me he'd once been in the army but he didn't like talking about it. After that day was over, I could understand why. He swung his blade and a gray piglike head went tumbling in a splash of red. Purple-white intestines spilled between slippery club fingers trying to hold them inside. I swung the sword and caught one of the creatures in the back of the leg. It collapsed and tried to grab hold of me with black claws. I waved my sword blade, an instinctive action, and the hand landed to my left, the claws slowly closing like a dying spider.

Other villagers were joining the fight, taking up rusty arms against the attackers. My father glanced back to check on me, a split second, then turned back to fight a winged monstrosity with four arms and as many swords.

We moved on, taking cuts and slices as we went, our home ever closer and now in sight. My left arm hung useless by my side, paralyzed by a lucky back-hand swing. I looked down at it once, saw a red-lipped wound grinning at me with teeth made of bone, and didn't look again.

And then my father was at the open door. He ran inside, fearful that some of the creatures had beaten us, shouting my mother's name. I think I heard her reply. I'm not sure, because at that moment I was looking down at a sword point that had just punched through my stomach.

I thought to myself, *That's my blood,* then the sword was yanked from my back with a curious sucking sound and blood bubbled from the wound.

I couldn't speak. I looked up at the empty door, thinking that if I could just get inside everything would be all right, that my mother would fix everything. I tried to walk, but my knees gave out and my face hit the rocky ground.

The last sound I heard was a guttural grunting noise from somewhere behind me.

I woke to the sound of creaking harnesses and the quiet *chuffing* of horses breathing into the air. I opened my eyes and stared up at the gray sky moving slowly above me. I opened my mouth to call for my mother, but all that came out was a dry croak. I felt the horses slow down, then stop completely. My father's face appeared above me. I was shocked by how worn he looked. His face was deeply lined, as if charcoal had been ingrained into all his wrinkles. Dark shadows ringed his eyes. I'd never seen him looking so frail. He tried to smile at me, but it faltered and he had to catch his breath.

"Welcome back, son," he whispered, and that was when I felt the pain. It was the color of fire and felt like ragged glass that crunched and splintered with every breath. I cried out and my father held a water skin to my lips. I felt the moisture sucked away like a droplet on drought-stricken earth. He poured some more, then took it away. "Easy," he said. "Not too much."

"What—?" I croaked

"Don't talk. They're gone, son. We beat them."

"Oh." I licked dry lips. "Did I do good?" I whispered.

"You made me proud, my boy. You made us both proud."

I stared into his eyes. It was as if I saw his fears written plain upon his face. I knew then that things were looking bad for me.

"They got me."

"Aye, son," he said softly. "They got you."

"Where are we going?"

"To the city. A healer there will take care of you."

I nodded wearily and closed my eyes. I slept again and woke to my father changing the dressing on my wound. I saw him wince at the acidic smell it gave off.

"It's getting worse, isn't it?" I whispered.

"No!" he said, too quickly. "Another day and we'll be there. That healer will fix you right up."

I didn't say anything. I was scared that if I opened my mouth I would say what I was really thinking. That it was too late for healing, that I could feel that the poison had already gone too deep.

I must have dropped off again, because I opened my eyes to darkness and the most intense pain I had ever felt. It was like someone had taken a hot coal from my father's forge and laid it in my wound. I cried out. My father was there instantly, holding my hand. He made meaningless noises and stroked my brow. When the worst of the pain had gone he went to the fire and brewed me some kind of foul-smelling concoction that seemed to dull the pain. I watched him walk the perimeter of the camp, checking on the talismans he'd laid out. I don't know why he bothered, though. The ones at the village hadn't worked.

I could actually smell the poison through the bandages the next morning. I watched my father stoke the fire in the early morning mist and surreptitiously probed my stomach. The pain had spread well beyond the initial area. I sighed. I'd heard about stomach wounds before. They took a while to kill you, but kill you they usually did. Anyone who thought otherwise was fooling himself.

I watched my father collect the talismans, then sit down and pull out some hard bread and cheese for breakfast.

"Dad," I said. He put down his breakfast and looked at me. "I know this is hard, but you know and I know that I won't recover from this."

He just stared at me, then lowered his eyes to the ground.

"I think I'm all right, though," I said. "I think this was meant to happen. I would never have been content with life. Not . . . not after what happened."

He looked up at that, and I went on to tell him of the events that had so drastically changed my life.

"I want to go back, Dad. To the Goddess. I want to say good-bye."

He said nothing for a while. Then he slowly shook his head. I could see the pain he felt. "Boy, you don't know what you ask."

"I do. What good will traveling to the city do? I don't want to die scared in a place I don't know. I want her to be there."

"How do you know she will be?"

I hesitated, then. How did I know? I wasn't sure, but it just felt right. "She'll be there," I said. "I feel . . . I feel like she's calling me."

By the time we arrived at the copse of woods where I first sighted the tower my wound was so hot that it made my whole body sweat.

"We have to walk from here."

"Crispin, you can hardly sit upright. How can you walk?"

I started to climb from the cushions and blankets. I slipped and fell. The pain shot up my spine so hard that I blacked out for a moment. When I came round again my father had his arm around me and we were walking through the grass.

He was making strange noises, and when I looked over I saw that he was crying, tears streaming down his face. He sensed my movement and looked down at me.

"I'm losing you today, boy. By the Goddess, I'll never see you again."

That nearly broke me, right there. Seeing him cry like that. My father, the one person who was always supposed to be strong for everyone else. I tightened my grip around his waist, and in some strange way, we almost seemed to switch places. It felt like I was holding *him* up as walked through the still, winter-brown grass. Like I was the one who had to be strong. It was there that I knew for truth what before I had only suspected. Whatever happened today, it was what I had been born for.

She was waiting for us when we arrived. Somehow, I knew she would be. I left my father standing some way back. He refused to come any closer, staring at the ground instead of laying eyes on his Goddess.

"I've been waiting," she said as I approached.

"You knew."

"I saw the possibility." She reached out and touched my stomach. The pain fled instantly. I stood upright again, took my first clean breath in days. "I can heal you, Crispin. You can go back to your family."

I looked down at my wound. It was still there. She had only taken away the pain. I looked up at her again, stared into her gray eyes. "No," I said. "I feel this is . . . right. Something has been missing ever since . . . what happened. I think that there is a reason for what happened to me, then *and* now. But I thank you for giving me the choice."

"I cannot see your future, Crispin. I know you are an important thread in the Weave but I cannot see how. The choices you make will affect not just yourself, but others also."

I bowed my head. I did not say anything. It was her decision now. She knew what I desired, had known even before I had.

I felt her hand on my head, and then I was *inside* her mind. I saw the potential held in every decision ever made. I saw the world as a tapestry, and every thought, every action, every word, made up its thread. Here was blackness, but it was surrounded by gold. Here was silver and love, but it was cut off by angry red. It was confusing and meaningless up close, but then I saw the whole thing as if I was suddenly miles and miles away. I saw the Tapestry as a whole, saw how it all balanced out.

I felt the wings grow from my back. They thrummed gently in the air, like the wings of a newly born butterfly. My earthly life, my past, seemed to fade. It did not disappear, because it made me what I was, but it was pushed to the background. I felt my clothes slide from my limbs like old skin, felt the wind tingle my body and tell me stories of distant lands. I looked up again. The Goddess leaned down and kissed me.

"It is done," she said.

I turned to the being who had once been my father. His head was still bowed. I stood before him. "Look upon me," I said gently. "Tell your wife I have not died. I have gone on to a better place." He cried, great sobs that he was unable to control. I wiped his tears with my hands. "I will always watch out for you both," I said softly. "I'm sorry you were never able to be proud of me."

"Oh, son!" he whispered. "You're just a boy. Of course we're proud of you." He reached out and gripped my arm, looking hard into my eyes. "Know that, if you know anything. I could not be prouder."

Then he turned and walked back the way we had come, an old man bent with his loss.

I watched him until he mounted one of the horses and disappeared into the trees, then I flexed my wings and floated slowly into the sky, higher and higher until the earth below me looked like the tapestry I had so recently glimpsed. I closed my eyes and saw the Weave overlaid on my vision. I could see the glow that represented my mother.

I saw the black hole that was the creature who had run me through.

I concentrated, and I saw the glow that was Ser'ashen, gold and silver surrounded by a halo of darkness. I reached out and touched it. I had a sense of fire, walls of pulsating flesh, of wind tearing through the hollow eye sockets of thousands upon thousands of skulls, then I *pulled*. I heard a scream of absolute hate, and then something more, something that froze my heart: a laugh of triumph.

I opened my eyes and looked at my hands. I held a softly glowing bead.

"I think I should take that."

I handed it over to the Goddess, unsurprised that she was there. She looked at it carefully. "With one act the future of the world is changed," she said. She searched my eyes. "I think I knew what you planned, even though you yourself did not. He was waiting for this, Crispin. I have trespassed onto his lands now. All the rules have changed."

"I only wanted to help her."

"I'm not saying you were wrong. In fact, I think you could have acted no other way. Your ancestors, your parents, your upbringing, all of it brought you to this precise moment where you acted the way you did. The one thing that makes me think this will work out is that you acted out of love. That is something he does not understand anymore."

She drifted slowly to the ground. "Come. We must prepare."

"For what?"

She gestured with her free hand. "For that."

I turned my head to see what she was pointing at. Darkness filled the sky to the south, a foul wind blowing before it. I could make out individuals in the mass, horrible, twisted faces and broken wings. I felt fear then, such as I had never felt before, but there was something else as well. I felt hope. When this was over, somehow I knew the Tapestry would be pure again, that the Weave would once again be as it should be.

*　　*　　*

We fought a war against God today . . .

The other image, the second one I will always recall when I remember the events of this terrible afternoon . . .

It was a brief glimpse I had through the thousands of fighting seraphs. A brief glimpse of Ser'ashen as she fought to cleanse the Weave of the world.

THE FINAL CHOICE

Irene Radford

Death sat at the bar wondering what he had forgotten to do. Eleven-oh-two p.m. December 31. There was something he had to do before midnight or the New Year would not arrive. Time would stop. Life would be frozen in an endless cold sleep. Souls would have no home.

Change would not continue to shape the universe.

Fates would not be fulfilled.

Death took a sip of his drink and concentrated on his duty.

The potential suicide in the corner vacillated in her decision. Her well-cut red suit looked too bright and cheerful for her mood. She twisted a diamond wedding set around and around her heart finger. Death shouldn't leave until she made up her mind.

Suicides always disrupted the schedule of appointments. He didn't like *last minute* changes.

But there was something else . . .

He checked his appointment book. The potential suicide wasn't listed anywhere in the last few pages. In two minutes, a man with a heart condition would run out of time. Death grabbed his staff of office and

211

left the bar. If the woman in the corner made her decision in the next two minutes, she'd still need two more to find a means and a place.

The little black appointment book with magnificent gold calligraphy on the cover burned in the pocket of his flannel shirt beneath a down parka. His staff of office, half again as tall as he, shrank to the length of a walking stick. The ebony end that curved back on itself to form a window for a huge black crystal dissolved into a knob with the winking crystal set into the end. No flowing black cape and skeletal hands for the heart attack victim. This candidate for death needed the reassurance of a familiar personage to make the transition quietly.

Death sidled through crowded Times Square. He appeared to be just another reveler on New Year's Eve.

His candidate jumped up and down, waving to friends and strangers alike. He paused in his excited dance only long enough to chugalug the whiskey in his hip flask.

Death tapped his shoulder.

"Hi! I'm George. Who are you?" The candidate greeted Death.

"Hello, George. You have an appointment."

An overweight, middle-aged body collapsed on the sidewalk. George turned to look at his former shell. "I guess I have to leave now. Before the New Year."

"Yes, you do."

"Pity. I've never actually been here on New Year's Eve when the ball dropped." He looked wistfully at the great ball of light atop a nearby building. "I guess now I never will. Can't I stay a little longer, just until the ball drops?"

"Sorry, George. Eleven-oh-seven. You are precisely on time. You can't linger, even to see the New Year."

George looked back at his former self, one last time. A Good Samaritan had already begun CPR on the limp body.

"He might revive me."

An ambulance siren wailed in the distance.

"He can't revive you, I have touched you. Your fate is determined. If you choose to wait, or refuse my escort now, you will wander aimlessly as a lost soul for all time. Your choice."

"Some choice." George looked back on his body with longing in his eyes and posture. Then he nodded in quiet acquiescence. Death took George's elbow and led him out of the crowd.

Two minutes later, Death blinked his eyes and transported back to the bar. Little Miss Indecision was still dithering, still twisting her rings, occasionally tugging at them. They wouldn't come off easily. She'd worn them long enough that her finger and knuckle had grown thicker. Death pulled out the appointment book once more. A little book now with only a few names left. The page with George's name dissolved under his gaze.

"Who's next?" he asked the book.

At year's beginning the book had been a huge tome that had gradually dissipated to this thin reminder. Not many names left. Not much time before one year faded into the next. Choices and change had to continue. Unless . . .

Death ordered a drink. He took a sip, remembering when alcohol tasted good, made him feel good.

Strange, he wasn't supposed to remember life, only his duties as Death.

Time. Eleven-twenty-six. There was something he had to do. The appointment book heated up again. A child dying of cancer. A child ready for the release of pain. Too bad his parents weren't ready to let him go. They had made all of the child's decisions for him. This last choice had to be his alone.

Death walked into pediatric intensive care at Mercy Hospital dressed as a teenage candy striper, the staff of office now only a small syringe with a black crystal plunger on a tray. The family of the candidate hovered around the bed. Tears and aching hearts filled the room with an aura of misery.

The candidate smiled at Death. "Hi, I'm Mike. About time you showed up."

"Hi, yourself, Mike," Death replied in his feminine voice.

Mike's body convulsed and gasped for breath.

"No. You can't die. I won't let you." Mike's mother threw herself onto the little boy's body, oblivious of tubes and machines. The woman looked up directly into the eyes of Death. "Take me instead. He's so little. He hasn't had a chance to live yet. Take me!"

Time stopped until a choice was made. Fate required a death.

"Can you do that? Change the appointment?" Mike asked, eyes wide and wondering. Momentarily he was free of the constraints of his body. Only his soul knew what transpired.

"Fate dictates that my appointment is in this room, at this time," Death announced to all those present. "The name of the candidate is not known until the actual moment of death. Anyone here may accept the fated death."

"Take me," the mother said resolutely. "Spare my little boy."

"No, Mom." Mike looked around at his loving family, frozen in time until the choice was made. "Think of Dad and the family. Julie and Tom need a mom. Dad needs his wife. They'll learn to get by without me. Life will be a lot harder on them without you than me. Let me go. I'm tired of hurting. I'm tired of watching you hurt because of me."

Emotions flooded Death. He remembered pain and how love lessened it. Getting involved with his candidates was not a part of the job. But Mike was so strong, so adult, he reminded Death of . . .

Death refused to remember life. Change and a choice of fates belonged to others now, not him.

Mike climbed off the bed, leaving his body behind. "Time to go. Good-bye, Mom. Bye, Dad, Julie, Tom."

Time resumed. The family clung to each other in sorrow.

Death and Mike walked slowly toward a swirling circle of light, leaving life behind.

A car accident diverted Death's attention on his transport back to the bar. Smashed metal, flying glass, the smell of hot gasoline ready to ignite. Agony! Desperate pleas. Death put aside the memory. Those terrible things must have happened to someone else.

He checked the most recent victims. Serious injuries, but no one needed his guidance to the other side yet. He made a note in his appointment book to check back with the five passengers and three drivers once they reached the hospital.

The little black book didn't accept the note. The accident victims would not face a final choice within the remaining minutes of this year. What would happen to the book at one second past midnight? Death did not know.

Or could not remember.

Which?

Death looked at the last page of his book curiously. He saw an appointment listed for eleven-fifty-nine and fifty-nine seconds. The assignation hadn't been there earlier in the evening. No place, cause, or name followed the time. Strange. What did he have to do in the last second of the Old Year to make certain the New Year came? The thought of all the souls of humanity drifting homeless for eternity made him shudder. Time must continue. People must experience change and make choices. Fates must be fulfilled.

He returned to the bar, drawn there as if by a magnet. His staff glowed brighter as he approached. The appointment book suddenly felt heavy. He checked, but no new appointments had been added past the cryptic one in the last second of the Old Year.

The bartender took Death's order for another drink. Automatically Death assessed the man's condition: arthritis, right shoulder and knee; weak arteries; and swollen feet. Six months tops.

A newcomer opened the door of the bar. The noise of the New Year celebration in Times Square filled the shabby drinking establishment with a moment of lively joy. The potential suicide wavered a moment in her decision. The door closed and the noise died. As the Old Year was dying.

Death hefted his little black book once more. "I need time to look in on the pope. I have to keep tabs on all the assassination attempts and a few great musicians and artists. There isn't enough time. Something I have to do . . ."

Death sipped at the drink that was supposed to taste good or make him feel good but did neither. He watched himself in the mirror behind the bar. He looked like any other generic, middle-aged male, not too prosperous, nor too downtrodden, his staff of office hiding as a black umbrella propped against his stool. The persona fit this neighborhood. He was used to the instant changes in his appearance. He didn't like terrorizing people—except some of the truly evil personalities. When Mother Teresa finally passed on, Death had chosen to be another elderly nun so as not to frighten the woman. But that determined lady hadn't been frightened by life. Why should Death in any guise scare her?

Eleven-forty-three. A sense of desperate need tickled his senses. The potential suicide in the corner passed her crisis and decided to give Life one more year.

Death followed her onto the street. He had too much to do in the last seventeen minutes of the year.

His long staff appeared in his hand, keeping its proper shape and size—nine feet of shining ebony, slender top curved into a full circle. Thousands of facets from the crystal reflected tiny pinpricks of light. His black-hooded cloak folded around him. He became one with the shadows, seeking the source of that last appointment. Only when the candidate, location, and circumstances were chosen would his guise take shape.

His hands tingled with the power encased in his trappings. His staff glowed in the reflection of street lamps. Aware, not fully active. Yet.

Out on the street, Death turned the staff right and left, seeking. A faint glow emanated from the crystal

when it faced right, up ahead. A very dark alley.
Streetlights shot out, garbage piled high. A haven for
vagrants, criminals, and violence.

The appointment book burned with impatience.

"Just another mugging," Death sighed. "I'd hoped
for something spectacular to close out the year."

The crystal glowed brighter, taking on red tones.
"Odd. Red indicates a death of great importance,
someone who will stop time if his, or her, destiny goes
unfulfilled." That had happened with Princess Diana
as she clung to life for agonizing moments, but others
had stepped in to continue her work. One instance
when the victim became more powerful dead than
alive.

While the world mourned her passing, people continued to make choices and grow through change.

Death followed the crystal with increasing urgency.
For the sake of all lost souls, time had to continue.

The woman who had chosen life over death walked
ahead of him, head high, shoulders back. She had chosen life and her posture reflected reawakened joy and
confidence. Her high heels tapped a rhythm onto the
sidewalk akin to the song of life.

Grunts. Cries for help. Scuffling feet and thumping
bodies. The woman gone.

Death hurried.

He rounded the corner into the alley. Three Lives
standing. One desperate Life sprawled amid piles of
junk and empty boxes, right leg twisted unnaturally
beneath her. The skirt of her red power suit hiked up
immodestly, torn at the side seam. Blood spilled on
the pavement.

Eleven-fifty-eight and forty-seven seconds. In the
distance the shouts from Times Square increased.

Close up, one of the standing Lives lifted a gun and took aim at the Life who waited. A feral smile grew around broken and rotted teeth. All four Lives were fully conscious. All four knew that Death awaited one of them.

"Should have given us the diamond ring along with the purse right off, yuppie bitch. We'd have let you off with a sore head," the youth with the gun sneered at his victim.

The diamond on the woman's left hand winked in the weak light, almost as brightly as Death's black crystal. A cherished wedding ring. A promise of love. The muggers had broken her leg while she struggled to protect the ring.

There was still time for Death to offer choices.

All four Lives froze in a tableau that screeched of man's violation of his covenant with Life. The black crystal in the staff passed from red to blinding white. The appointment book grew heavier and hotter yet.

Eleven-fifty-nine and forty-five seconds. Time stopped.

Death looked anxiously from the crystal to the Life who awaited his touch. Time awaited the next candidate. Who? The book didn't tell him.

"Don't kill me!" the woman who had left the bar filled with renewed purpose yelled at the three muggers. "You've got my purse and my jewelry. I can't run away. My leg is broken. Leave me alone."

No one moved. Nothing moved, not even the freezing wind.

Death waited. A curious sensation of warmth engulfed him. He'd been cold so long he'd forgotten what warmth was. Not exactly warmth, an absence of heart-chilling cold. But with the warmth came pain too. Sharp pains filled his leg in empathetic sharing with the woman. Curiosity and dread warred with fear for mastery within him. His heart raced and then seemed to stop. This was the last appointment in his book and he would be an active participant instead of an escort after all the choices were made.

Fate had caught up with him at last.

"Help me, please. I don't want to die," the woman called to Death. Her hand reached out in entreaty.

Death heard himself issuing the same plea a year ago. He remembered fear and its copper taste on his tongue.

He shook off the memory and the residual tremors. He had a duty to perform.

"I have an appointment with someone in this alley. One of you must go with me." Death's voice echoed around the alley, like a bronze bell. The three muggers remained frozen in time. Not so much as an eyelash twitched among them.

"Take one of them." The woman pointed to the tableau of criminals frozen in the act of theft and murder. Her hand wavered and almost pointed directly at Death.

Death tried to retreat within the folds of his hood. "They are outside this decision, ma'am. Only you and I are here." Her name eluded him. Why? This had never happened to him before . . . before he became Death.

A year ago he had wanted so desperately to live that he had chosen to become Death rather than accept his fate. And now he was faced with another Life in the same dilemma. One of them must die.

He planted his staff in front of him. The glowing black wood gave him authority and confidence. Someone in the alley had to die. Time would not resume unless Death escorted a candidate to the other side. He still had a choice.

"I'm not volunteering to die," the woman screamed. "I'm not ready to die! I just decided to live. Please let me live!"

"I can't give you that choice," Death lied.

"Do something." The woman grabbed the staff and shook it in desperation.

Death jerked back on the length of wood in panic. "The staff is my badge of office. Only I may touch it." His hood fell back. This time he knew his appearance was the classic personification of Death, a skeletally thin face, pasty white. Deep-set eyes that looked into eternity.

The woman held tight to the staff, shaking it again.

"You. Must. Let. Go." Death grabbed the black staff with both hands, trying to wrest his tool away from her. "You. May. Not. Touch. It."

"If you won't help me, then let me have it to save myself." She clung to the staff as if it were Life itself; a Life she desperately wanted. Now. A few moments ago she'd almost thrown it away. "I can use this as a weapon to save myself!"

Power raced up and down the wood binding her to the staff and to Death. He almost let go. Desperation kept him glued to the wood.

If he let her live, what would happen to him? Someone had to die or time would not resume.

Who would it be?

What choices were left?

The only way to cheat fate and Death is to become Death, another voice had told him a year ago.

Death stumbled. The woman twisted the staff and

tripped him with it. Death dropped to his knees. His cloak fell away, revealing a red woolen suit, the same cut as woman's. Same blouse. Same scarf around the neck. His skeleton took on flesh but remained pasty white.

"Who are you?" The woman rolled to her left, away from the collapsing body of Death. She stood up in one fluid motion with the staff in hand, as if her leg hadn't been broken a moment ago. Her shoulders hunched and she aged a thousand years in a moment.

"There is something I have to do before midnight." Death's voice remained deep and solemn, echoing and reverberating around the alley. Which one would die? His right leg twisted unnaturally beneath him.

The muggers came back to life.

A mighty roar rose from Times Square. *"Ten."*

Three shots rang out in rapid succession.

"Nine."

The muggers turned and bolted from the alley.

"What do you have to do? There isn't much time." Shock made the standing woman's words weak and squeaky. She bent low to catch Death's words, feeling for a pulse, trying to stop the flow of blood from his chest. She didn't have enough hands, or medical knowledge to save him.

"Eight."

Death grabbed her lapel and pulled her closer yet. His clawlike hands seemed incredibly strong for someone who'd just been shot in the belly, the heart, and the lung.

"Seven."

"Tell me what you have to do. I can help," she cried.

"There is a way for you to survive this encounter."

"Six."

"I have survived; you're the one who is dying."

"One of us must die at the stroke of midnight. You have taken the choice away from me. The only way to cheat death is to become Death." He repeated the words spoken to him a year ago. A lifetime ago.

Everyone was fated to die. The choice of when fell to only a few.

"Five."

"Become Death? You mean I'll die, too. Who are you?"

"Four."

"I am your destiny, your fate. Life or Death. You must choose. As I chose a year ago. I loved life too much to give it up. I still do. But I no longer have the right to make that choice." Choice and change belonged to the living. Everyone had to die. Fate determined when and where. No choice.

Except for the last death of the year.

"Three."

"If it means living, I'll become Death, I'll become Santa Claus or whoever it takes. Just so I can live. I decided not to kill myself over my husband's infidelity and a mangled career because I realized that life is too beautiful to waste."

"I thought the same thing last year at this time." A fiery car crash, pain beyond enduring, and still he had clung to life rather than let Death take him. "And now I know that all Life is beautiful. If one of us does not die then time will cease, taking all Life with it. Life must be preserved."

"Two."

"Then why must I become Death? I'd rather be alive."

"Death, like change, is a part of life. If Death does not walk the streets then all Life will cease. The choice is yours."

"What is that supposed to mean?"

"You'll find out."

"One! Yeah! Whoopee. Yahoo!"

The body of a young man, who had refused to die in a car crash the year before, took on the last vestiges of the woman wearing a red suit. He/she collapsed in the alley. The last page of the old appointment book dissolved.

A skeletally thin old hag, dressed in tattered red and black draperies, with eyes that burned clear through to eternity stood up and retrieved Death's cloak, without dropping the staff. All memory of her life, her decision to live, her wrestling match with Death, faded. She was Death now, with duties to perform.

From the folds of black cloth fell an enormous book bound in black leather. The gold calligraphy on the front was fresh and new, spelling out one word.

"Appointments."

"Let's see. Victims of an automobile accident. Mercy Hospital," the old hag cackled. "Five passengers. Three drivers. Four of the eight need an escort in two minutes. A musician is shooting a bad batch of drugs in Central Park in six minutes. The pope can wait a little longer."

She morphed into a young nurse wearing bright turquoise scrub pants and a white tunic with tumbling turquoise teddy bears. The staff of office coiled around her neck like a stethoscope, the black crystal blocked the metal bell at one end.

Death popped into the emergency room of Mercy Hospital, ready to escort those who needed her.

A diamond on her left hand winked in the bright hospital lights as she escorted the first death of the New Year into the swirl of light.

THE PROPHECY OF SYMON THE INEPT

Rebecca Lickiss

"**N**o!" she bellowed. "Bastard son of a whoring slug, I will not." She emphasized her point by planting her foot solidly in the midsection of the man on her right, her brother Mark, bending him neatly in half. In the gathering gloom her brother straightened himself and stood rubbing his midsection for a moment.

Lord Leopold Smallpenny watched from a safe distance. "Sorry, dear, but this must be."

He was a smallish man, rail thin, with weasely features. Lady Patience Smallpenny, née Tillman, was a woman of large and generous proportions. Her current delicate condition would have prevented any other woman from physically domineering all and sundry, but not her. She wasn't the sort to allow anyone or anything to get the best of her. Lord Smallpenny had learned to fear her more than anything else in the world.

Having managed to get this far seemed rather remarkable. Lord Smallpenny suspected that she wasn't entirely set against the necessities of this night. It was just that certain aspects of the coming ordeal, while romantic to contemplate over a cup of wine by a roaring fire, were decidedly unpleasant when confronted in substantiality.

"You fool-swilling, toad-warted, beetle-witted, mangled, bootless miscreant!" Lady Smallpenny lay half in the wagon, clinging to the side with fierce determination. "I will NOT give birth in a stable."

"Yes, dear," he responded automatically without thinking or meaning. He motioned to her brothers to continue their efforts to get her into the stable.

"Cowardly curs. I'll see you flogged for this!" She struggled against her four brothers as they slowly dragged her enormous, resisting bulk from the wagon.

To Lord Smallpenny's way of thinking, his wife's brothers were all cut from the same generous mold, big as moose, strong as oxen, fierce as bears, and about as intelligent as your average goat. With odds of four against one you'd have thought they were a sure bet to win. Problem was, they were unaccustomed to contradicting the females of their family. For the last ten months of Lord Smallpenny's acquaintance with them they'd shown him no sign of any thoughts or ambitions in their minds, other than what was put there by their mother or sister. They were willing enough to go along with his schemes, as long as Mother said, or their sister supported the idea. Now with all her shouting and cursing, that looked in doubt. The youngest, John, looked to Lord Smallpenny for support.

"Get her inside!" Lord Smallpenny had spared nothing for this moment, and he wasn't about to have it ruined by a gaggle of foolish louts. "Remember what we are doing this for. You'll be princes. Hurry. It won't be long."

"You sniveling, beslubbering, pribbling, addle-pated, beetle-brained, sparrow-headed boar-pigs," she shouted at her brothers as she slid from the wagon to the ground. Her kicks had knocked Mark to the dirt, where he nicely cushioned her fall.

Matthew, the eldest brother, in a sudden fit of intelligence, grasped his sister's knees, one in each hand. He pulled her behind him as if she were a wheelbarrow he was dragging. Mark and Luke each grabbed up an arm. John covered her eyes in an attempt to calm her. However, what works for a horse generally doesn't on an extremely enraged woman. She nearly knocked them over at the door of the stable.

The midwife, Prudence Marblepot, looked on disapprovingly. "She'll be wanting her mother."

Lord Smallpenny smiled. "Mother was . . . unavoidably detained. It's unfortunate that she won't be able to join us."

Her mother was currently locked in a windowless tower of the castle. Lord Smallpenny could not have controlled the situation if both women were loose. More important, the Tillman boys would've long since lost their nerve. He could hear the vile things she would currently be shrilly howling without even being there. Pity she usually freed herself in less than a day.

"It won't be long, will it?" Lord Smallpenny asked Prudence pointedly.

"Not long at all. She's been trying to deliver for a week now." Prudence's mouth puckered, as if tasting something sour. "I doubt you'll be able to get a pint to drink before the child is born, let alone finish it. But know this, the child may be a half-wit. What with all the potions used to keep the lady from confinement till now. You've only got yourself to blame."

Lord Smallpenny fixed her with an icy stare. "Go. In. Deliver my son. Make sure he is born before midnight. Do you understand?"

She fixed him with an icy stare of her own. "Oh, I understand. I understand all too well." She snorted, adding under her breath, "Midnight," then motioned for her assistants.

Prudence Marblepot could adequately deliver a child with nothing more than a paring knife to cut the cord. However, she believed in the mystique of midwifery, and anything that would make her position more important. For an ordinary peasant birth she would have three assistants: one to boil four gallons of water and heat three blankets, another to sharpen to a razor's edge two knives and stand around looking important while handing over the contents of the Midwife's Bag, the last was to comfort the mother. For this birth she had fifteen assistants. Following directly behind her was her chief apprentice, carrying the Midwife's Bag. Behind her chief apprentice were two other, younger apprentices, each carrying a large stack of blankets. Behind them, two ornately dressed bourgeois gentlewomen each carrying a large red velvet, gold fringed pillow cushioning a sharpened saber. Following were two of the village young women carrying swaddling clothes. Next, another pair of young women with a woven baby basket between them. After them were two stout goodwives each hefting a large steaming bucket. The next two matrons carried bowls and basins. Bringing up the rear were two girls carrying woven baskets containing herbs. Prudence led the procession to the stable, muttering about foolish lords and silly prophecies.

Shortly after the midwife entered the newly built stable, the lady's brothers hurried out. Lady Smallpenny's shout followed them, "Fetid drool of a pox-faced donkey! Get away from me!"

Lord Smallpenny hoped that the sounds that followed could be associated with birth, though the last time he'd heard most of them had been during battle. One noise particularly reminded him of the sound of a fist pounding flesh. The only good thing about his wife's currently enlarged swelling bulk was that she wouldn't be able to leave the stable under her own power. She'd finally become too cumbersome even for herself.

"Let's get a drink," Lord Smallpenny said to his brothers-in-law. "And see if the midwife's prediction is correct."

As they walked into the Vanishing Moon tavern, the dusk gave way to dark. On the far horizon clouds banded together in preparation for an assault on the ground. This pleased Lord Smallpenny greatly. He gave a happy sigh, and with great satisfaction pulled the cord to make the moon on the inn's sign vanish. All would be well.

Matthew went behind the bar, nodding to his pleasant wife, Anne. She smiled back at him from the hearth where she tended the fire. Mark, Luke, and John sat uneasily at a table not far away, nursing their drinks. Lord Smallpenny appropriated a table away from the heat of the fire, and motioned for food and drink to be brought him.

The door opened, and Lady Smallpenny could be heard saying, "—puke-eyed, empty-chested, yellow-gutted, slug-limbed, swamp-reeking—"

Two girls from the midwife's entourage hurried in carrying the buckets and some of the blankets. As they spoke with Anne, Lord Smallpenny knew the delivery of his meal would be delayed.

The women set about getting the water on to boil, setting the blankets by the fire to warm, chatting and laughing and doing whatever other dawdling they could think of. Lord Smallpenny considered pulling rank, but decided in the end that since the interruption aided the birth of his son he would allow it, and bank his carefully cultivated patience. He'd been working toward this goal for a long, long time.

As he sat stoically he compared his preparations to the prophecy, the old soothsayer's prediction of the birth of the one who would unite the warring factions of Killgully. Even though he was a child when the prophecy was announced, his ambitions had caused him to immediately seize upon it. He had memorized it, treasured it, and manipulated it.

He could still hear his father reading the prophecy when it was published.

> When Lording takes a peasant shrew
> A common thread of life to hew
> They a royal line will make anew
>
> The first fruit of the Goodwife's labor
> Born in the stable of her kin and neighbor
> A warrior child's life-cord cut by saber.

Royal birth under the vanishing moon
On the night of the midsummer June
Hope for the kingdom, to be united soon.

For the child of this birth so royal
All princes, lords, and vassals loyal
Shall all enemies bury in soil.

                    Symon the Inept, Soothsayer

"Old fool," his father had laughed. "The meter is off, the rhymes are forced . . . it's complete and utter nonsense. I've said for a while old Symon was not what he used to be. In his younger days he would have been ashamed to predict such drivel. He's getting old and senile, and while we must tolerate his lunatic ravings, a man would have to be insane to believe this hogwash." He had looked down his patrician nose in disgust as he tossed the notice in the fire.

Leopold Smallpenny knew his father better than to indicate he took the prophecy seriously. By waiting until his father's death he managed to choose his own bride. He had scoured the countryside for a shrewish peasant girl, with the intention of marrying the worst he found. His quest had been endless and unfruitful until the day his manservant Kermit returned from a little hamlet at the western edge of the country.

"Oh, she's the one. Meaner than a wolf, with a mouth a harpy would envy. Her four brothers live in fear of her tongue. She scolds and chides and nags the whole day through. Her mother is the same and taught her well. Life with her would be a miserable, eternal hell."

Her name had been Patience Tillman. His courtship had lasted long enough for the flowers he'd brought to end up in the muddy street. Her mother, however, realized his intentions and what coming up in the world would mean for her. She had a short talk with her daughter, and the engagement began. He insisted that the marriage take place in September. His son had to be born at midsummer.

Of course, there were a few other prophetic demands that had to be arranged.

Matthew was set up at a local inn. Marrying him to the old innkeeper's daughter, and bribing them to rename the inn the Vanishing Moon was actually the easiest part of the whole plan. Especially since his mother-in-law had insisted on new positions for the whole family as befitted their new rank. He'd even had two new signs made, one for the inn and one for the stable attached to it. That way the stable belonged to her kin and neighbor, and the boy would be born under the sign of the Vanishing Moon.

Then his wife, recalcitrant termagant, started delivery much too early. He'd had to force the midwife to use her skills and her herbs to delay the birth. It was now the night of midsummer. The midwife had been cautioned to cut the cord with the saber he'd provided, and nothing else, under pain of death. There was nothing more he could do but wait for the prophecy to be fulfilled. His son would be king.

Thunder heralded the arrival of the storm. Peasants streamed into the inn from their midsummer revelry, dripping rivulets of water on the floor. Lord Smallpenny always provided generously for the midsummer festival. It insured the continued cooperation of his peasantry. He hushed their grumbling at the interruption of the festivities by buying a round of drinks for all.

His pint finally arrived without the midwife. Lord Smallpenny considered quaffing its contents just to prove her wrong, but drink had a tendency to go right to his head, and he wanted to be particularly alert tonight.

Rain beat down on the inn's roof and thunder shook the walls. While the storm may have ruined the festival for the common folk, it made Lord Smallpenny's heart glad. For now the moon really had vanished behind a curtain of clouds. There was nothing now that could tarnish this night. The omens for the birth of his son, who would one day be king, were perfect.

At the height of the storm, about an hour before midnight, one of the midwife's apprentices hurried in to say the birth was imminent, and to gather up the hot water and warmed blankets waiting at the fire. Lord Smallpenny was forced to endure the sly grins, goodwill toasts, and overfamiliar back slaps of the excited horde. Even knowing everything was perfect couldn't reassure Lord Smallpenny. Why was it taking so long?

In the midst of the excited merrymaking an inhuman scream could be heard from the stables. It was followed by something rather like, "Day-old dung of a putrid skunk! He'll never touch me again!"

Anne turned to Matthew and winked. "It won't be long now."

Lord Smallpenny sat impatiently at his table, nursing his pint. Waiting. His son would be king. His son would be king! His SON WOULD BE KING.

As the storm subsided, so did the crowd's excitement. Eventually, some drifted out into the disappearing drizzle for other, more private, camaraderie. At midnight, Lord Smallpenny headed toward the door closest to the stable, intending violence.

When he opened the door he could see the mid-wife's assistants gathered in the open stable door. They looked like a group looking for a messenger to deliver bad news. As he approached them some of the braver ones ran into the covering darkness of the village.

"Well, what news?" he hollered as he approached them.

"The lady is well," one volunteered, then dis-appeared.

"And . . . ?" he bellowed as he had heard his wife do.

"And she's recovering quite nicely." She quickly followed the first.

"And . . . ?" He had reached the group by now.

"And . . ." this one twisted her hands round and round, "she's very happy." Several looked like they wished they were somewhere else, like running off in the dark, but none of them dared.

"And my son?" he roared.

"And the child is fine," the midwife pushed through her few remaining loyal, but nervous assistants. "A strong and healthy brat. Would you like to see?"

There was something about her smile that unnerved him. He pushed several assistants aside and sauntered into the stable. Behind him he could hear running feet, and the midwife's laugh.

He walked down the aisle of stalls until he came to the last one.

It had been specially prepared for this occasion with a low couch. Strewn about were the midwifery tools and extraneous implements brought by the midwife's entourage. The reek of the bloodstained straw over-powered the other ordinary stable smells. Reclining on the couch was the Lady Patience Smallpenny. At her breast was a baby, squirming and sucking vigorously. The baby had managed to wriggle out of its swaddling clothes. Lord Smallpenny could see its pink wrinkled feet and small hands pumping in the air. Fat, healthy, vigorous, everything everyone claimed to want in a baby.

"I've done it. The prophecy has come true." Lord Smallpenny was invigorated by his victory. He couldn't help grinning and pumping his own fists into the air. "Yes, my son will be king over all!"

Lady Smallpenny smiled at him in the same way the midwife had. "Would you like to meet *my* daughter?" The baby shrieked its rage as Lady Smallpenny detached her, and rolled her over for him to see.

Daughter! Ruin crumbled Lord Smallpenny, literally, to the ground. As he knelt in the filthy straw, shocked, his mind would not accept defeat. He had come too far, worked too hard to surrender now. This could not be.

The words of the prophecy flowed through his mind. Each one standing out clear and crisp. He had satisfied every particular; he would not, could not, be thwarted at this point.

Rage overfilled him. He stood up, raised his fist to his wife, and . . .

"Don't you dare!" she shouted, and flung a wad of bloodstained rags at him. "You bird-brained, snake-faced hog's rump."

He collapsed again, ruined, defeated. This couldn't be happening. He'd done everything right, arranged everything. He looked up at the obstinate, captious woman who ruined his world.

Lady Smallpenny bundled up the screaming baby, and gave it what it wished.

"Think on it, you old goat-faced, spit-spattered, mouse-mucked, bewoozled, sorry excuse for a husband," Patience Smallpenny said. "She will rule all. As a woman she will have advantages in uniting the kingdom that a man would not."

He rose again. "Yes, yes, dear. Whatever you say." Then he turned, and walked out the door. As he stood just outside the stable he whispered to himself, "What have I damned this kingdom to?"

He could hear her inside, crooning to the misbegotten wench.

"Eat, my puny-footed baby. Your father is a silly one, but then again, he is a man. No matter, I see the greatness in you, and after all you do fulfill the prophecy." Lady Smallpenny cooed quietly for a moment. "When we get back to the castle, you will have silks and furs. Your grandmother and I will teach you how to rule over men. You will rule with an iron fist."

Far off in the forest, an old soothsayer laid down his looking glass and his life with a long and hearty laugh.

CHOICE OF THE ORACLES

Kate Paulk

The great looms stood silent, strands of Scylla-silk glimmering in semidarkness above the completed weaves. Air heavy with the acrid tension of electrical discharge sparked and crackled with each of my cautious steps.

The rounded shape of a cable met my probing toes, sending a thrill of fear through my body and clenching my stomach. Delicately, I twisted my foot, my toes questing for the next safe step.

Without Scylla-silk, Delphi died, and the Oracles with her. The Founders would not thank me for dooming their descendants, not when they had risked worse than death to escape the Old Earth Empire.

As loom engineer, I had the responsibility of repairing the great looms after each firestorm. The fate of my people rested on my shoulders.

My foot found clear floor. I eased forward, transferring my weight to my right leg. My body flowed into its new posture, the crackling air transforming the normally simple act of walking into a prickling dance. Too fast, and I would generate a current that could destroy the great looms.

I carried no metal, and Scylla-silk covered me head to toe. Still, an accidental discharge could fry any number of critical components in a heartbeat. The prickling on my skin, the crackling air . . . I needed no instruments to tell me I walked in the heart of a firestorm barely quieted.

Barely five meters separated me from the main consoles. They stood in the island between the looms, lit only by shafts of light from viewplates in the wall behind me. Even in that faint light, I could see enough.

The boxy shapes of the Weavers were gone, replaced by an amorphous heap of melted, scorched metal and plastics. The Weavers were dead, and my life's purpose with them.

Cool, sterile air met me as I passed through the Scylla-silk iris into decontamination. The taste of ash lingered in my mouth as every trace of the spores was sterilized and destroyed.

I shifted from foot to foot, restless, anxious. What future would the Oracles ordain, now that the Weavers were gone?

Without the Weavers, Scylla-silk was nothing, mere strands of filament that shone and glittered in the sunlight. Only when woven and sterilized did it become valuable. Nothing else worked as well for electrical and EMP insulation. Not even Delphi's firestorms could touch something wrapped in Scylla-silk.

With a brush of air, the decontamination unit opened to Delphi's habitat dome, spilling me into a crowd of people anxiously waiting to know what the storm had done to their livelihood. My livelihood.

The answer must have shown on my face as I stumbled through the iris into the corridor beyond, for the crowd drew back, their buzzing speculation silenced in my presence. I looked for Diarran among the familiar faces, found him. His square face held nothing I could read. As always, he was a mystery to me, but he was the one the Oracles had determined I should wed.

The cool voice of the Oracles scattered my thoughts. "Engineer. Report." As always, it was impossible to guess which of them had initiated communication.

I swallowed, pressing my hands against my thighs to keep them from curling into fists. My head rose to face the nearest monitor as though I faced one of the Oracles themselves. "The Weavers are beyond repair." My voice cracked. I dared not say anymore.

Silence. I could hear every breath, every tiny shift of fabric. My hands ached with tension. Fear crackled in the air, as potent as any firestorm.

Finally, the Oracles spoke again. "This is unacceptable. You are fated to maintain the looms."

My lips drew back into a snarl. "So tell me how to repair melted sludge!" For all their power, all their monitoring links, the Oracles needed human eyes and hands to work with the great looms. They could not even communicate with the Weavers.

Delphi's ever-present spores and the static they carried blocked communications lines, and risked discharge. Scylla-silk lined the habitat dome to protect all of us within it, but the thread could not be woven inside the dome. Attempts on small looms produced cloth. Nothing more.

The Oracles' analyses determined that sterilized dead spores were integral to Scylla-silk's properties.

Unless the thread was woven in the presence of spores, it was of no more use than any other cloth.

"Insubordination is not merited, Engineer." The Oracles never expressed any emotion. "You have twenty-four hours to reconsider."

My mother's voice was the first to rise after the Oracles fell silent. "Chandra! How could you?" She was somewhere to my left, beyond my range of sight.

I turned to my right, and stalked away, my heart a tight pounding knot. Each footfall measured my fate. If I apologized to the Oracles when they next asked for my report, I might receive nothing worse than flavorless rations for a time, or a pain sequence. If I did not . . . the Oracles ruled. They could sentence me to anything they considered suitable for my offense.

It was only fair that they should govern our actions, for they protected us from the dangers of the spores and the firestorms. Without them, the human settlement on Delphi would have died in the first firestorm to thunder past the dome.

I saw no one in the too long walk to my quarters. They were adequate to my station, three small, stark rooms with bare fiberpress walls. The main room held nothing more than the minimum furnishing allotment— a chair, a low table, and a stool, all fiberpress. The bench along the right wall had a catering unit set into the wall beside the personal terminal.

The terminal blinked green, indicating that I had unread messages. I ignored it.

The door to my bedroom slid into its recess in the wall as I approached, then closed behind me with little more than a whisper. I saw the bareness, the bleakness as if with new eyes. The narrow bed with its undyed coverings, the tiny closet holding my uniforms and the two threadbare dresses that were my only leisure outfits. Both had faded to the same gray as the walls. The chest of drawers holding my underwear. My two pairs of gray work boots and one pair of faded strap sandals on the floor of the closet.

I pulled off my insulation suit's gloves and tossed them on the bed. After unwrapping the tail of my hood, I pulled it off and threw it on top of the gloves. The rest of the suit joined it as quickly as my fingers could pull the ties loose. The Scylla-silk piled on the bed, shimmering with iridescent colors that seemed to light the room. Strange that something so lovely could cause such grief.

With a sigh, I reached for the coarse polysynth fabric of my uniform shirt, and pulled it over my head without bothering to unbutton it. It hit the wall by the bathroom door and dropped into the laundry hamper with a satisfying thump. The rest of my clothes followed as quickly as I could strip them off and throw them.

Naked, I padded the handful of steps to the bathroom. My fingers traced the well-known outline of scars as I walked. The long ridged line from left breast to knee I gained when a laser-guidance cable came loose and scored its path in my skin. The hashing of hair-thin stripes earned when a snapped frame sent its threads scything into anything unfortunate enough to be in the way. Each scar was a mark of honor, a peril of my fate I had survived and conquered.

And now, lost.

Diarran sat in my main room when I emerged from the bedroom. I wore a clean uniform, but my feet were bare, and I had not tied back my hair. It curled around my face and into my eyes though I tucked it behind my ears to keep it from getting too much in the way.

He stood when he saw me. "Chandra! I . . . are you well?" His dark hair stood upright, as though he had been running his fingers through it.

"Well enough." I shrugged. "Thank you." I moved toward the stool so that he could have the chair.

Diarran did not look away from me. His dark eyes seemed too bright against his pale skin. His hands clenched into his uniform pants. "Are the Weavers really . . ."

"Yes." There was little else I could say. Diarran's destiny lay in the hydroponics section: he knew little of the great looms.

He swallowed. The muscles of his jaw tightened. He raised fisted hands, let them drop. After a long moment, he turned away from me. "You must go to the Oracles, and beg their advice."

"I know." The Oracles guided every aspect of life. If they could not offer an answer, there was no answer. Questioning their authority as I had done might be insubordination, but asking their advice was not. Perhaps if I asked, even begged, they might show mercy toward me.

They would need my skills to repair the looms, even if the Weavers could not be rebuilt. I had no apprentice, and my own teacher had died three years before. The Oracles said there was ample time to choose the right parents and select sperm and egg. I was young and healthy, and there were more important places to fill.

Places like Diarran's, maintaining the hydroponics

systems that kept us all fed. Or like my mother's work in the atmospherics unit, ensuring that the air we breathed remained clean. Delphi was only barely self-sufficient, so the Oracles rarely chose to increase our population.

Diarran rubbed his chin. He turned to look at me with troubled eyes. "Chandra . . . please think before you speak. The Oracles . . . they prefer considered, reasoned words."

I nodded. Emotion was alien to the Oracles; they knew only the benefit of Delphi. My outspoken ways had earned me punishment cycles before. Blurting out the unwanted truth damaged morale. "I promise I will."

He stepped forward, caught my hands briefly in his. "And say nothing of the Founders." His intense gaze held me. "Father tells me they dislike the old legends, especially those of the Watchers."

I blinked, startlement showing on my face before I regained proper control. "But why? What harm can legends do?" Old, old stories said that the Founders had left treasures in safe storage near their colony ship, with sleeping crew members to guard them and watch over us.

Even if such a treasure had been left, it had surely been lost to the firestorms long ago. There could be no reason for the Oracles to dislike the stories.

Diarran's stare seemed to hold me in a steel vise. "Are legends logical? That alone is reason enough." He shook his head. "Be safe, Chandra." With that, he released my hands, and left me to my thoughts.

Within an hour I stood as close to the Oracles as any human ever came. Here in the bare metal Request Room I could place my petitions and beg for mercy.

I took a deep breath and knelt facing the blank screen that was the room's only decoration.

"I seek advice and offer apology for my words earlier, Oracles. I should not have risked morale."

Silence. The air in the room seemed to press heavily on my shoulders as I waited for the Oracles to determine the priority of my request.

Finally, the cool, sexless voice spoke. "Your apology will be taken into consideration when punishment is determined, Engineer." The Oracles never inflected their speech. "State the items for which you desire advice."

I swallowed again. My hands sweated against my uniform pants as I stared at the viewscreen. "Can the Weavers be rebuilt? Can the great looms?" My voice broke and a shudder ran through my body. "Delphi's economy depends on Scylla-silk—if we are unable to weave it, how shall we survive?"

With my interwoven fears spoken, a weight seemed to lift from me. Whatever happened now, it was the decision of the Oracles. My fate was in their hands: I had done my part.

Then the Oracles gave their verdict. "Delphi lacks the materials to replace the Weavers or the looms. Survival will require reduction in personnel to bring consumption to self-sustaining levels. Nonessential personnel will be scheduled for termination."

My eyes burned, my heart tightening around a knot in my chest. I had asked: now I knew. I could see the future of Delphi closing around me, its fate determined by the logic of the Oracles. Population would fall, driven by the ever-decreasing ability to produce the necessities of life, until at last only the Oracles would survive. All for the good of Delphi.

I could not believe that the Oracles could see only that choice. "Surely that will eventually destroy Delphi?" The words fell from my mouth before I could stop them. I hastened to minimize my error. "Each new problem will force further reductions with fewer personnel to mend them. Is there no alternative?"

The pause before the Oracles replied told me they had at least considered my question. "There is no alternative. Current stocks of Scylla-silk are insufficient to purchase replacement units. Continued existence of the settlement dictates the selected course of action."

I could not sleep. The knowledge that my fate was decided, that I along with all other surplus colonists would soon be dead . . . there could be no rest for me.

Diarran's words about the colony ship, the legendary treasures guarded by sleepers, worked upon me, driving me to wonder if there might be some miracle there. I could not wait quietly for death—I had to act, even if that meant a foolhardy chase for a legend none truly believed.

The evening firestorms had passed and the stillness of full night lay heavy in the air as I stole through empty corridors to the Weaving annex. The iris opened for me, admitting me to the decontamination unit though the Oracles were undoubtedly aware that I was breaking curfew. Perhaps they thought it considerate of me to remove myself from their aegis and spare them the resources required for termination.

My Scylla-silk insulation suit whispered with each movement as I walked through the inner iris to the Weaving annex.

My breath caught in my throat. Spores danced in

the air, light sparking between them in a flickering dance of miniature lightning. The half-finished Scylla-cloth glittered with spore light, making the huge room almost as light as it was when the lights were powered up.

I felt my way through the room, not caring if I sparked a firestorm. There was nothing left to destroy. The greasy feel to the air and actinic taste told me how much static had built up, static the disconnected grounding rods no longer drew away from the precious looms.

As I passed beneath the massive plas-steel structures, I did not even look up. They had been my life: now they were nothing but twisted shapes in the night.

At the far end of the annex, I felt along the wall until my gloved hands found the door to the cocoon bay. The plastic latch snicked as I turned it, the door scratching along the floor when I pulled it open. Electricity jumped between the floor and the nearest spores in a shower of blue-white light.

A step, and I was outside, or nearly. The cocoon bay was no more than an enclosure of stone walls set against the Weaving annex. Perhaps thirty man-sized cocoons lay scattered about the enclosure, each the home of a Scylla-grub partway through its transformation into one of the immense butterfly-like Scyllae.

Here, grubs could sleep safe from whatever predators roamed the rest of the world. The noises that came from the annex combined with the two-meter walls to ensure that few creatures other than the grubs ever entered the cocoon bay. Until they slept, there was an ample supply of decaying fiberpress to feed them and give them the energy to spin their cocoons.

The cocoons glittered in the night; their coating of spores sending out tiny sparks as new spores drifted closer.

The wall was almost as old as the dome, and lacked any protection from firestorms. Charred black streaks marred the pale stone blocks, while deep shadows showed where stone had crumbled away.

I set my teeth, and began to climb.

It was easier than I had anticipated—I was not even out of breath when I reached the top of the wall and looked out over Delphi.

A seething moil of fungi met my eyes. From the edge of a wide swath of seared, glassy rock, fungi grew so fast I could see weird shapes swelling into familiar bulbous spore pods, spore-catching vanes spreading and thinning, even fungal spires as tall as the dome. Chittering and hooting sounds that surely came from animals offset the crackling rustle of fungal growth. I could see no animals, though in that great sea of life even a giant might be hidden.

I swallowed and dropped from the wall to glassy stone. This must be the perimeter the first settlers had made, back when they still had working plasma weapons.

A darker line winding through the forest of fungi caught my eye. Curious, I walked toward the line, my nose wrinkling and my eyes watering when the smell of vegetable decay caught me.

I paused to rearrange my hood so that a fold of the silk covered my nose and mouth. It could not protect me from that awful stench, but it did soften the effect. I swallowed down nausea as I tied the hood in place.

The dark line was a path of seared rock. It led into the seething forest, apparently without end. .

To the Ship? Or perhaps it led to the legendary

treasures of the Watchers. Either destination was worthwhile and taking the path was a far better choice than circling the dome in search of a clearer way. I swallowed, and stepped forward.

Fungal growths made fans and umbrellas, partly shadowing the glassy stone on which I walked. Glittering light from insects kept me from utter darkness. Despite the stench, I stared around, entranced.

Surely there was hope to be found here. Surely the Oracles were wrong. That such beauty could be of no use was unthinkable.

The explosive opening of a spore pod warned me of approaching dawn. Around me, spore pods filled, straining.

I dropped to the ground and covered my head with my arms. Each pod blasted open as though explosives had been set within it, fungi straining to send their spores as far as they could. Meaty ripping sounds marked where spores were driven through fungal flesh, then another explosion as a fast-flung spore tore through an unopened pod sent the whole spore release cascading on.

All I could do was hope I was below the spore range. Spores that could not escape the shading fans drifted to the path, layering the smooth surface of the path with shimmering light.

Finally, I could hear no more explosions. I climbed to my feet, trembling. The gray light robbed the fungi of their magical lights and colors, drove them into themselves, to shrink and shrivel as sunlight approached.

At least it was safe to walk. The spores could only grow on dead vegetable matter, and then only at night.

As I trudged forward, the fungi receded, wasting away, until I could see clear to a distant silvery speck. The Ship? Curiosity stirred within me, and I walked a little faster.

The first rays of sunlight gave no warmth, only clear, golden light. That light triggered another transformation in the Delphian wildlife: plants began to push aside the withering fungi, straining toward the light.

My mouth sagged open. The sound of plants growing crackled through the air, bringing with it a rich, earthy taste. I watched as a single round leaf pushed through the dying fungi, then shot sprouts as it grew to top my height in less than a minute.

Not until I saw the growth of flower buds did I realize my danger. Exploding spore pods would not clog my lungs and swell my throat shut. The pollen likely to erupt from the plants would.

I ran.

I staggered up a rise, my feet slipping on rock slick with pollen and spores. My eyes were too swollen for me to see, though they still streamed tears. Every wheezing breath burned my chest. My nose streamed, and I could not pull enough air through my mouth.

Stumbling, I fought my way to the crest of the rise. The ground tilted beneath me and I began to descend. My feet skidded, the Scylla-silk insulation suit offering no purchase on pollen-coated stone.

My arms flailed as I fought to keep my balance, to keep from tipping back. If I fell now, I would die.

The ground tilted further, the path growing steeper. My feet shot out from under me, and I landed hard, pain shooting from my tailbone. Even that was not enough to slow my slide. I scrambled to try to stop myself, to grasp fast-growing plants I could not see. Nothing met my straining fingers.

The ground beneath me ceased to exist.

I reached for something, anything that could stop the inevitable fall. My hand brushed something hard, but it was gone before I could grasp it.

Air I could not breathe rushed past me as I fell. My heart throbbed once, twice.

Solid ground slammed into my body, and I knew nothing more.

I awakened to warmth and comfort. When I opened my eyes, I saw that I lay in a cave of treasures. Golden light filled the cave, radiating from globe-shaped lamps attached to the walls. Computer parts lay scattered around as though worthless, sharing the floor with hydroponics equipment and things I could not name.

I lay on a thick mattress of some synthetic material, a white computer beside me. It had a multitude of appendages: grippers, scanners, fine knives, needles, and other things that seemed purposeless to me. The arms were motionless and folded.

It was not until I sat that I realized I was in no pain. My eyes were no longer swollen and I could breathe without difficulty. Was the system beside me a legendary autodoc?

I shook my head, but my confusion did not clear. Nothing in this cave of parts gave me any indication how I had come to be here. I could not have landed on the mattress. This cave had no holes in the roof, no gaps I could have slid through. The only entrance I could see was a door at the far end of a cleared path from the mattress. It stood open, silent.

There was only one thing I could say with certainty: this was not the colony ship. There were signs that at least part of this cave had been smoothed out with plasma cutters, but it remained indisputably stone. The air had a faint tang of oxidation, far weaker than I was accustomed to.

Footsteps echoed, growing closer.

My chest and stomach tightened, and I pressed my hands against my thighs, striving to appear properly calm. I should not be here.

All pretense of calm fled when a giant of a man filled the doorway. He had to duck his head to enter. I stared as he approached, realizing first that he was no one I knew, then that his clothing could not have come from Delphi. We could not produce such deep blues, such brilliant gold ornamentation.

He smiled as openly as an infant. "Ah, good. You're awake." His voice was open, too, lacking any of the restraint I had thought was normal for adults. Despite his accent, he was easy to understand. "The autodoc had to wake me to put together an evac unit for you."

I blinked, trying to make sense of his words. He had found me and brought me here?

"It was a close thing," he added as though he had not noticed my reaction. "You did yourself plenty of damage with a massive allergic reaction and then the fall into the caves." He shook his head. "Why in the world didn't they give you a breather?"

I swallowed. My eyes burned, and I blinked several times. The damning emotions would not be held back. "Why would the Oracles do that? I am surplus to requirements." Nothing could keep bitterness from my voice. I needed all my control just to keep from crying.

The man's eyes opened wide and his mouth fell open. "Surplus to . . ." He swallowed. A muscle along his jawline twitched. His hands clenched into his shirt, unclenched slowly. "I think perhaps you need to tell me what's been happening at the dome."

"You do not know?" I gulped, my hands clenching into my pants. I should never have allowed myself such an undisciplined outburst.

He raised one eyebrow. "I've been in suspended animation since a few months after we made landfall. It's a little hard to keep up with current events when you're on ice." Amusement laced his voice, telling me he either had not noticed my transgression, or was choosing to ignore it. "So, what's this with the Oracles making the rules? They were supposed to help the colony, not control it."

The cave and its treasures seemed to spin around my head. That the Oracles ruled for the greater good was a fact of life as solid as the rock beneath my mattress. And yet . . .

I shuddered, feeling tears scalding my face, the man's arms holding me as a father might comfort a child. What had my people done? What had we become?

Eventually the man—Medical Officer Jared Aldreth—brought me from the treasure cave to a much smaller cave furnished with chairs and tables, and set a meal in front of me.

While we ate, he asked question after question of me, his mood growing darker with each answer I gave. The pent-up anger within him held until I told him why I had fled the dome.

"Damn it, are you all sheep?" His hands clenched

the tabletop. "Your ancestors risked *everything* to escape being controlled like this."

I flinched from his words, shame burning within me as I bowed my head. "I apologize, officer."

He shook his head. "Just Jared, Chandra. I don't need fancy titles."

I looked up in time to see him close his eyes briefly. "And it's me who should apologize. This mess isn't your fault."

I picked up a grape and popped it in my mouth, savoring the cool smooth shape of it for a moment before biting down to release the sweet juice and flesh. Food like this was a rare luxury: most of the hydroponics section was given over to the enhanced soy plants we processed into normal rations. Plants like grapes, which gave so little nutritional return, could only be considered when the needs of the colony were met.

Thoughts spun through my mind. The colony was doomed if the Oracles were not stopped. They had saved Delphi, but they had also destroyed us, draining our souls until we were mere shadows beside our ancestors.

I swallowed another grape before I asked, "So what happens now?"

Jared sighed. When he laid his hands flat on the table they seemed so much larger and stronger than any of the people I knew that I could not help feeling like a child beside him.

I swallowed, tasting the last of the fruit in my saliva.

"I can't solve this one for you." His eyes were very blue and open, so different from Diarran. I could not look away. "You and the other colonists are going to have to work that out for yourselves." His shoulders dropped and he leaned forward, his eyelids falling to free me from his gaze. "If I fix it for you, I'll just be another thing for you to worship, you see?"

Disappointment ebbed as his words sank in. The Oracles had indeed conditioned us to worship them, to leave all decisions for them to make. But we did not have to stay slaves to our own weaknesses.

I sat a little straighter. "Can you help me do something?" I had already defied the Oracles once. Once more could not be so difficult.

They would not welcome my interference. Reasoning with them would surely fail—I was certain now that the Oracles knew of this place and chose not to use the resources here—but they held so much knowledge, so much power "Could you help me shut them down, and replace them with ordinary computers?"

He smiled, the corners of his eyes crinkling. "Now that, I can do."

My stomach clenched tight as I tied my insulation suit closed. The once-sleek lines of the skimmer beside me now bulked out with the assortment of computers, hydroponics equipment, and seed stock Jared and I had loaded onto it.

An ancient insulation sheet covered and partially concealed the load, less effective than Scylla-silk but better than nothing. It could not conceal the plasma cannon we had mounted on the steering mechanism.

The plasma pistol I wore on my belt bulged against my insulation suit. An uneasy thrill slid through my body each time my arm brushed past it. I tried not to think about having to use it.

"The storms have passed." Jared's soft voice did

nothing to calm me. I pressed my hands flat against my thighs, feeling the silky smoothness of my suit.

A deep breath, in, out. "I should start." My voice trembled. "Thank you."

He nodded, weariness showing in his slumped posture, the strain around his eyes. "Good luck." Jared blinked and wiped his arm across his face. "I need to go back to sleep. They warned me before I volunteered that any forced wakes would play hell with my system, but I didn't realize they'd be this bad."

"Being brought out of suspended animation for me?" I hazarded. While Jared's accent and speech patterns were not difficult to follow, his terminology confused me.

"Yeah." He leaned against the wall. "Waking up's supposed to be done over two to three days. The drugs they pump in to bring me up in under an hour . . . once they wear off, I'm useless."

I winced. "The systems here can close up after me, yes?" If Jared fell unconscious, I doubted I could carry him anywhere, much less to wherever he was supposed to sleep. He was starting to tremble.

He nodded. "Yeah, the systems handle that without a hassle."

"Then please, go." There would be enough on my conscience by the time this night ended. "I can manage here."

I watched as Jared stumbled away. If I dared take the time, I would have helped him. My eyes burned as I reminded myself that if I did not act, and soon, the Oracles would begin killing my people. They might have already begun.

"Be well, Jared," I whispered.

With a deep breath, I climbed onto the skimmer.

Its controls were simple even for one who had never used such equipment. A power button, a thumb tab on the right to control speed, another on the left for height, and the steering arm for direction. The synthetic fabric on the handlebars held even my Scylla-silk gloves in place.

I pushed the power button. Green light shone on the steering arm, a gauge that seemed to indicate that the skimmer was fully powered. It rose gently, so gently I felt nothing and only the movement of the walls relative to me told me I was rising. A soft chime sounded, and another section of the steering arm glowed with light. This one seemed to be an indicator of speed, for when I touched the right thumb tab, it rose as the skimmer moved forward, the color changing from dark blue to bright green as my speed increased.

Cool night air caressed my face as the skimmer passed from the confines of the holding area and into open air. I pushed the height tab up, and the skimmer angled upward, climbing until I released the tab.

Below me, fungi writhed and flourished, filling the air with their magical light. There was no greasy overload of static in the air, no sparkle of discharge around me. Unlikely as it might have seemed, I was above the static, and the air smelled fresh and clean.

I breathed deeply, throwing back my hood that I might fully experience it. As I thumbed the skimmer's speed up, the breeze grew until it lifted my hair and plastered my clothes to my body. I grinned, heedless as a child. My heart seemed to lift and swell with pleasure until I thought I might cry for joy.

The silvery blue glitter of the habitat dome shattered my joy as surely as the storms had destroyed the Weavers. Now it was time for me to decide my fate, and the fate of my people.

I left the bulk of my cargo on the skimmer. The insulation cloth concealed most of my treasures, though nothing could conceal the hole I had made in the wall. The Weaver annex had not been designed to allow vehicles to enter.

For tonight, I needed only the pistol in my belt and a handheld electromagnetic pulse generator and circuit locator. The most important knowledge the Oracles held had come from the original colonists. The datacells from the systems on the skimmer held that same knowledge.

I slipped through the glittering darkness to the entry iris. A single pulse fried the circuits, allowing me to pull the iris apart and step through into the quiescent decontamination unit. The same process took me from the decontamination unit into the habitat dome.

The still, sterile air seemed lifeless as I padded through featureless corridors. In my insulation suit, I ghosted through pathways familiar only because my journeys through them had become habit.

The Oracles no doubt monitored my every move, though it was unlikely they divined my intention. Perhaps they thought I had returned with a solution to restart Scylla-silk production.

The corridor opened to the market square, a large, open room where we bartered for the few luxuries Delphi possessed. Here, the dim night-lights shone on atrocity.

Bodies lay sprawled on the floor, over tables and chairs, wherever they had fallen. The light was too dim for me to see their faces. My chest tightened and my eyes burned. Too many of the fallen were children, too young to be productive.

I swallowed in a throat tight with suppressed grief. The Oracles could not be allowed to take any more lives. They had stolen too much from us already.

My feet shuffled against the floor as I ran from the market square, half blinded by unshed tears. My lips curled back from my teeth in a grimace. Never again.

Only crashing into a wall stopped me. I blinked; catching my breath while my head stopped spinning. This was nowhere familiar to me. Dust lay thick on the ground, inactive spores glimmering with faint static.

My left hand tightened around the EMP generator.

The spores sparked and faded. Beside me, a door I had not seen slid open, its lock deactivated by the generator.

I rubbed my nose to keep from sneezing, and stepped inside.

An alarm flashed red. "Unauthorized intrusion." The words must be intended to warn any intruder to flee. I took another step, peering into the flashing darkness. If alarms were going off, I was close to the Oracles.

Distant alarms wailed, intruder and attack alerts. The possibility that Delphi's tiny security force had been terminated as surplus to requirements made my lips curl in the tiniest of smiles.

Metallic shapes emerged from the shadows, great looming bots with cutting tools on their arms. I hit the EMP generator again and ran forward, not waiting to see if I had fried their circuits.

The toneless voice of the Oracles echoed from more speakers than I could locate. "Rebellion is not tolerated. Surrender now, or face the consequences."

I sped into darkness, trusting my instincts to keep me from falling. The circuit location function of the EMP generator showed a massive cluster of circuitry not far from me. It had to be the Oracles.

Voices, human voices, behind me. "Great Oracles! How can we serve you?"

So the Oracles had not terminated security. I was less surprised than I might have been just days before.

Light blazed, making me squint into a room suddenly brighter than daylight. The Oracles stood perhaps twenty meters from me: too far for the EMP generator to damage them. A great chasm gouged from the stone beneath the dome surrounded the Oracles, a protective moat too wide to jump. If I did not jump, I would not be able to kill the Oracles.

My right hand fumbled for the pistol in my belt. My gloved fingers closed around smooth metal, and I drew the pistol out.

"The intruder must be terminated."

My death sentence hung in the air. With no hope in any other direction, I sprinted for the gap, wincing as blasts of superheated air shot past me. I would destroy the Oracles as I fell.

"Aim for the *woman*, fool!"

"This is no firing range!"

My feet touched the edge of the chasm and I leaped. Mid-leap, something crashed into my back, pushing me forward. I smelled charred fabric, and the air around me burned. I had a moment to realize that I had been shot, that only my insulation suit had saved me, then I slammed into the floor, skidding along the dust-slicked surface. Sparks flew around me, spores giving off their static.

I wondered how many years had passed since spore-borne static first corrupted the Oracles. How long had we followed the orders of insane AIs?

Breathing hurt. My lungs burned, but there was something I must do.

My left hand tightened around the EMP generator, and held.

The death of the Oracles was not accomplished in a shower of sparks, as storytellers like to relate. They simply fell silent, the purr of their drives silenced. Around them, the bots froze, and all through the habitat dome lights flickered on and doors opened as ancient emergency backups powered on.

I hauled myself to my feet to find the security crew kneeling, their heads bowed. When I tried to speak, I managed only a croak.

One of the men lifted his head. I recognized Diarran's father, but his face was twisted with emotions I could not begin to name. We stared at each other for what seemed like eternity. I wanted to speak, to apologize for destroying everything he had known, but the words would not come.

"The Oracles," he said at last. "You . . . you destroyed them."

I nodded. "They would have killed us all, like the children in the market square." Though I ached from head to toe, I found strength to glare at him. "Is that what you wanted?"

He winced with his whole body. "No! But . . . you *destroyed* them! Our only hope."

"No!" My voice cracked, echoing in the still air. "We still have hope." I blinked to clear my eyes. "I brought old datacells from the cache the Founders left for us. Everything we need is there. We have generators, Scylla-silk, hydroponics. We do not need the Oracles."

His jaw worked. He looked so like Diarran that my heart tightened. Surely Diarran had not been among those terminated. Surely not. For a moment, it seemed that he would argue, then his shoulders sagged and he bowed his head in submission.

I longed to scream, to protest what I could see about to occur, what Jared had refused to become. Weariness and emotion stilled my tongue.

His voice was dull, empty, when he asked, "What is your bidding, Great Oracle?"

CAMELOT'S GREATEST HITS

Laura Resnick

The boy who pulled the sword out of the stone that summer's day was, if I may be candid, something of a disappointment to me.

(Don't look at me like that. He had ample opportunity to tell the story *his* way, after all.)

He was young at the time, just as the most popular songs and stories about him (most of which *he* wrote, by the way) indicate; but he was hardly the stalwart, fresh-faced lad of noble spirit and unstained soul that most people suppose.

However, in the interests of accuracy, as well as whatever honesty I may owe to posterity and to the heavenly rest that awaits me (God willing), I will admit that the spin put on his image over the years was not entirely devoid of my influence. In the beginning, as you will no doubt realize, it made sense. Indeed, it seemed downright necessary. It was only later on that the fiction took on a life of its own, hurtling through time and space in a thousand-legged body of exaggerations and fabrications that were not, to put it mildly, always in the best possible taste.

But I digress.

The day he pulled the sword out of the stone, I foresaw no hint of what was to come.

Since I am a famous prophet, you can perhaps imagine what a huge admission this is for me to make. However, I merely foretell the future as it is *meant* to be. What actually happens, what flawed mortals choose to *do* with this information—that's another department entirely. In my defense, I say only that I did my best with the material that I found in my path. Can any wizard do more?

And such *un*promising material it was, too, on that fateful day! He was skinny and pale, with poor posture and long, unkempt black hair. His clothes were slovenly and ill-fitting, and his overall manner was that of an unprepossessing adolescent of the lower orders.

Nonetheless, fate cannot be denied. So when I recognized that my destiny had come for me, my disappointed hesitation lasted only, I assure you, a brief moment.

"Hail, young squire!" I cried after that (truly) brief moment, my long white hair and dark robes flowing in the summer's breeze as I made my way across the village square to the lad who had just performed the long-awaited and supposedly impossible feat of withdrawing that famous sword of incalculable value, known as Excalibur, from the massive stone in which it had been firmly lodged up to the hilt for so long.

"*Whoa!*" said the lad, examining the gleaming sword. "Awesome!"

"Thou hast freed Excalibur!" I cried. "As foretold in prophecy—er, mostly *my* prophecies, if I may forego modesty in favor of truth—a young man of noble but obscure birth has come forth to seize Excalibur, which he will now hoist overhead to drive our enemies from British soil forever!"

"Huh?" said the boy.

"You are the great war leader we have awaited, lo these many dark years!"

"You talkin' to *me*?" He looked around, as if thinking there might be *two* boys in the square who had just withdrawn swords from stones.

"You have come at last to lead us and to save the Britons from annihilation!" I proclaimed.

"Whoa, dude," said the boy, blinking. "Get a hold of yourself. You're, like, totally tripping out."

"Your coming was foretold. I realize this may be hard to absorb all at once." I took him by the shoulders and leaned close to him, peering hard into his vacuous blue eyes.

He gripped the sword more firmly and backed away rather quickly. "Hey, bro, look, if you're one of those Greek types, that's cool, no problem, but that's just not my scene. Dig?"

I glared at him, offended.

He added, "Anyhow, you're a little old for me, dontcha think?"

"I do not have abhorrent proclivities," I said frostily.

"Hey, I wasn't trying to imply anything about your health, dude. Just saying I don't play that side of the street. So are we cool now?"

"Let's start over," I suggested after a long moment of consternation.

"Sure, man, we got off on the wrong foot," Arthur said amiably. "No hard feelings?"

"I would not be sane if I had not by now learned to overlook the mistakes of mere mortals."

"Great. Put 'er there." He offered me a none-too-clean hand. "Name's Arthur. Arthur Pen."

"And I am Merlin, the prophet and sorcerer," I announced.

"Prophet? No kidding! Is there any dough in that?"

"Dough?"

"You know. Bread. Moolah. Shekels."

"It's a living," I said. "And, as it happens, I'm custodian of one of the most important prophecies in history."

"So I guess you've got job security?"

"You and I were destined to meet."

"Is this, like, a fortune-telling?" he asked warily. "Because, if it is, dude, I can't pay you. I'm skint."

"By pulling Excalibur from the stone, Arthur," I said patiently, "you have set your foot upon the road you were destined to travel."

"Yeah?"

"Indeed."

"I had a feeling," the boy said, looking excited.

"You sensed your future embracing you?" I asked eagerly, hoping to get things on track at last.

"Yeah! I saw this sword, that's been left sitting here, like, *forever*. And I thought, hey, you know, that is one *good*-looking sword, I'll bet it's worth something."

"It is worth a nation's fate and history's adulation," I assured him.

"So I can get something for it?"

"Pardon?"

"I figured I'd take it to the market, see if I could sell it," Arthur said.

"*Sell* Excalibur?"

"Uh-huh."

"For *money?*" I cried.

"Well, unless someone's got a really good lute to trade for it."

"A lute? To *trade?*"

"But I'd rather go for the money," Arthur said. "This sword looks pretty valuable. I'll bet I could get enough dough to outfit the whole band, don't you think?"

"*What* band?"

"Well, okay, I don't have a band yet. That's in the future. I figured I'd go on the road alone first, build my rep, get some steady gigs, and then acquire the band. I'm going to call it Arthur Pen and the Dragons. What do you think?"

"*What?*"

"Or maybe just Arthur and the Dragons. Or Arthur Pen's Dragons? I dunno yet."

"We have to talk," I said urgently.

"Another time, bro. I need to go down to the market and sell this sword."

"Wait!" I cried in my most thundering voice. "You cannot sell that sword! You're making a grave mistake!"

"No time to talk now, dude. Catch you on the flip side."

"*Stop!*" I used my mighty power to freeze time and space for a few moments, so that I could talk some sense into this boy.

Arthur looked around at animals frozen in mid-stride and villagers frozen in mid-sentence as the universe came to a sudden halt upon my bidding.

"Whoa, dude! *Awesome!*"

* * *

"Well, first of all," the boy said, after I had explained his destiny to him, "I don't think I like what you're implying about my mom."

"But Igraine was beloved of a great king!"

"If he was so great, how come the country's in such a mess?" Before I could respond, the lad continued, "Besides, that's not the point. The point is, you're saying she was, like, you know, *untrue* to my dad."

"Uther *was* your dad."

"Unfaithful to her husband, then."

"Whom you've never even met, so what does it matter?"

"Dude, wise up. She's my *mom*. So you really want to quit that whole 'she lay in adulterous union with a king' rap, and you want to quit it right *now*. Dig?"

I sighed. "All right, fine, I di . . . er, I comprehend." I had neglected to consider how touchy boys his age could be about their parents. God forbid that his mother had ever been a young woman with passionate needs. *No.* In a teenage boy's worldview, his mother was necessarily an asexual being who existed only to clean up after him and feed him.

But I asked curiously, "What did Igraine tell you about your father?"

Arthur shuffled his feet. "He's doing ten to twenty upstate for stealing horses."

It seemed a rather unsatisfactory alternative to telling the boy he was the illegitimate spawn of a liaison with the late King Uther, but I decided to let it pass.

"In any event," I said, "you are the stalwart young man who hath pulled Excalibur from the stone, so you're definitely—"

"No *way* am I this war leader you're looking for,

man," Arthur interrupted. "I, like, *hate* war. Totally! I'm a lover, not a fighter."

"But—"

"I'm a *musician*, bro. An artiste!"

"You *were* a musician, but now you're destined to unite Britain under a strong monarchy and usher in a Golden Age," I explained.

"No, I want to be the court minstrel *singing* about the Golden Age. Which, frankly, can't come soon enough, as far as I'm concerned. With things being so bad these days, it is *incredibly* hard to start a career as a bard."

"Arthur, there is no escaping your destiny."

"Mom wants me to settle down to something steady, like agriculture or brewing. But what can I say? I've got ballads in my blood."

"And I'm sure music will make a nice hobby," I said firmly, "while you're changing the world and carving your name into history for all time."

"How about this?" Arthur suggested. "What if I give you the sword and you go find someone who *wants* to wage war against the Saxons? I'll write a song about every battle! How about that? You could give me a nice new lute in exchange for the sword."

"Arthur, no, *you* have to wield the—"

"Or you could take the sword for free," he said, pushing it into my arms and trying to get rid of me. "I'll pick up some extra work at harvest time to pay for a new lute. Or maybe I'll just go on the road with the old lute, it's not really that bad. One string is missing, and the—"

"I will *create* the finest lute in the land right now and give it to you, if you'll just shut up and cooperate," I snapped.

Arthur paused. "Really? You can create a good lute?"

I sighed and muttered, "The things I do for destiny."

I am forced to admit that Arthur was a most creative and versatile musician, and it cannot be denied that he had considerable technical skill. His music was not to *my* taste, of course. I prefer the classics. But there is no denying that, once I put a worthy lute in his hands, his musical influence quickly grew—and, indeed, *grew*.

His war skills, however, were pathetic beyond the power of mere words to describe. When it came to slaughtering Saxons, his heart simply wasn't in it. Our first battle was an embarrassment. Our second was a total disgrace.

Then Arthur came up with his master plan for the third battle against the Saxons. We had very few warriors left alive and in one piece, and I was thoroughly demoralized and all out of ideas. So, although I thought his plan was half-mad and doomed to certain failure, I didn't oppose him. If we were going to go down, we might as well go down singing, I supposed.

Thus it was that, on the eve of Arthur's third battle against the Saxons, he and a select group of warriors, whom he now called the Dragons, sang the epic ballad that Arthur had spent the previous month composing and rehearsing with the men. It was entitled "The Bloody, Gory Tragedy of the Doomed Saxons" and was performed in four-part harmony, with a nice little lute solo for Arthur just before the big finish. It told the tale of Saxons perishing by the thousands in their first and second battles against Arthur, only to return foolishly for a third battle, in which the rest of them died most horribly.

I thought the fact that *we* had died by the thousands during our first two battles against the Saxons, while they had come out of those confrontations with most of their army intact, would make that ballad the laughingstock of the Saxon infantry that night. However, Arthur assured me that there is nothing more powerful than a good story well told—particularly when it's accompanied by a catchy tune.

And he proved to be right. Arthur Pen's Dragons sang about the bloody, gory, could-have-been-avoided-if-only-they'd-used-their-heads-and-turned-back-while-there-was-still-time deaths of thousands of Saxons during the third battle for Britain . . . and by morning, we discovered we couldn't actually *fight* the third battle, because the Saxons were busy fleeing back to Saxony as fast as their bony feet would carry them. The only Saxons who had remained to fight us were a few tone-deaf Bavarians, whom we quickly took as prisoners and held for ransom.

The ransom we got helped finance Arthur's purchase of some superior musical instruments from the Continent, and he used these in an elaborate composition that ensured victory in our fourth battle against the Saxons. It was a mourning song wherein (supposedly) Saxon women wail for the men who would never return home from this battle, so mighty and undefeatable was the massive British army. The (real) Saxons, listening to this ballad, grew so overcome with grief at their own imminent deaths and guilt over the women they had abandoned back home in search of vainglory, they surrendered at dawn, weeping copiously and crying phrases which our translator interpreted as, "Tell Mom I love her," and "I left my heart in Freiberg."

This was actually the end of the Saxon wars. But you know how it is once you've got a hit on your hands. The public just keeps demanding more. Thus it was that Arthur wrote several more ballads, right up through his "ninth" battle with the Saxons. By then, he felt burned out on ballads of military victory and Saxon doom.

"I'm an artiste, Merlin," he said to me. "If I keep covering the same ground over and over, I'll grow stale and my muse will desert me."

I didn't object, despite the tremendous acclaim the immortal "battle ballads" had won for the young King Arthur (who was crowned, by popular demand, after his first battle trilogy went double platinum). I had too many responsibilities on my hands, since Arthur was not interested in *ruling* the country of which he was king, to quibble about his music. It's only in retrospect that I realize I should have taken a more active interest in the band.

How was I to know that two new additions to the group would eventually change everything? Their names were Lancelot and Guinevere.

Guinevere had auditioned to be in the wailing chorus for "O Ye Women of Saxony, Lament Your Lost Loves," the smash hit that had ensured our victory in the fourth Saxon battle. Arthur had been so taken with her lilting voice (not to mention her long blond hair and generous curves) that he wrote a solo especially for her. After the battle was over, they became inseparable. Before long, they were living together.

Being very *modern*, they never actually married, though she was crowned queen. She also brought some mismatched furniture to the relationship, including a large round table that came from her ancestral home. Yes, *that* Round Table. Arthur composed most of his ballads at that table, though its real source of fame can be found in one ballad in particular, "The Knights of the Round Table," a wholly fictional composition in which well-meaning aristocrats (hah!) pass laws and mete out justice while assembled around the Round Table. (It wasn't round to create the illusion of equality, a nonsensical bit of legend that lingers from the song, but rather because it was cut from a massive fallen tree in Wales and, in its natural state, fitted perfectly in some lesser king's watchtower along the border.)

Arthur and Guinevere bought an estate in the West Country which they called Camelot, and they began an ambitious series of renovations that they never did manage to finish. The rehearsal studio was the only portion of the whole place that was ever fully completed, and they spent most of their time there. Arthur was entering a new phase of his development as a troubadour, and he spent several years working on a complex and obtuse set of compositions collectively known as the "Green Knight" ballads. (You may recall the work? His nephew Gawain plays a major role in one of the pieces. He wrote the boy into the song as a sort of christening present. However, Arthur's half-sister Morgan, whose musical taste was always conservative, promptly feuded with him over this, and things were never again the same between them.)

I, meanwhile, kept trying to interest Arthur in things like, oh, *ruling the nation*. But, well—have you ever tried reasoning with a musician? Sometimes I simply tore my beard out in sheer frustration.

It was during the "Green Knight" years that Lancelot appeared in our midst. Or as he laughingly called it, our "mist." He never did get used to British weather.

He'd been experimenting with percussion instruments that had made their way into the Aquitaine via the Iberian peninsula, and when he heard about the interesting work going on at Camelot, he packed up his drums and came to our little corner of the world to join Arthur's band. Arthur was immensely taken with the young man, hugely enthused about his musical input, and filled with admiration for his improvisational abilities.

"I'm telling you, Merlin," Arthur said to me one day, "this French fellow is the finest drummer in all the land!" This undisguised favoritism caused some resentment among the king's musicians, sour feelings which would eventually contribute to the disintegration of the band.

Arthur and Lancelot became close friends and started writing new ballads together. Since many of these songs required only male voices, Guinevere felt a little left out; consequently, she and Arthur started growing apart. Meanwhile, in his solo work, Arthur created a new character in his ballads, a noble knight named Lancelot who won every joust and could slay every beast. This new cycle of ballads turned out to be Arthur's most popular work yet, and his dear friend became a huge national star, second in popularity only to the king himself. Several of the chorus members started drifting away from the band, feeling their own talents were being neglected, their own contributions overlooked.

However, the unparalleled success of Arthur's "Lancelot" ballads led to a fresh burst of raw energy in the King's creative drive, and he soon began work on his most ambitious song cycle ever, the "Quest for the Holy Grail." It was such a huge hit that I agreed with Arthur's decision to go on tour for the first time since his coronation.

"My fans are clamoring to see me, Merlin," he said. "I can't disappoint them."

"I'll run the country until you get back," I offered. Why not? I'd already been running it for *years*. Though no one gives me credit for that, thanks to all those spin-off ballads about what a dedicated monarch Arthur was.

Well, the "Holy Grail" tour was such a success that he extended it, then extended it again, and then *again*. Lancelot, however, had lost some popularity after a much-publicized breakup with the Lady of Astolat, whom he had treated rather shabbily. There was even some booing in the crowd when the band played in villages near Astolat. So when Lance came down with food poisoning in Scotland, Arthur saw that the long tour was taking a heavy toll on his favorite musician. He decided to send him home to Camelot to recuperate.

Call me prophetic, but I thought that any supposed "genius of the human heart" (as one critic described our king, after seeing his standing-room-only performance in Londinium) should have been able to foretell what would happen when he sent a drummer to stay with his disenchanted wife while he remained on tour.

Arthur always suspected that Morgan started the gossip, never having forgiven him for whatever unspeakable things she thought the "Green Knight" cycle implied about Gawain's soul. Other people said the source was Mordred, her youngest son. I've always suspected a third party, possibly the spiteful Lady of the Lake, since I cannot imagine that either Morgan or Mordred, difficult personalities though they were, would have started that (wholly untrue) rumor about incest, which somehow became inextricably linked with the whole tale. And that's all I'm going to say on that distasteful subject.

Lance himself said the rumors were started by jealous members of the band, musicians who thought his own popularity had prevented them from gaining the limelight. And maybe that was so.

In any case, it wasn't long before Arthur, still on the road and playing to sold-out houses, heard that Guinevere was involved in an illicit liaison with Lancelot. Fame and fortune and coronation cannot change the human heart, and Arthur was crushed by the news. He even canceled a portion of his tour and retired to Sir Galahad's estate, where he alternated between drinking himself senseless and writing angry, accusatory letters to Guinevere.

And although I don't believe that Mordred started the rumors, there is no denying that he quickly took advantage of the tale. He'd wanted to join Arthur's "Holy Grail" tour, but the king had said that he wasn't ready, that he needed more rehearsal. An impatient and rebellious lad, Mordred now formed his own band, Lot's Sons, and went on the road. They had a new kind of sound, harsh, aggressive, antiestablishment, and atonal. And their first big hit was a direct challenge to the monarchy: "The Queen Is Having It Off with the King's Favorite Drummer."

This discordant and treasonous music appealed to a new generation, to young people who suddenly started saying that Arthur's best work was already behind him, that the "Holy Grail" cycle, until now the king's biggest hit ever, was just rehashed old stuff from his early years, dressed up with a little foreign percussion.

Realizing that his career—nay, his entire musical legacy!—hung in the balance, Arthur pulled himself together enough to take his dispirited band back on the road to finish their tour. But the tide was turning in favor of Lot's Sons. Arthur Pen's Dragons were now playing to half-empty houses, and the new reviews were tepid.

Meanwhile, the Saxons, having heard of the crisis in the British monarchy, were again marching against us. (Those damn Saxons! Don't they *ever* quit?) I tried to rally the king to write another battle ballad, but he was in creative freefall. With no feasible alternative, I went to Mordred, the uncrowned king of music in our country now, and begged him to write a song to defeat the Saxons.

"Don't be silly," Mordred said. "*Singing* the Saxons into submission is the old way. We need a fresh approach. I say we raise an army and kill them all."

Recalling our previous battles against the Saxons, I said, "That may not be such a good idea. Arthur is no war leader or military general, but he did invent an effective strat—"

"He's also no king or ruler," Mordred said contemptuously. "I mean, after twenty years of the king devoting himself entirely to his band, look where we are today! The king is on tour with some rehashed old material—"

"Actually, the 'Grail' cycle is really rather—"

"—while the Saxons march on our country! It's a disgrace! And has the king even, oh, passed a *law* in twenty years of rule? Has he ever bothered to show up at court since his coronation? Does anyone even remember where the Treasury *is* anymore?"

There was no denying that Mordred had a point. Arthur was not precisely the king I had foretold. He was more like the court minstrel who should have sung *about* the king.

"Oh, dear," I said, realizing that perhaps I had not managed destiny quite as well as I might have done. "I wonder if it could have been some *other* sword that some *other* lad was supposed to pull out of a stone?" I mused.

"What are you babbling about?" Mordred said.

"Never mind. It's the Saxons we need to focus on right now."

"I'll go raise an army and kill them all."

"All right," I said, giving in. "Let's try it your way."

"And when I come back, I insist on being crowned king."

"Er, um . . ."

"Face it, Merlin. My 'King Arthur Is a Cuckold' cycle is already more popular than anything Arthur's ever written. My time has come."

"We'll talk about it after the Saxons are all dead," I said.

"You bet we will."

•

Unfortunately, Mordred was not much more of a war leader than his uncle was. He *was* every bit as influential a musician, which turned out to be a huge problem. Mordred's music was mean-spirited and divisive. It didn't bother the Saxons at all, but it *was* successfully dividing the Britons and speeding up the collapse of our society. After Arthur inexplicably disappeared from the touring circuit, Mordred's "This Monarchy Sucks" became the most popular ballad in Britain, followed immediately by his darkest composition yet, "Your Parents Never Really Loved You" (in which the repeated refrain was, "Get over it, get over it, get oh-oh-oh-oh-OH-ver it!"). Clearly we were entering a very Dark Age in Britain.

Then one day, as we were packing up the court and preparing to flee from the Saxon invaders, the king showed up.

"Where have you been?" I demanded.

"Rehearsing the new battle ballad!" Arthur said.

"Oh, thank God! You know Mordred's losing the war?"

Arthur sighed and shook his head. "I keep telling him he's not ready for public performance yet. But does he listen? *Teenagers*. Was *I* ever that irritating, Merlin?"

"Never mind that. Can you win this war without Lancelot and Guinevere?"

"You don't need to worry about that. We're all back together again, and the band is better than ever!"

"Really?" This was a surprise.

"I went home to Camelot and worked on my relationships."

"While the country was being *invaded*?" I demanded. "You're the king, damn it!"

"Hey, I'm no good to the country if I've got writer's block," Arthur said. "I had to get my personal life in order before I could focus on the Saxon invasion."

Musicians.

"Well, now that you're focused," I said, "please, go

out onto the battlefield and start singing! Otherwise, Britain is doomed!"

Well, you now how it ended. Or, that is to say, you probably know as much as I do.

Subsequent reports from the front were very confused, since we were busy being conquered at the time. But it seems that I made a fatal error when I put two rival bands on the battlefield at the same time. When Arthur started singing, Mordred couldn't stand the challenge to his artistry. He stopped fighting and launched his new ballad right then and there. Arthur lost his focus and, instead of singing the Saxons into submission, he concentrated on outsinging Mordred. This battle of the bands fully occupied all the Britons, who scarcely seemed to notice that the Saxons took the opportunity to slay or enslave everyone, burn everything in sight, overrun the country, and make us all start speaking Saxon.

Of course, by the time I was learning to conjugate Saxon verbs so that I could negotiate our unconditional surrender, Mordred was dead, Lancelot had been shredded by the critics for his subpar performance, Guinevere had fled to a nunnery, and Arthur, mortally wounded, had been carried to Avalon. The Golden Age was over, our court lay in ruins, Camelot was abandoned, and the fickle public had already embraced a new musical form called the polka that the Saxons had brought with them.

Once the surrender was completed, I went to Avalon to visit Arthur on his deathbed. Despite his pain and delirium, he'd been working on a new composition.

"I don't think this polka trend can last for long," he said to me as he gasped for his final breaths.

"In case you were wondering," I said, "we're ruled by Saxons now."

"I think there'll eventually be a revival of a truly Celtic sound," Arthur rasped. "And I swear to you, I'm going to make a comeback. I'll reunite the band, and . . ." The thought ended in his death rattle.

"Prophecy or no," I said, "I should *never* have tried to work with a musician."

JACK

Dave Freer

*N*ow you see me . . .
    Now you don't.

But I'm out there, oh, yes. You all just keep looking for me, my little darlings. Peer out into the dark. There are always things that skitter in the night. Twigs that crack in the silence. A hint of movement where all should be grave-still. Ha. As if a grave is ever really still. I've spent enough time in one to know that. You haven't. Yet.

A muffled shriek at midnight. It could be an owl.

Or it could be me.

Tch. Keep looking out, silly ones. Stare hard into the shadows under the wind-gnarled trees. It's very black over there.

Now you see me . . .

Now you don't.

Which is all really very odd because I'm in here, in the circle of firelight, with you. I DO so like it when you look for me out there. Stopping myself from giggling is the hardest part. And it is nice and warm here by your fire. The things people will believe. As if that

would keep me away. Your cold iron could kill me,
but that is a chance I must take.

Gray dawn is a fair way off, still, and before then
my mischief and damage must be done. I'll have to slip
off and to go to earth then, before the sunlight comes.
It is such a lovely foxy way of putting it, "to go to
earth." Appropriate, too, for me, even though I can't
say that it is too accurate. But it has a better ring to it
than "to go to the mound." A pity, that. My kind are
rather obsessed with accuracy.

Magic requires it.

She huddled into her hooded cloak and leaned
against him for security. The child was shivering
slightly. Well, they all were, probably, and not from
the cold. Terrible tales were told of Gnita Heath. Of
the dragon, of the ring of old misshapen rocks which
were strangely bare of the lichen that grew on the
other stones out here. Of the doom that overtook
those who wandered too far onto it.

Or, in other words, about Jack.

"It'll be all right. We're ready for anything. We'll
see him coming," said Hrolf, trying to keep even the
hint of a quaver out of his voice. "And there are lots
of us."

She smiled at him. There was a quick flash of white
teeth in the shadows of the hood. "You're so brave."

In his heart of hearts, Hrolf Ragnarsson did not feel
it. He had come here to die, seeking the death that
had been foretold when he was barely three months
old. The wise women, the chanter of *galdr*, and mis-
tress of *seid* had spoken with his *fylgja*— his fetch. He
would die on Gnita Heath. A part of him wanted that
death but not yet, not now. Not at the hands of a

night-monster. Not overtaking the others with him.
"We warriors are not afraid of anything," he said with
all the stoutness he could muster. The poor mite was
so frail. What did the king think he was doing, sending
a waif of a girl out here?

"Not even a ghost that drinks blood and sends men
mad?" she asked.

Her teeth were very even and very white.

Did she have to mention that story? That was almost worse than Jack.

*I suppose it is rather nasty, enjoying watching him
shake. But some things need to be kept from humans.
Some things are holy, and fragile. Anyway, I like doing
my job.*

Jack . . .

Jack o' lantern . . .

Jack o' shadows . . .

Jack o' bedlam.

*The redcap of the heath. It's quite a job. Quite a
responsibility.*

*I do wonder why the humans think I'm male. My
kind never are. There are some tasks we females do
better than male-kind. The princes of Faerie find that
an affront too. But thrones and powers mean little to
our charge.* *And she is our sacred trust.*

The girl-child snuggled into him. Looked up at him
with big green hazel-flecked eyes. "We could slip off
somewhere together," she said quietly. "Just you and
I. There's a little dell just beyond the firelight. They'll
never know we're gone."

Hrolf blinked. "Are you mad? We're keeping watch
for Jack."

"You said that there were lots of us keeping watch. And you're surely not afraid?" she said archly, rubbing her cheek against his shoulder. "Not a great warrior like you. You could protect me." She smiled ever so . . . admiringly. Or was that a hint of mockery? A hint that Hrolf Ragnarsson was maybe not man enough, and should prove it?

"You're a child," said Hrolf roughly. "You should still be thinking of children's games, playing with dolls, not slipping off into the darkness with men."

It was her turn to blink those big eyes of hers. They really were too big for that elfin face. "I'm not that young."

He could see the soft swelling of her breasts now. He hadn't noticed them before. Perhaps she'd pushed back her cloak or something. It was a very fine cloak, he noticed. What was this girl-child doing here? "You're younger than my daughter would be if she were still alive. Go and lie down by the fire and behave yourself," he said, turning away. Looking out into the darkness again. He wouldn't show this little temptress the tear starting down his cheek, brought by memories that had been best left undisturbed. Little Bryn was dead, and Helga, his precious Helga, with her. She'd died trying to protect their only chick.

So, now he was out here on Gnita Heath, seeking out his fate, with this bunch of hirelings and guttersweepings that King Heimir had sent after the rest of the treasure. There wasn't a decent shield-brother among them. It had seemed fitting to go and meet that fate now that there was nothing left to live for. Now he found that, despite the sorrow, he was not ready to die.

* * *

I am really not accustomed to this! Do my powers fade? Dolls? Dolls! I was old when he was playing with a wooden sword. Still . . . there is something about him that made me choose him first. If he had been taken, the rest of them would have broken and fled. I'll try another. The vain-looking blond one. This Hrolf is only one man. But then Sigurd was only one man. And between him and Reginn, they killed our guardian. Fafnir the dragon failed. Reginn, who would have done well to guard the hoard, fell to Sigurd. I cannot fail. Only Sigurd's greed and stupidity saved us and our duty last time. This Hrolf may not be so obliging.

Perhaps blond Thorvard will do.

Hrolf looked out into the darkness. Right now it was a shield hiding his face from the others. His eyes were so blurred he couldn't have seen Jörmanrekk's horde, let alone the redcap. There'd been nothing but night-noises, really. And you couldn't see much anyway. The night-mist had crept in and was shrouding everything.

"Thorvard is missing," said Vikar, from behind him. "Have you seen him?"

Hrolf rubbed his eyes hastily. "He was here just a little while ago. Maybe he went to make water."

"Stupid fool," said Vikar irritably. "If I find he's just gone off to sleep, I'll have his guts for bra . . ."

A terrible quavering scream came out of the darkness. Far off in the darkness. Those few who had managed to get a little sleep were all awake now. Swords in hand, eyes peering into the dark, uneasy words on lips. More kindling on the fire made it flare a little. Not that it made much difference in the misty dark.

Hrolf saw that the girl was among them. She looked suitably scared now. Too scared to try her charms. Just as well. That could have been her, and him, if she'd not been so young and reminded him so much of Bryn.

She looked at Vikar and said, in a quiet voice that somehow cut through the fearful hubbub. "Why is there blood on your collar?"

To his horror Hrolf realized there was also blood on Erp's cheek, and Bikki's neck.

"The ghost who drinks the blood of men and sends them mad," she said. "Which of you is as big as an ox, and has a baleful eye? I saw such a shape stoop over those three."

The hardest part is always not to snigger. All that panic for a nick with a bronze knife, no worse than a man might give himself shaving. Well, they'll not sleep anymore tonight. And in the morning they'll find Thorvard's blood-stained clothes. And no trace of him.

Well, no trace, unless, like that fool a few years ago, he gets lost. Instead of running away that one had somehow blundered in a full circle in the mist. He'd come running into camp, screaming, as naked as the day his mother birthed him, with no more than the few little cuts it had taken to provide me with a bit of blood for my work. It was a good thing that his companions had thought him a fylga—a fetch—and killed him. Then, of course, when they'd found out that they'd killed their own, they'd blamed Jack.

That suited me perfectly.

And now the others would be eyeing the three of them out of the corners of their eyes, waiting for the

*moment they went berserk-mad from the bite of the
blood-drinking* draugr. *Sooner or later, the victims
would snap and flee. If they managed to get away
from their own companions they'd be lucky. Or, as
I'd seen often enough before, one of them would
make some innocent but untoward movement. A
hand trailed on a sword hilt, a hand too close to a
dagger, or something like that. And then it would be
bloody mayhem. Sometimes they'd bind them and
leave them here, usually promising to return. Ha. It
was always left to me to deal with them in the end.
Not that they appreciated it much. Some really were
mad by then.*

Hrolf saw how the frightened eyes of his companions darted around, staring at the *draugr*-victims and
then to the darkness of the heath. And how they
paused, just for a moment, as they looked at him.

He was not as big as an ox.

But he was the largest man there.

Dawn was still a fair way off, and it didn't look as
if it would bring much cheer.

He still longed for it.

They huddled in their cloaks, backs to the fire,
swords out, waiting. Swords out except for Vikar, Erp,
and Bikki. "We can't take a chance on you three,"
Erik Big-Belly had declared. "Give us your swords.
You tend the fire."

For a tense moment it had looked as if the three
would choose not to. But, reluctantly, Vikar had
agreed. He was the nearest thing to a leader that this
group had had. So now they tended the hungry flames
while the rest of them stared into the darkness. With
occasional nervous glances at the fire tenders, who

kept that fire burning bright. Hrolf knew that they had precious few more bundles of firewood on the pack-ponies. Fuel was scarce out here, on the high and bleak heath. What trees there were, were little more than bushes, twisted by the almost relentless wind. Mind you, when they'd had a lull in the wind, the midges nearly drove them all mad, never mind the blood-drinking *draugr*.

It was a long wait, made longer by the fear, until Hrolf realized that the mists were paling. Dawn had crept up on them like a thief—or a ghost—in the night.

"What are we going to do with these three?" asked Red Gunnar, named thus for the color of his hair rather than his sword, pointing at the victims of the blood drinker. In the pale light of the new morning the three men looked wan and fearful. The wounds on their necks were still there, although they'd all tried to rub the dried gore away. Vikar's once white shirt, that he'd boasted of taking from a chieftain's hall on a Viking raid to Ireland, was the worst testimony to the attack. The rusty brown stain was an abject re-minder of the terrors of the darkness. Hrolf wondered how the girl had weathered it. He couldn't see her right now.

"Kill them before they kill us," said one of the men. The Southerner. Hrolf hadn't got his name and didn't care if he never learned it.

"We can't do that," protested Big-Belly. "Bikki's a friend of mine."

"A better reason to kill him, if you ask me," mut-tered one of the others, but not too loudly. Big-Belly was a kin-slayer who'd sought refuge and employment at King Heimir's halls. There were not a few of them here that Heimir might just be grateful to rid his kingdom of.

"Bind them and leave them here," said one of the others. "We can take them with us on our way back."

Hrolf knew that would be as much of a death sentence as they'd been given by the Southerner. Worse, it was a cowardly way of imposing that death sentence. "No." he said grimly, stilling the nodding heads, turning them to look at him. "Sigurd was six days traveling across Gnita Heath from Fafnir's lair before he came to Heimir's halls. We cannot leave them here, on the heath, bound and unarmed, at the mercy of Jack. What kind of men are you?"

The doubtful looks told Hrolf that whatever else they were, they were men who did not want three men infected with *draugr* madness to be in their midst. Looking at the three, all a little wild-eyed and tense, ready to fight, Hrolf could understand their point.

"Give us our swords and our horses and let us go," said Vikar. "If we ride west we should be a long way from this accursed spot by nightfall, and into King Gjuki's lands before morning. That's where I should have run to when I first heard about being sent here."

Hrolf was shocked. But he had been born and bred under King Heimir's rule; Vikar had not. But surely this hire-sword had some loyalty? It would appear that it was not so.

"And have you turn back when the madness takes you, and attack us? I think not," said Red, standing well back from what would be knife-work at the least.

"Bind their hands and put them on their horses," said Hrolf. "We'll take them along."

No one had any better ideas, so they agreed to that.

But they laughed when he suggested getting the woman to watch them.

"No bites on his neck are there?" asked Big-Belly. "He's mad enough. Let's have some ring-bread and some ale and then ride on. Not that I don't know if Vikar's not right about the direction."

It was then that they discovered that they had ale . . . but no food. One pack was missing. Stolen in the night.

In the cool darkness, here, where in the daylight hours I take my rest, I pondered that big man. Hrolf. I'd set doubt among them. It could be that by nightfall he'd have been attacked and pulled down by the man-pack he ran with. He would have to go. He saw too much, even through the glamour. Perhaps the old blood ran in his veins. Such men were dangerous.

Anyway, I would see about it at nightfall. I was tired after my labors. We can go far and fast compared to humans, walking the low roads that they cannot see. But I had traveled far to get to the resting place I shared. My host didn't mind my using his tomb. He had been the sort of man I'd not minded sharing with. We'd raised a good mound for him, but there were more of us around here then. He'd placed honor before ring-gold, which is why we laid him here in that honor, with his sword, his dagger, and a coat of mail. I'm not fond of cold iron, but I don't let it keep me from my sleep. It's not as if he's going to use it anymore. A pity, actually. We could use such a defender again.

"We need a defensible camp," said Hrolf, pointing at the stones. There weren't many other features out here. Just grass, heather, and a little gorse. Little

boggy gullies. Occasionally a few scrubby trees in
hollows, where they'd found some shelter from this
wind. Unfortunately the midges also found shelter
there.

Big-Belly shook his head. "That did us no good.
We should just ride on. Maybe we can outrun Jack
and the blood-drinker."

Hrolf shook his head. "That's the ale talking, not
common sense. The horses need to rest." Ale, tiredness, and lack of food was making for a fractious
party.

"True," said Big-Belly. He turned in the saddle to
shout to the others. "Ho. Where is Red? And . . . and
Hogni and little Erik?"

Turning, Hrolf realized that he was right. The
three tail enders in the column were missing. "I'd
guess at half way to Huldaland by now," said Vikar
sourly. "Where we should be. Or among the Jor-
danes."

"Shut up. You can stay sitting in the saddle for
that," said Big-Belly, dismounting at the stones.
Climbing off his horse, Hrolf saw that they were
worked stone. It was a ruin of some kind. Perhaps a
shepherd's croft. Not that anyone had kept sheep here
for many centuries. Fafnir had seen to that. Dragons
liked sheep. And shepherds, too, for that matter.
There was a twisted lime tree here in the shelter of
the ruin. It made a good place to tie the horses. And
to off-load some of the ale. They said that beer was
liquid bread, but Hrolf would rather have had the
solid kind. Anyway, this was well-bounced ale, and
none too good to start with. He had a feeling that
more than one of them would go down with the flux.
They'd seen—and brought down—only one hare all

day, and it wasn't going to go far between the remaining fifteen men. That Hogni was a better archer than Hrolf would have guessed.

"Hoy! Stop them!" yelled Big-Belly, looking up, and wetting his boots. Vikar, Bikki, and Erp, left sitting in their saddles, had taken the chance to flee, tied hands or no. You couldn't blame them. Things looked black for them. Actually, things looked black for all of them.

Hogni had taken his bow with him when he dismounted. He drew and loosed while the other men were still untying horses.

He was as good at shooting men as he was hares. The last of the three peeled out of the saddle. No living man bounced like that.

"That was Bikki! You've killed Bikki," said Big-Belly, grabbing Hogni's bow.

"You told me to stop him," said the jowl-faced Hogni sullenly.

"Not by shooting him, you *nithing*. Why didn't you shoot the horse? But you've no brains above your balls." Big-Belly smashed the bow against the rocks.

With a choked snarl Hogni pulled his knife from his belt and stabbed upward into the largest part of the man who had just broken his bow. Big-Belly seemed to have trouble believing it. He grabbed Hogni by the throat, as the man stabbed again and again. He had big, meaty powerful hands, and by the time the two were pulled apart, it was too late for Hogni. Too late also for Big-Belly. His face was ashen, and he slumped against the gray stones, coughing blood. He looked up at them, but it was plain by what he said that all that he saw was his own murdered kin. The others backed away. Only Hrolf stood close, holding his sword-hilt, wondering if he should give the man battle-mercy. But death spared him that decision.

The bodies were laid around the far side of the scrap of wall, out of sight, if not out of mind. They were down to ten now, and three more bundles of firewood, with a long night ahead. She poured foaming ale for all of them. There was more ale than fire-roasted hare.

Hrolf blinked at the slight woman handing out ale horns. Where had she been earlier? It was on the tip of his tongue to ask when he had to knock two heads together to stop another fight. Fighting like rats, when they faced death. He shook his head. It was almost as if they•were being torn apart from within, let alone by the redcap of Gnita Heath. He shook his head again. She really was very like his Bryn, or Helga, when she was younger. And, like the taste of this ale, there was something wrong with that. He poured the ale out, quietly.

Well, my little ones, you have got farther into Jack's lands than most people do. Most blunder around in circles. There are less of you than there used to be, though. Still peering faithfully into the dark, I see. And choosing such a good place for me to work my glamours. So kind. Even though I am sure you don't mean to be, hee hee. Beside cursed ruins and a holy tree. The lime has always been good for my kind.

I must bind the dead that you have provided for me onto their horses. The horses will go home, and not along the winding routes you humans send them on. It does do such a lot for my reputation when the bodies come back from the heath. I am strong, far stronger

*than most mortal men, but the task of lifting that one
onto a horse will be hard. Poor beast. At least he won't
be using spurs on you.*

*I think it must be tonight. You are too close. Yes, I
will act tonight, in the small hours, when you are full
of ale and fullest of fears. It is always odd that they
never notice the ale I add to the supply. A triumph of
human optimism, I suppose: the hope that the drink
will not run out, against the certain knowledge that it
will. With my help, hope wins, for once. And the buck-
bean I put into that ale will send some off to squat in
the dark. I do find it funny to take them with their
breeks down around their ankles. Childish, I know. But
in some ways we never really grow up.*

Jack came just before moonset. Just after they had
found out that Nidud and the Southerner had taken
the choice between soiling themselves and just step-
ping out of the circle of firelight, and had made the
wrong choice. The fire was low now. They had very
little fuel left, and the green lime branches would not
burn. Now there were eight of them left. The drink
the girl kept plying them with might have given them
some courage, but the tiredness seemed to cancel it.
No one, no matter how mazed, dared sleep.

Jack was as bad as all the tales of the evening made
him out to be. The moon shone on his red cap, dyed—
and still dripping—with the blood of men. He stood
as tall as a mounted man. Sharp tusky teeth snaggled
in his cruel smile. He was clad in a mail shirt cobbled
from the flat-beaten breastplates of dead warriors,
hung with the pelts of wolf and lynx. His arms were
long and covered in a mat of black hair. In one hand
he held an iron-studded club and in the other a cruel

hook-bladed knife. He laughed as he strode forward
out of the dark, and a rank foxy odor blew off him.

His laughter was as cold and sharp as the cracking
of ice.

Hrolf raised his shield, and held his sword before
him . . . It had come at last. And facing it was better
than the waiting.

And his companions screamed, and, as one, turned,
and ran for the horses.

For a moment, Hrolf nearly joined them. Then he
raised the sword point as Jack strode closer out of the
dark. "Come back you cowards!" he yelled. "Come
and die like men, at least."

His answer was the sound of iron-shod hooves. He
wondered briefly if they'd even left his horse or the
pack-ponies. Well, no matter, now. He took a step
toward Jack.

The redcap halted. Lowered the club slightly. In a
gravelly voice full of menace it asked, "Is the gold
worth dying for?"

Hrolf looked at the monster, its bulk that of four
men. "No," he said, truthfully. There was no one to
lie to here anymore. "I don't think I really came for
the gold. But if I fight you, then the others and the
girl-child may get away."

Redcap snorted. "They're oath-breakers and hire-
swords. Not worth your dying for either."

"True." Hrolf nodded. "But there is the girl. She
may be a slut, or even a *draugr* of Gnita Heath. But
she reminded me of my daughter. And *that* is worth
dying for. I was not there to defend my own child
when the raiders came. I have looked for meaning and
purpose since, which I have not found in war or in
the service of the king. This may not be much of a

purpose. But it is the first one I have found in all the years since Bryn and my Helga died. And I am fated to die here."

Redcap put the club on the ground. "Run," it said in a quiet voice. "I will not hurt them. And the woman is not what you think she is."

Hrolf did not move. He knew that this was his chance. He should attack now, lop off the thing's ugly head before it could raise its treelike club again. He would be the hero of Gnita Heath. Renowned, like Sigurd, in poem and song. Wealthy and famous. Instead he too put his sword point to the ground. "What is she, then?"

The redcap looked at him in silence. In the distance he could hear the rest of the party riding hard. Away. "She is Jack," answered the Redcap, finally.

"But you are Jack. The Redcap."

"We are many. The monster who dyes his cap in the blood of murdered victims. The *draugr* that drinks blood and brings madness." The huge figure blurred and faded in the last of the moonlight and the girl-child stood there, eyes large and sad in her elfin face. "But we are also only one. I have no need of your defense of me, Hrolf Ragnarsson. Go now. I will not harm you or even the others. I never do."

Hrolf felt his legs go weak. He sat down. It was better than falling, even if it made her smile. At least the ground felt solid. "You have bespelled me. You are the monster, Jack."

Now her smile turned to a snort of laughter. "I wish I could. My skills are small. A minor glamour is all that is really in my power. And it works badly on one such as you, Hrolf. You see me much as I am, unless I exert every grain of my will on you. I can only do

that for a short time. Not one of your party questioned
what a young woman was doing in your midst. Or
should I say none of them except you. None of them
remembered me by daylight. Except you. Go now. I
will not harm you or even the others. As I said, I
never do."

Hrolf shook his head. He began to see his duty here,
as little as he liked it, with Jack in this form. "You
have killed many. All that dare to venture here."

"I have never killed any man. Have I killed any on
this expedition?"

"Thorvard."

"Did you see his body?"

Honesty compelled Hrolf to admit that he had not.
"But then what happened to him?"

"He fled from me onto the heath. After that I don't
know. The cold or his own fear may have killed him.
But not me. That would be against our compact and
my nature. Besides, you are all shielded and armed
with cold iron that would kill me. I only have my
illusions and your fear to protect my sacred charge."

"But many expeditions have set out to seek the rest
of the dragon's hoard ever since Sigurd came back
with part of it. They have all disappeared. Bodies . . .
and ponies have returned, with the riders savaged
and killed."

"Some of them were killed by each other. I have
always returned the bodies. As for the others, those
who disappear, well there are a dozen little kingdoms
all around here. The chances are against them all ending up in the same one. And humans being what they
are, they're unlikely to tell a true tale when they get
back. I am a precise Jack. There have been twenty-
three expeditions to find the rest of Fafnir's gold.

There must be ten 'sole survivors' of each of them out there, and many more who do not admit that they ever ventured onto Gnita Heath."

"Then why do you do it?" asked Hrolf. Something about it all rang true. After all, what she had said about their own expedition and her glamour did seem correct.

"It is my work," she answered. "A part of my appointed task. I do enjoy it a lot, I admit. They're many. I am one and weak against the daylight and cold iron. It's a challenge." She smiled, her face foxy with mischief. "It keeps me from being too bored. The watch is a long and lonely one."

Well. As a bored young guard he'd once tied his fellow warriors' boots together with thongs, and then woken them. "So you keep those who search for Fafnir's hoard away by trickery and illusions?"

She pulled a face. "Not all, no. But greed killed the one group that did find their way there. They fell to fighting among themselves. Their bones lie with those Fafnir devoured."

She was a creature of night and darkness. But she looked like his daughter might have done, if she'd lived. "So why do you guard the dragon's hoard, or what is left of it?"

She shook her head. "Say rather that the dragon guarded things for us. A dragon sits on his hoard. He does not use it. And Sigurd took that which he could. He had to choose, and he chose gold and rings, and the gold-hilted sword Hrótti, the gold-embossed helmet of terror, and the golden mail shirt. But he was too blinded by gold to see quite what we had given the Dragon to guard. There was a more dangerous thing than the helmet of terror, and a more precious thing

than the cursed ring-gold. Now there is no more
dragon. Only me."

"Why are you telling me this?"

She stood and looked intently at him with those
hazel-flecked green eyes. "Because, just as I remind
you of one you once loved, you too remind me of
someone. Someone I trusted. I had forgotten how
much he meant to me. It has been many years." She
took a deep breath. Gestured with a hand, and his
horse, with all its tack in place came out of the darkness. "Gnita Heath is bigger and less big than it seems,
especially by night. Come. Ride and follow me and I
will take you to the cave of Fafnir and the mound of
Hedin Vidarsson."

Whatever magic she could, or could not do, she
could get a restive horse tacked up. And Grani trusted
her. That was enough testimony for Hrolf. He
mounted and followed as she ran through landscapes
that blurred and swirled around him as if dimly seen
through the mist. Sometimes he heard the sounds of
the chase in the distance, and the far-off blowing of
horns. But he paid them no mind and followed her as
she ran, light of foot, fleet as any fox.

The sky was paling when they came at last to a
valley through which a stream laughed its way across
the rocks and a black cave-mouth looked out from
under the twin hills, just as Sigurd had described. In
the valley stood a long barrow-mound, mightier even
than that which had been raised to rest King Budli.

She led him past the bones of Fafnir, into the cave,
past the unburied and still helm-clad skulls. She kin-
dled a brand and Hrolf gazed on the fabled hoard.
Sigurd had left what he could not carry. He would not
have needed many more pack-ponies. There was very

little left, and not much of it was gold. The dream of Fafnir's hoard was little more than that. Words spoken with the bragarful cup, and taken as truth, that had sent men to scour Gnita Heath.

She pointed. "There are two things here. One must lie here until the Time. The end itself. We cannot unmake it, we cannot return it, and we cannot let it loose again without its rightful wielder. The other waits until after the Time. She waits for Baldr. Her father. She will not wake until he comes."

Hrolf looked at the great plain steel sword which was called Head, and once the weapon of Frey. A sword which would make any king more mighty than the Huns themselves, more mighty than any king. The other—a sleeping child in a simple cradle.

He nodded. "There are things more precious than gold. I suppose there is a need for a day guard too."

She nodded. "That was Hedin's task, before Fafnir. Men who can see that truth are rarer than dragons, and more valued here, in the place where all times and all places meet."

He's soft, really. Few of them die anymore. I question the wisdom that says that only one of my sex is a fitting guardian in case the child wakes. I can wet-nurse her, yes. But the dog-wolf watches over the sleeping pups as diligently, even if he has no milk to give them.

Fewer come searching these days, as the memories grow dim, and the legend of Jack o' the Heath grows. And I must admit that I like the company, even if he's not as given to nasty practical jokes as I am. Besides, with us all being female, we do have to find mates from outside. Perhaps, this time, there will be children. A new redcap—we grow old too, eventually—or, well,

*there are seldom boy children. It does happen. I think
Hrolf is of the line of one such. Not exactly the line of
kings, as is sometimes claimed among men. They make
poor kings. They lack the greed and the ambition, and
have too clear a vision. But they make good men as
a result.*

*Yes, he will die on Gnita Heath, as foretold. I will
raise a mound for him as I and my sisters did for
Hedin. The* fylgjur *did not lie.*

ABOUT THE AUTHORS

Daniel M. Hoyt's influence in the science fiction/fantasy field is not yet seminal, but he hopes it will be one day. After Dan's first short story appeared in *Analog,* he sold several more to other magazines and anthologies. Most recently, his work appeared in *Cosmic Cocktails.* Along the way, Dan also found time to be a small press publisher and editor and an anthology editor. Dan takes a break from his writing and editing with rocket science, math and piano, all of which he inflicts on his family—and any unsuspecting guests in his Colorado Springs home—with surprising regularity.

Canadian author and editor **Julie E. Czerneda** has been a finalist for the John W. Campbell Award for Best New Writer and the Philip K. Dick Award for Most Distinguished Science Fiction Novel, as well as the winner of three Prix Aurora Awards, the Canadian version of SF's Hugo, for her novel *In the Company of Others,* her short story "Left Foot on a Blind Man," published in *Silicon Dreams,* edited by Martin H. Greenberg and Larry Segriff, and as editor of the anthology *Space Inc.* Julie has published eleven science fiction novels with DAW Books, the most recent being *Reap the Wild Wind*, first of her Stratification trilogy. She's edited *Polaris: A Celebration of Polar Science* and, with Jana Paniccia, *Under Cover of Darkness*. Her next anthologies will be *Misspelled* and, with Rob St. Martin, *Ages of Wonder*.

Mike Resnick currently stands first on the all-time short fiction award list, according to *Locus*. He has won five Hugos and a Nebula, plus other major awards in the United States, France, Japan, Spain, Poland, and Croatia. He is the author of more than fifty novels, two hundred short stories, fourteen collections, and two screenplays, and is the editor of more than forty anthologies. His work has been translated into twenty-three languages.

Barry N. Malzberg began publishing short stories in 1967, novels in 1970, and became known as a prolific writer of fiction that took a sardonic view of the meaning—or lack thereof—in individuals' lives and undertakings, to the point of occasionally being labeled anti-science fiction in his outlook. Notable novels include *Beyond Apollo* (1972), winner of the first John W. Campbell Award. He lives with his wife, Joyce, in Teaneck, New Jersey.

Sarah A. Hoyt is the author of the acclaimed fantasy trilogy consisting of *Ill Met By Moonlight, All Night Awake,* and *Any Man so Daring* that undertakes a magical reconstruction of Shakespeare's life. She has also published over three dozen short stories in magazines that include *Analog, Asimov's,* and *Amazing*. Her shifter novel, *Draw One in the Dark,* has recently been published as has *Death of a Musketeer,* the first of her Musketeer Mysteries (written as Sarah D'Almeida). An upcoming trilogy takes place in the far-flung reaches of a magical British Empire. Sarah lives in Colorado with her husband, two teen males, and a pride of cats and is furiously at work on her next dozen books.

Alan Dean Foster's sometimes humorous, occasionally poignant, but always entertaining short fiction has appeared in all the major science fiction magazines as well as in original anthologies and several "Best of the Year" compendiums. His published oeuvre includes more than one hundred books. The Fosters reside in Prescott, Arizona, in a house built of brick salvaged from a turn-of-the-century miners' brothel, along with assorted dogs, cats, fish, several hundred houseplants, visiting javelina, porcupines, eagles, red-tailed hawks, skunks, coyotes, bobcats, and the ensorceled chair of the nefarious Dr. John Dee. He is presently at work on several new novels and media projects.

Darwin A. Garrison lives in northeast Indiana with his wife and three children, a dog, and a cat (the squirrels don't count as they feed themselves and don't require lawn scooping). He began writing in his teens but gave it up as a bad bet after getting one story published in his college journal. Two decades later, after almost dying of boredom while treading water in the great cesspool that is corporate America, he again took up the word processor. Thanks to the existence of the Internet, this led to meeting many wonderful people and not a few outright scary ones. On the whole, however, it allowed him to network with some wonderful mentors and learn to write fiction that people could actually read without vomiting (occasionally and with adequate preventative measures such as prophylactic Dramamine).

Barbara Nickless sold her first short story to *Pulphouse* and has since appeared regularly in other magazines and anthologies. Barb holds a BA in English with additional degree work in physics. She is a classically trained pianist who hopes someday to master Grieg's Concerto in A Minor. She lives in Colorado Springs with her husband and two children.

Nebula Award–winner **Esther M. Friesner** is the author of thirty-one novels and over one hundred fifty short stories, in addition to being the editor of seven popular anthologies. Her works have been published in the United States, the United Kingdom, Japan, Germany, Russia, France, Poland, and Italy. She is also a published poet, a produced playwright, and once wrote an advice column, "Ask Auntie Esther." Her articles on fiction writing have appeared in *Writer's Market* and *Writer's Digest* books. Besides winning two Nebula Awards in succession for Best Short Story (1995 and 1996), she was a Nebula finalist three times and a Hugo finalist once. She received the Skylark Award from NESFA and the award for Most Promising New Fantasy Writer of 1986 from *Romantic Times*. Her latest publications include *Tempting Fate*; a short story collection, *Death and the Librarian and other Stories,* and *Turn the Other Chick*, fifth in the popular "Chicks in Chainmail" series that she created and edits. She is currently working on two YA novels about young Helen of Troy, *Nobody's Princess* and

Nobody's Prize, as well as continuing to write and publish short fiction. Educated at Vassar College, receiving a BA in both Spanish and drama, she went on to receive her MA and PhD in Spanish from Yale University, where she taught for a number of years. She is married, the mother of two, harbors cats, and lives in Connecticut.

Kristine Kathryn Rusch is an award-winning fiction writer. Her novella *The Gallery of His Dreams* won the Locus Award for Best Short Fiction. Her body of fiction work won her the John W. Campbell Award, in 1991. She has been nominated for several dozen fiction awards, including the Mystery Writers' Association Edgar Award for both short fiction and novel, and her short work has been reprinted in six *Year's Best* collections. Before that, she and her husband, Dean Wesley Smith, started and ran Pulphouse Publishing, a science fiction and mystery press in Eugene, Oregon. She lives and works on the Oregon coast.

With a name like Robert Anson, it was fated that **Robert A. Hoyt** would eventually write fantastic fiction. He lives in Colorado, where he enjoys reading classic science fiction and designing strange machinery. He is of the firm opinion that everything and anything can be found in New York City.

Jay Lake lives in Portland, Oregon, with his books and two inept cats, where he works on numerous writing and editing projects, including the World Fantasy Award–nominated *Polyphony* anthology series. Current projects include *Rocket Science* and *TEL: Stories*. His next novel, *Mainspring,* will be released in 2007.

Jay is the winner of the 2004 John W. Campbell
Award for Best New Writer, and a multiple nominee
for the Hugo and World Fantasy awards.

Paul Crilley was born in Scotland in 1975 and
moved to South Africa when he was eight years old.
He was rather disappointed to discover that Africa
was not at all like the Tarzan movies he watched on
Sunday afternoons and that he would not, in fact, have
elephants and lions strolling through his backyard.
When he was eighteen he met Caroline, and they have
been together ever since. They have a two-year-old
daughter, Isabella-Rose, who is a stubborn little bun-
dle of joy who they both love to bits. He and his
family live in what was once a small village (but is
now rapidly being invaded by rich people from Jo'-
burg) called Hillcrest. They have two dogs and seven
cats. He is currently trying to finish the first book in
his fantasy series, The Sundered Land Cycle.

A member of an endangered species, a native Ore-
gonian who lives in Oregon, **Irene Radford** and her
husband make their home in Welches, Oregon, where
deer, bear, coyote, hawks, owls, and woodpeckers feed
regularly on their back deck. As a service brat, she
lived in a number of cities throughout the country
before returning to Oregon in time to graduate from
Tigard High School. She earned a BA in history from
Lewis and Clark College, where she met her husband.
In her spare time, Irene enjoys lacemaking and is a
long-time member of an international guild.

A passionate reader, **Rebecca Lickiss** began telling
stories at an early age. She finally decided to write

them down for publication, since it was better than cleaning house again. Her husband and her children humor her; otherwise they're making their own dinner. Her husband also writes, because he doesn't want to clean house either. In addition to her short story publications, Rebecca's most recent novels are *Never After* and *Remember Me*. Just to keep herself busy, Rebecca has gone back to school to get her master's degree.

Kate Paulk takes interesting medication. This explains her compulsion to write science fiction and fantasy and also means you'll be seeing a lot more of her in the future. Her friends would fear for her sanity, but she claims not to have any. She's been published in *Crossroads* and is hard at work on a novel. She lives in semi-urban Pennsylvania with her husband and two bossy lady cats. Whether this has any effect on her sanity is not known.

A music lover and longtime fan of Arthuriana, **Laura Resnick**'s current fantasy novels include *Disappearing Nightly*, *Doppelgangster*, *The White Dragon*, and *The Destroyer Goddess*. You can find her on the Web at www.LauraResnick.com.

Dave Freer is a South African of half Scots, half Yorkshire and half Afrikaans descent, which explains a number of things: his logic, his mathematical skill, and his attitude. Dave lives in KwaZulu Natal, Mount West (which is a white painted rock three miles farther in from the middle of nowhere), a remote, high altitude extensive farming and timber area. It's all dirt roads and very few people. Around there "log on" is adding fuel to the fireplace. And "Internet" is what happens to fish that do not swim away from the net. The locals—those that matter anyway—mostly speak Zulu and regard computers with distrust or as very boring TV. Dave has fourteen novels written, collaborated on (with Eric Flint or Mercedes Lackey), or upcoming. He can be found hunched, red-eyed and gnomelike, staring at his computer screen while working on his next novel.

MERCEDES LACKEY

Reserved for the Cat

The *Elemental Masters* Series

In 1910, in an alternate Paris, Ninette Dupond, a penniless young dancer, recently dismissed from the Paris Opera, thinks she has gone mad when she finds herself in a conversation with a skinny tomcat. However, Ninette is desperate—and hungry—enough to try anything. She follows the cat's advice and travels to Blackpool, England, where she is to impersonate a famous Russian ballerina and dance, not in the opera, but in the finest of Blackpool's music halls. With her natural talent for dancing, and her magic for enthralling an audience, it looks as if Ninette will gain the fame and fortune the cat has promised. But the real Nina Tchereslavsky is not as far away as St. Petersburg...and she's not as human as she appears...

978-0-7564-0362-1

And don't miss the first four books of
The Elemental Masters:

The Serpent's Shadow	0-7564-0061-9
The Gates of Sleep	0-7564-0101-1
Phoenix and Ashes	0-7564-0272-7
The Wizard of London	0-7564-0363-4

To Order Call: 1-800-788-6262
www.dawbooks.com

P.R. Frost

The Tess Noncoiré Adventures

"Frost's fantasy debut series introduces a charming protagonist, both strong and vulnerable, and her cheeky companion. An intriguing plot and a well-developed warrior sisterhood make this a good choice for fans of the urban fantasy of Tanya Huff, Jim Butcher, and Charles deLint."
—*Library Journal*

New in Paperback!
HOUNDING THE MOON
0-7564-0425-3

Now Available in Hardcover
MOON IN THE MIRROR
0-7564-0424-6

To Order Call: 1-800-788-6262
www.dawboks.com

DAW 70